GLORIA

GLORIA

MARK COOVELIS

POCKET BOOKS
New York London Toronto Sydney Tokyo Singapore

This book is a work of fiction. Names, characters, places, and incidents are either products of the author's imagination or are used fictitiously. Any resemblance to actual events or locales or persons, living or dead, is entirely coincidental.

POCKET BOOKS, a division of Simon & Schuster Inc.
1230 Avenue of the Americas, New York, NY 10020

Coovelis, Mark.
Gloria/Mark Coovelis.
p. cm.
ISBN 0-671-73578-0
1. Sisters—United States—Fiction. 2. Murder—United States—Fiction. I. Title.
PS3553.06327G57 1994
813'.54—dc20

First Pocket Books hardcover printing April 1994

10 9 8 7 6 5 4 3 2 1

POCKET and colophon are registered trademarks of Simon & Schuster Inc.

Printed in the U.S.A.

for Fae Myenne Ng

For generous support during the writing of this book, I thank the San Francisco Foundation's James D. Phelan Award, George Mason University's Rinehart Prize for Fiction, the Djerassi Foundation, the MacDowell Colony, the Virginia Center for the Creative Arts, and the Corporation of Yaddo.

GLORIA

ONE

Her name was not Gloria at all. It was Elizabeth and she was named after our mother. But Gloria was the name she died with because that's what the kid called her when he led the police out to the ditches and raised his handcuffed hands and pointed at the soft earth between the water and the exposed root of an oak and said, that's where we put Gloria.

So in Lauren's book and the movie they made of it, my sister is always called Gloria. Lauren loved that name so much—the dark, low tone of it and its bright, ironical promise of glory—that when her book came in the mail, I was surprised she hadn't called it *Gloria*. It came straight from the publisher, and there was no note from Lauren, so I don't know why she decided to call it *Quick Blood* instead. Now I'm just as glad she left the better title for me.

My name is Marvin Stone. I own StoneS, a restaurant and bar at the bottom of University Avenue. My sign revolves on the roof, shining in the shadow of the overpass. Its blue haze pours through the skylight into my office. I'm here now, at my desk. It's a little after three in the afternoon; it's still raining. Downstairs, my people are preparing to open. Before the customers come there's a kind of calm in the place, and now it's so quiet I can hear the hushed swoosh of traffic on the avenue.

Yesterday, driving down to StoneS, my wipers working against a steady downpour, I noticed *Quick Blood* on the bright marquee of the U.C. Theater. Three young women were buying tickets. Their hair glistened under the bright lights, the shoulders of their coats were dark with rain.

Quick Blood. Why the college kids like it so much, I don't know. I've never seen it. I didn't go when it first came out, three, four years ago, or when it started to come back to the revival houses. As you can imagine, the last thing in the world I wanted to see was a movie about my murdered sister.

But it always comes back. A temptation. Part of me wants to park, feed a meter, and hurry through the rain to the ticket booth. Part of me wants to see it. To know.

I go to that theater all the time. On slow nights I often duck out of my place for an hour or so to catch a glimpse of an old movie. The girl who sells tickets knows me by sight. I'm the tall, gray-bearded, balding man who buys his ticket during the middle of the movie, who often leaves before it's over. And I know her. She pouts as I lay my five in the wooden slot; she pushes a dollar and a torn ticket back at me. Her hands—plump as a child's, nails bitten—remind me of my sister's hands. The day I let Lisbeth go, she sat picking at the ragged fringe of a bandage. She just kept picking. And now I can't let the memory go, like my mind keeps picking at it, remembering.

So I know this ticket girl. And I like to think there's a kind of intimacy between us, as though she knows why I watch the movies for only an hour at a time, why I like to sit for an hour under the focused light, in a darkness as safe as sleep.

Yesterday, I didn't stop at the theater. I resisted temptation and drove on to work. It was that hour of the afternoon when the lights of passing cars suddenly flash on, and when I parked behind StoneS the streetlights glowed in the branches of the city trees. I came straight up here to my office and hunted through my desk for Lauren's book. It was in the bottom left-hand drawer, locked up with the ledgers, stuffed in the padded brown envelope it came in. I read through the supper rush. Then I asked my barman, Ronson, to bring me up some soup and bread and a cup of coffee, and I kept on reading.

I'd read her book before—the day it came in the mail—skimmed it really, looking for glimpses of Lauren, for some sign she might still love me. I didn't much care about her portrait of Gloria. Lauren and I were lovers when she wrote *Quick Blood.* (This is only one of many facts omitted from her book.) I lived with her in her student-ghetto one bedroom apartment where we went to sleep serenaded by sirens and where I woke up alone in bed listening to Lauren tapping the quiet keys of her computer. As she worked, she grew paler and thinner, more distracted, more beautiful. Sometimes she read her work out loud to me. I remember her voice—a soft, serious monotone—and the shy and hopeful way she looked up at me when she finished reading. I would hold her head in my hands, kiss her hair, tell her how good her writing was, even though I usually didn't listen to the words themselves, but just to the serious sounds they made.

Lauren wrote her book in Berkeley from March until the

September of the following year, and some time during that second June she stopped asking me about my memories of my sister or my theories about the motives of Gloria. She stopped reading to me. Late at night, when I came home from StoneS, I'd find her working. One night, near the end, I remember lying alone on the bed watching television while Lauren wrote away and the sky outside the window slowly lightened to blue. Then when the college kids were moving their skis and stereos into our building, Lauren loaded her dented Datsun and headed for Hollywood.

If you never read *Quick Blood,* you might want to go out and get a copy. It was a bestseller and I still see beat up copies of the paperback in the used bookstores in Berkeley. It's blue and it says *Quick Blood* in raised red letters. By Lauren Ogilvie, it says, in black. My sister's picture's on the cover, the famous one that was in the papers of her sitting in the sun with her hair blowing back. She's smiling. She's wearing a tank-top, and there's a curved black shadow between her breasts. (But that's not what she looked like. My sister could look different in every picture you took of her, and I've got pictures at home that would break your heart, knowing what happened.)

You can usually find Lauren's book among the other used true-crime exposés. If it's not there, you might try Sociology or the Women's Studies section. Once I found it among the mysteries. *Quick Blood* sounds like a mystery story; I can see how a hurried clerk could get fooled.

I finished reading close to midnight last night. My place was closed, I could tell, because Ronson had turned the tape player up. As I looked through my desk for a blank ledger, I could hear Percy Sledge singing down in the dining room. I wrote the first two paragraphs of this straight out. Then I stopped. I was too keyed up to concentrate.

Ronson knocked and I closed the ledger, slid it into my top drawer. I told him to come in.

He held the black pouch in his hand. "You all right?" he said.

Ronson's tended bar for me for almost ten years. In that time I've never stayed alone in my office all evening long. I told him I'd been reading, that I'd fallen asleep. He put the pouch on my desk, started gathering the dishes: my bowl, my cup and saucer. I asked him how business was, and he shrugged, meaning, what did I expect on a rainy Wednesday? Ronson's a black man who wears his face like a mask. He stood in the blue light from my sign, holding my dishes in one hand, watching me from behind his quiet-tired-after-work face.

"You want anything?" he asked.

I told him no, and he left me alone. I unzipped the pouch and dumped the bundled bills and receipts on my desk, found my current ledger and started counting. And recounting. It often happens lately—I remember things; I lose count, like it's not numbers I'm adding up but moments and people I've known and loved and lost.

TWO

The first time Lauren showed up at the restaurant, I was behind the bar. Late afternoon—it must've been four-thirty, quarter to five—and I was behind the bar helping Ronson get ready to open. He was in the cellar with his list, rooting around in the dark. I was pouring house wine. Six empty liter bottles on the bar, an orange plastic funnel stuck in one of them, a gallon jug, heavy and cold in my hands. I heard her knocking and looked up and there she was at the window. Behind her, cars flashed by, bright as the cars of a carnival ride. She cupped her face to the window, peered in.

A waiter was setting the tables Ronson had pushed away from the cellar door. He glanced at me to see what to do. I reminded him we opened at five and he held up his hand and showed her five fingers.

She called through the window: "I want. To talk. To Mister Stone."

Maybe she was looking for a job, maybe she was a customer hunting for a lost umbrella. Whatever she wanted, there was no sense talking to her about it through the window. I said all right, and the kid pointed his handful of forks at the back door.

It's hard to separate how she looked that day from my general memory of her. The only thing that sticks in my mind is that she was wearing a black turtleneck sweater, like my waiters. I teased her about it later. I told her I thought she was trying to trick me into hiring her by dressing the part of a waiter, like waiting tables was a matter of costume. The turtleneck was pure coincidence. But if it had been a trick, it wouldn't have worked. Lauren lacked a certain waitress-like quality. Call it grace. She was tall, awkward, gawky almost. But pretty. Skin like milk. And something about the way her hands were connected to her wrists made me think of birds. It was the bones. They seemed fragile, maybe even hollow. Her hands had a way of flying up to her face when she talked. Nervous, bird-like hands.

She came to the bar and put her briefcase on a stool and smiled at me. I noticed her small, even teeth, the high, blade-like bridge of her nose. She said, "You must be the easiest man in Berkeley to find." Then her hand flew up; she pointed at the ceiling. "Your name lights up the sky."

"I'm running a restaurant here," I said. "I'm not hiding from anybody."

She smiled at me again and then looked out at the dining room where the kid was lighting candles and closing the curtains, bringing the darkness in. The other waiters sat in a booth on the mezzanine, folding napkins, smoking, drinking coffee. Ronson crawled out of the cellar, a case of wine in his arms, his list in his teeth. We were almost ready.

What could I do for her, I wanted to know.

"I want to talk to you," she said. "It's personal."

Ronson heaved his case onto the bar, gave the strange woman a glance. "All right," he said, meaning you're crowding me here, I got work to do.

I slipped out from behind the bar. "Personal?"

She looked at Ronson who was sliding bottles into the racks overhead. "Can we talk?"

I said, "What are you selling?"

"I'm Lauren," she said, "Ogilvie."

I waited for an answer to my simple question.

"You're Marvin."

My friends call me Stone, like my sign says, and I told her so, but I was getting impatient. Like an itch, I could feel five o'clock creeping up. There's something holy about opening time, the still moment at the beginning of the night. In a minute my doors would be open. You never know what kind of trouble can come pouring in.

"What do you want?" I asked her.

"To talk to you."

"Stone." Ronson had found my keys by the register. He was holding them up for me to see, so I nodded, and he tossed them over the bar. I remember the glittering cluster flying toward me. I remember snatching it out of the dark.

"About Gloria," Lauren said.

I didn't say anything. I turned away from her, leaving the word Gloria hanging in the air—a cluster of anger and fear and confusion—arching toward me. It was straight up five o'clock and I had my keys in my hand. I had something I had to do—open my restaurant—and I didn't have to stand there talking to her.

In the mirrored vestibule, I worked the lock. It was bright in there where the mirrors caught the light and I could see myself hunched toward the glass door. I thought, I'm opening my place, the thought forming into words, pushing the thought of Gloria away. I was doing this very simple thing, inserting a key, turning it, feeling the bolt slide. Here was something to take refuge in. A moment. Slowly, deliberately, with all the seriousness of a ritual, I pushed the door open. Traffic rumbled on the overpass. I flicked the doorstop down with the toe of my shoe; the rubber tip caught the sidewalk, held. I was open.

Inside, Lauren was still standing by the bar, but I avoided looking her in the eye. I watched Ronson, who was at the register counting the bank. I watched the teller-quick flick of his wrist.

I said, "I don't know anybody named Gloria."

"Your sister," she said. "Lisbeth."

I gave her a look. "Why'd you call her Gloria then, if you knew her name?"

"It was the name she wanted. I respect that."

To me, Gloria was just a name in the papers. By the time she started calling herself Gloria, Lisbeth was lost, gone. "She's old news. I thought you guys would've forgotten about her by now."

"I can't forget," Lauren said. "Neither can you."

My sister's murder is the central fact of my life, and I live with it every day, like a blind man lives in the dark. Lauren had some nerve walking into my place clear out of nowhere, saying that name. But her briefcase, her bird-like hands, her black turtleneck sweater: they added up to something. I liked the way she looked. It wasn't every day a pretty young woman walked in off the street wanting to talk to me so badly. She seemed shy and aggressive at the same time and so earnest I couldn't help being a little interested. Part of me wanted to talk to her. Part of me wanted to know.

* * *

I took her down to Brennan's Pub to talk because I wanted to get her out of StoneS. I learned a trick soon after I took over the place. Those days things were touch and go, but as soon as I installed my own sign and turned on the light, old co-workers and half-forgotten friends started to drop by expecting dinner or maybe a drink or two on the house. I learned to walk the guy down to Brennan's and buy him a beer with cash-money. That lent an element of realism to the transaction and disabused him of the notion that just because I owned a restaurant I was some sort of cornucopia of food and drink. Often he'd buy me a drink in return. Things balanced out nicely and the only thing I lost was time. After a beer or two, I'd glance at my watch and announce that I had to go back to work. Instead of being trapped behind my own bar, I was free to walk out the door with the clear conscience of a man of responsibility. That's how I planned to deal with Lauren. I'd talk to her, but I wouldn't give anything away.

She'd been in Brennan's before. She told me that when she was a graduate student she and her friends would come down slumming on Friday nights to drink Irish coffee. She'd even been in StoneS before, when it was called The Depot. I told her I was probably behind the bar, but she didn't remember me.

We took a table against the wall and I went to the bar and bought her an Irish and me a regular cup of coffee and carried them back to her, her glass hot in my hand. She sipped and then licked the cream off her lip. She told me she'd been living in Santa Cruz for the past few years teaching sociology at the U.C. there, but if she ever wanted to get tenure she had to write a book, so here she was back in Berkeley with a year off and no apartment. She'd spent the night before sitting in a Golden Bear Motel room eating takeout Chinese and watching stupid stuff on TV and hating herself for being such a coward she couldn't get in her car and drive to StoneS. She stared at her drink, her head bowed. She said, "I was afraid you wouldn't talk to me."

I looked at the part in her hair, the bone-white scalp, thinking, *she's scared of me.* Meanwhile, I was sitting there bone-scared of what she knew about my sister. Things seemed to have balanced out. I watched her stir her Irish, watched the cream slowly pale the coffee. She looked up at me from under those eyebrows and said, "You understand how important Gloria is?"

Anger flashed through me. The woman was my sister; of course I understood.

"Her case has endless ramifications," Lauren said.

"For your book," I said. "For your tenure or whatever."

But she begged me to listen. What could I do? I listened because she was talking about something I had a serious interest in. According to Lauren, Lisbeth was a victim twice. Tunney killed her and then he crucified her with his story. Lauren had done a lot of research into these kinds of cases, and she had a theory, a thesis. My sister's case was unique. She said experts say women rarely do what Tunney said Gloria did, and her own research proved it. Women didn't. Tunney said Gloria helped with the others just to lessen his own responsibility, to dilute his own guilt.

The others. The girls. Near where they found Lisbeth's body they found those three girls who'd been missing. But she never touched them. She was as innocent as they were. I told Lauren I didn't need to read a book to know Lisbeth never hurt those girls.

But everybody else in the world believed Tunney. That was Lauren's point. The newspapers, television. Nobody said, *Wait a minute* but the judge, and he only did because it was irrelevant; Gloria wasn't on trial. Officially. But Tunney talked. The judge never stopped Tunney from talking. Now you ask anybody in California—or the whole country for that matter—about Gloria Rose Simpson and Arthur James Tunney and they'll tell you they're the ones who killed those girls. The two of them together.

Lauren said it was always the same. We only hear the man's version of these kinds of crimes, and men never admit it's only men who do these things. So they let Tunney turn all the hatred on Gloria. Lauren said she didn't know if Tunney was smart enough to know what he was doing. She didn't know if he knew people would be more outraged by a woman killing those girls—or even just helping—but he probably sensed it.

He was more than smart enough, if you ask me. He was some talker, Tunney. And handsome. I used to study his pictures in the magazines, trying to see something that would help me understand. But he looked like a TV actor with his careful haircut, his white teeth. One magazine printed a series of photos of Tunney and he looked different in every one of them, like an actor in different roles.

So Lauren's theory was that most of the outrage was focused on Gloria. Tunney's story made sure of that. She'd discussed it with her classes, men and women both, and it was Gloria they hated the most. She said, "A woman killing girls like that is unnatural. It goes against human instinct." So Tunney's story took on the power of a horror story. Witches. That's what Gloria's story reminded Lauren of: a witch hunt. "But it's a myth," she said. "It never happened. And that's why I want to write my book. I want Gloria's side of the story. I want to find out what really happened. But I need your help. I want to know about your sister, everything you can think of to tell me."

"Sorry," I said. "I couldn't do that. I'm sorry." Call it fear of the dark.

"So you want Tunney to have the last word?"

No, I didn't want that.

"Well?"

I didn't know what I wanted.

"Do me a favor," she said. "All right? Just think about it."

That's where we left it: with me thinking about it. As we walked back to StoneS, Lauren was quiet, letting me think. My lot was almost full. Cars drove slowly down the rows hunting for parking spaces, their headlights dim in the dusk. We found Lauren's car, a mud-colored Datsun, and she tossed her briefcase on the passenger seat and got in and rolled her window down. She said, "Promise me you'll think about Lisbeth."

As though I could keep from thinking about her. I promised. Then I made her promise to come in for dinner some time. On the house.

THREE

When I told Ronson that Lauren wanted to write a book about my sister, he shook his head. "Tell her forget about it." He said any woman who wanted to write a book about his dead sister would get no help out of him. She might even get some trouble.

StoneS was closed and everybody had gone but Angel and Herbie and Ronson and me. Those days, Ronson was in his Billie Holiday phase. He liked to put *Billie's Blues* on the tape player at closing time and turn it up. I sat at the bar listening, and it was quiet except for Billie and the murmur of Spanish voices drifting out to the kitchen.

Ronson knew enough of my life story to know I wouldn't enjoy reciting it to Lauren. He knew how I came to own the restaurant, how Barbara, the woman who owned the place before, just gave it to me. I was the barman then; Ronson, a waiter. The day before Barbara got married she handed me her keys. She told me, now it's your problem. Ronson knew she gave me her place for favors rendered over the years—sexual and otherwise—and because it *was* a problem, a run-down restaurant under the freeway. Under capitalized. Worn carpets, broken chairs. An air of seediness bordering on the forlorn.

Ronson and I became friends during the years Lisbeth was lost. I was married to Donna then, and we lived in San Lorenzo, so Ronson often hit me up for rides home to Oakland. Most nights I just dropped him off on some dark corner: West MacArthur or High Street or the Oakland end of Telegraph Avenue. But twice or three times, I drove him to a converted warehouse called Michael's Place. He knew some people with coke. He scored and we drove to my house and sat up all night in my bright kitchen, doing it.

Donna and I weren't getting along very well those years. She didn't like me bringing Ronson home in the middle of the night. She didn't like me sleeping all day. Then after my sister was murdered, I started sleeping with Barbara, which pretty much put an end to my marriage.

I miss Donna more than I can say.

One night soon after Gloria was on the news, Barbara stayed later than usual, after everyone else had gone. Playing the bartender, I offered her a drink, lit her cigarette. I watched her head as she leaned toward my lighter. Barbara had a lot of gray hair for a thirty-eight-year-old woman. It flowed away from her part, catching the dim bar light. I'd never slept with a woman with gray hair. It promised something sweet for its very lack of sweetness, like cinnamon.

I burned across my shoulders and down my legs. I was dead tired, but I knew I wouldn't sleep. For a while after I let Lisbeth go, I could sleep after making love with Donna, but then drinking became easier, and I curled up with my back to her, enveloped in the warmth of four vodkas, and pretended to sleep until sleep came. After my sister died, I let Barbara put me to sleep. That's what I remember best about that first night with her, the sweet sleep in her strange bed.

Ronson knew I had secrets to lose sleep over.

I told him, "She's got some ideas I'm thinking about."

"What's there to think about?" he said.

"She thinks Tunney told a story."

"You know that already."

"Maybe she can shed some light, is all I'm thinking."

"Too much light's been shed already. It's over. Let it be."

"People remember," I said.

"Nobody remembers nothing. You're the only one who remembers. Even I already forgot."

He hadn't forgotten any more than Lauren or I had forgotten. I didn't like him lying to me and I told him so.

He said, "I'm telling you the truth. Leave this lady alone. Forget about her."

But I couldn't forget about Lauren. Friday night I waited for her to come in for her free dinner. All evening I worked the floor exhilarated by a waiting list that at one point must've been a dozen parties long. While Angel set the tables, I swung into the bar, calling out the names with a kind of confidence I only have on busy nights when the voices of the customers drown the taped jazz and blend into one pleased voice. I looked for Lauren's face in the crowd of faces that turned toward me. She was never there. I hoped she'd come later, around eleven, but when I got all the waiting people seated and the crowd around the bar thinned out, there was only old Eli, my most regular of regulars, perched, glass in hand, on the first stool.

Saturday night we were even busier. But I worked with the

sure knowledge that at some point during the evening I'd look up from my clipboard and see Lauren sitting at the bar sipping wine. It never happened. I didn't mention my disappointment to Ronson, and he never brought it up, but once in a while I'd catch him watching me from behind his quiet face. He knew that every time I glanced at the front door, I was looking for Lauren to walk through it.

On my way home that night, I turned into the parking lot at The Golden Bear Motel. No Vacancy. A row of dark cars. I crept along until I found Lauren's Datsun. It was parked in front of number seven. No light behind her window: she must have been asleep at that hour. I watched her room by the light of my headlights.

I wanted to knock at that door. Seven. Lucky for somebody. Hadn't she walked out of the blue into my place? What if I knocked? Would she even answer? I'd say, you want to talk to me? Let's talk now.

Fifty-fifty odds she'd take me in. Her black turtleneck thrown over a chair. Chopsticks on the nightstand. A book facedown to mark her place. Her slept-in bed loose and warm. I craved sleep in a strange bed.

A flip of the coin, she wouldn't answer. If she was as smart as she pretended, she'd call the police, lock herself in the bathroom until they came. Or pull the curtain back and peek, see it's me. Talk through the window like the other day: *Stone! What do you want? Go away! Leave me alone!* Free me from my temptation to talk to her about Lisbeth.

Exhausted after a night's work waiting for her, I felt willing to let it happen either way. Heads, she took me in. Tails, she was out of my life forever.

But I never even cut my engine. I just crept out of the lot and drove home.

FOUR

□

I drove home thinking. Thinking about the first time I ever heard of Gloria. Another woman clear out of nowhere. Clear from Crescent City. This woman called me saying she was Ruth Haywood from the House of Haywood and she'd found my name in a box of things someone had lost or hidden or left behind in the women's room of her restaurant. She read some names off some envelopes: Lisbeth Stone, Beth S. Murphy.

"That's my sister," I said.

The woman wanted to know if I wanted the stuff. Some of it looked important; insurance papers, she said. I asked her to hold on to Lisbeth's box until the weekend when someone could come by. I told her Lisbeth had a husband and he might come. Then I called Earl in Grants Pass. Earl Jr. answered the phone and said his father was at a neighbor's house working on a car.

"Where's your mom?"

"At The Caves."

I made it clear I wanted his father to call me back. I said, "Even if it's late, hear me?"

Then I called The Caves. My father runs the concessions at the Oregon Caves National Monument. The Chateau, guide service, gift shop. Lisbeth and I grew up there.

Brenda answered. She's worked the front desk since my mother left.

"Is Lisbeth there?"

"No. She's at home with Earl. She went back on Friday. Or Thursday night, it was."

"She's not there. She's gone again, it looks like. Where's my father?"

"Oh, Lord, Marvin, I should've made her stay. But she doesn't listen to me. She just comes and goes, Marvin. You can't make her listen."

"I know, Brenda. Where's Dad?"

"Right here. Just a minute."

I could hear Brenda calling, "Curtis, Curtis. Lisbeth's gone again! It's Marvin. He's on the phone. He knows something."

My father came to the phone. "What's this, Marvin?"

"Lisbeth's in California," I said. I explained about the call from Crescent City and my call to Earl's. Then I told him that if I didn't hear from Earl I'd drive up to Crescent City to get Lisbeth's box myself.

"And try and find her, Marvin," he said.

I waited all that night and the next day for Earl's call, but it didn't come. Damned if I was going to hunt him down if he didn't care about his own lost wife.

On Saturday morning Donna woke up early with me, and we sat in the kitchen drinking coffee, talking in low voices so we wouldn't wake our baby, Daniel. It felt good to sit across from Donna so early in the morning. Her hair was tied back and her face was a little swollen from sleep. Donna's hair was as black as a Mexican's. I loved her hair, and even after the baby was born I discouraged her from cutting it. I lingered over my coffee. Donna spread jam on her toast and licked her finger.

She said, "I hope you find her. For Junior's sake."

"I'll find her," I said.

"I mean, how can she do that? Disappear and leave her son behind?"

"She likes to be by herself sometimes," I said. "It's like an urge or something."

"I'm sorry, Marvin. It's not natural. I can understand almost anything, but not that."

What could I tell her? I was as mystified by Lisbeth's disappearances as Donna was. "I'll find her," I said.

"I hope so. Or something awful's going to happen."

"What do you mean?"

"I don't know. I have a feeling about it and it scares me. That's all."

"Don't worry," I said. "She'll be all right."

Donna shook her head. "You just can't run away from your child like that. You just can't."

When it was time to go, she followed me to the garage. Outside, the streetlights were still on, and above the ball park across the way, the sky was changing colors like the inside of a seashell, pink and pearl-like and blue. Donna held the garage door cord with one hand and her robe closed with the other, while I backed out into the street. I rolled the car window down and said, "She's going to be the death of Brenda yet." And Donna smiled, waving good-bye.

Even though we were married for a couple more years, that moment feels like my last happy glimpse of Donna.

I arrived at the House of Haywood during the lunch rush and had to wait on a stool at the counter drinking beer while Ruth and the girls fed the crowd.

After things quieted down, Ruth led me to a booth carrying Lisbeth's box. She wore her hair in tight curls all over her head. Her arms were as white and blue-veined as marble.

"You're the brother," she said.

I told her Earl was in business, Honda cars, and he couldn't get away on a Saturday, which was true.

Ruth considered this for a moment, biting the corner of her lip. "Not the first time, I guess."

I explained that Lisbeth had sensitive nerves. Always did have.

"She asked for a job," Ruth said. "Waiting tables. Last thing in the world I need is a fragile waitress, you know?"

She reached into the box and brought out a sheet of Earl Jr.'s school pictures, wallet-sized, all eight of them intact. "Everything's in here. You know, her whole life's in here. Marriage certificate, the boy's report cards. Everything."

Out the window, I could see the sun baking the tall trucks. I thanked her for calling. Then I told the first of a whole long series of lies about Lisbeth. I said, "Her husband said to thank you. He's been worried."

Ruth tossed the pictures back into the box and slid it toward me. "It's not every day somebody leaves this sort of stuff behind."

I asked whether she had any idea where Lisbeth was headed.

"I told her about a place in Eureka called Great Days Cafe. Talk to Johnny. He may've hired her. She was pretty and God knows Johnny likes the pretty ones."

I took up the box. "Thanks."

"Yeah, any time," Ruth said. "And ask for Gloria. She didn't say anything about Beth Stone or Murphy. She said she was Gloria Rose Simpson and she had experience."

Lisbeth had a habit of changing her name. It seems to me being called Elizabeth isn't like being given a name at all, but a choice of names. Lisbeth ran through them all when she was growing up. But there, in the House of Haywood, was the first time I'd heard of her changing her name to something else altogether.

When Lisbeth was small, everybody at The Caves called her Sissy. Big Jim, the dinner chef at the Chateau, sat Sissy on a bus cart and taught her to sing "Strangers in the Night." At five, Sissy was famous with the waitresses for innocently mimicking Jim's drunken fat man's voice, for her little girl's version of his slurred words and sudden low tones. The prep and pastry cook, Tommy, made Sissy special miniature apple pies. You might say Jim and Tommy competed for her affections. They didn't like each other much. They were opposites in almost every way: the only things they shared were a love for Sissy and cases of Seagrams 7. Tommy was a jockey-sized guy no bigger than my twelve-year-old self. Somewhere on his travels he'd lost his thumb and forefinger on his left hand and his claw frightened and disgusted me when I was a kid. He used to twirl a burnt match between those three fingers while he talked horse racing. But Sissy loved him as much as she loved Jim. She was oblivious to their vices and afflictions and they loved her for it. That's what I remember about Sissy. When I came home from school, I'd find her in the coffee shop sitting on a counter stool eating Tommy's apple pie while he sat beside her in his whites, studying the Racing Form, drinking coffee spiked with bourbon.

When she was about eight or nine, she got tired of her baby

name and started calling herself Betty. Hank, our father's assistant, used to pick Betty and me up from school in a truck with a huge cave man painted on its side. He liked to tease us, tell us we were on his list. He'd pull a note out of his shirt pocket, smooth it out, study it. He'd say, "I've been to the post office and I got the paint and the flowers and the eggs and the meat and the liquor. Looks like the only thing's left is you guys." Picking us up was his job, but in a lot of ways, Hank was like a father to Betty and me. And his wife, Brenda, was like a mother.

Our mother never really took to life at The Caves. I remember her lounging in the lobby in a green dress and high heels, her red hair piled high on her head, a pile of bright magazines on the couch beside her. She spent most of her time up in her room on the third floor; we rarely saw her until dinner when she'd come down and drift through the dining room chatting with the guests. At bedtime, we'd find her in the bar, smoking. She'd give us smoky good-night lipstick kisses.

Our father was busy running the place, especially in the summer. The thing I remember most is his voice booming out of the loudspeakers in the heat of the afternoon: "First call for tour number twenty-two. All those holding tickets for tour number twenty-two, meet your guide at the cave entrance."

The summer Brenda was pregnant and too big to bend down to tuck the sheets under, Betty and I helped her clean rooms. I was fifteen that summer, so Betty must have been about to turn thirteen. She loved making beds, loved the stiff clean sheets, the way they billowed up and drifted slowly down.

That was the summer Mr. Spenser came to The Caves. I guess he stayed a few days in early June, but I didn't notice him until he returned in July and stayed a week, which was a rare thing for anyone to do. After people went through The Caves and walked the trails and ate a dinner at the Chateau, there wasn't much else to do, and they generally left. Nobody ever came back the same summer. So I was surprised when I recognized the powder blue convertible in the parking lot.

All week Mr. Spenser slept late and spent his afternoons on the bench near the mouth of the cave feeding chipmunks. He had short brushed blond hair. His face and arms were tanned. He wore sunglasses. When Betty and Brenda worked his room, they admired his leather luggage. His initials—RWS—were stamped in gold near the handles. Betty paraded around the room in Mr. Spenser's silk robe singing "Strangers in the Night."

After dinner he sat in the bar talking to our mother, and she introduced him to us when we went to say goodnight. "Say goodnight to Mr. Spenser," she said.

Just when we were thinking he was going to stay forever, we went to his room and found his luggage gone. We thought that was the last we'd see of Mr. Spenser. But late in August, he came back and stayed overnight. In the morning, my mother's luggage was in the lobby next to his. That summer's bellboy carried it all out to the convertible and packed it neatly in the trunk. My mother wore sandals and a skirt and a sleeveless blouse. I remember her pale, freckled arms in the sun. Her red hair was wrapped in a scarf. She kissed us good-bye in the parking lot while my father's voice boomed over the loudspeakers.

Mr. Spenser held the passenger side door open for my mother. She slid in. The blue car glided through the tree shadows on the road beside the Chateau and disappeared. It was like our mother had checked out of the hotel, out of our lives.

Brenda's baby was born dead in the fall, and Betty started calling herself Liz, our mother's name.

Then, when she was fourteen, summer became different. Liz seemed to feel the heat for the first time, feel it slow her blood. She moved into the third-floor room our mother had kept and stayed up there through the heat of the day, looking out her window at the green-shirted guides who sat on the benches near the mouth of the cave, and at herself in the mirror, trying to figure out if she was pretty like Brenda said she was, or bucktoothed like Hank said. She began to spend time with the college girls, the waitresses and maids and girl-guides who lived in the Chalet above the gift shop. She let them rat her hair and paint her face. She acted as go-between, delivering notes to the guys in the guide shack.

Up in the Chalet, Liz heard things about our father. He had a favorite waitress, a plump girl from New Orleans called Gail who would sneak out of the Chalet around midnight and walk through the empty Chateau lobby and upstairs to our father's room. In the morning, she went directly downstairs to work her breakfast shift at the coffee shop. "Bold as brass," Brenda said.

Every year our father found a new favorite waitress. (For all I know, he's still doing it.) He wasn't young or very handsome —being completely bald—and he had to compete with the guides and the bartender and boyfriends back home and even me, but he always found one rather serious, quiet, plump girl to keep him company for the summer.

Liz made it a habit to get as close as she could to those girls. What she learned from them, I don't know. I remember seeing her sunbathing with them on the flat rocks above the Chalet, eating supper at their tables in the staff dining room, hanging around the coffee shop during their shifts. I doubt they talked about my father much. His girlfriends probably had less to say about him to Lizzie than the other waitresses did. My guess is that she just wanted to be close to someone who was close to him.

But every September, most everybody went away. The top two floors were cold and quiet, closed. The dining room was closed, too, and what guests there were ate in the coffee shop. Big Jim lived in a room below the kitchen. Tommy went to California to cook at Santa Anita. Hank and Brenda lived above the gift shop, but the guides and waiters left, and the shack where they slept was deserted. All Lizzie's friends—the waitresses, the maids, the girl-guides—left too. It was the story of our lives; every winter, everybody went away.

The year I moved to California, Earl Murphy stayed the winter to take over some of my jobs, to help Hank drive the truck. I remember Earl as this tall, sullen character with a cave-guide's face—pale and squinty—like he'd spent all summer underground and he was just getting used to the light. I didn't give the guy a second thought until I got a letter from my sister saying she was going to have a baby and marry Earl. She signed that letter, Love, Lisbeth.

I didn't even know her, was what I was thinking when I parked my car behind my apartment house. What could I tell Lauren? My sister liked to change her name, like she always wanted to be somebody else. Between us, Lauren and I could come up with some fancy ideas about Lisbeth. Our mother checked out of the Chateau. Lauren would probably love that. Every year everybody went away, which would explain why Lisbeth liked to disappear every once in a while, why she disappeared for good in the end. We could come up with some kind of version of Lisbeth, Lauren and I, but it was like Lisbeth spent her life trying to make herself a mystery. The thing Lauren didn't know was that I wanted to solve that mystery as much as she did.

I'm not even sure whether I was aware of how desperately I wanted to know about Gloria until Lauren showed up asking questions. Now I think I was probably waiting for someone like her to come. If that's true, I'd been waiting for her at least since I'd left Donna, maybe even since I began sleeping with Barbara, doing coke with Ronson. Maybe that's what all that craziness was about: I wanted some answers, but I was still too confused to ask myself the questions.

I climbed my stairs and worked my lock and stripped out of my work clothes and pissed and washed up and fell into bed. When I closed my eyes, I could see Lauren's motel door. Number seven. I wished I'd knocked on that door.

FIVE

□

Lauren's call woke me the next morning. Sunday. What time was it?

"Late," she said.

Lateness is relative. I swung my legs out of bed and sat there, elbows on knees. So I could sleep through the mornings, I had heavy blinds on my windows, and only the faintest strip of white light bled in at the edges. But I could tell it was bright out there.

She said, "You're in the book. I'm surprised."

"Like I said . . ."

"You're not hiding from anybody."

"No, I'm not." I pictured her motel room, takeout cartons on the dresser. "You didn't come last night."

"You were busy. It was Saturday night and everything."

I decided to confess. I set the scene for her, gave her something to think about: two in the morning at The Golden Bear, me sitting behind the headlights in my dark car, watching her door, thinking about knocking and asking to come in.

"Then what?" she asked.

"That would've been up to you."

The phone sounded hollow as a shell; I could hear the rush of the sea.

"Are you serious?"

Yes, I was serious.

"But why would you do a thing like that?"

I told her why: I wanted to scare her away. I wanted to make her think I was a creep.

"That would've done it."

"So now you know."

"What? You didn't knock. What am I supposed to think?"

Didn't she think it was creepy I sat outside her room watching her door?

"Guess where I am."

"Room seven."

"Can you see Winchell's from your window?"

Suddenly that sea-sound sounded like traffic.

"Can you see me? I'm waving."

I couldn't see her; I lived in the back of the building, so she was out there waving up at nothing. She said she was looking at apartments, she was in the neighborhood.

I asked her to give me a half hour so I could straighten my place and wash up. My shower was short, but I was naked in there long enough to remind myself I was an old guy, at least ten years past my prime. I definitely had a gut. I had no discernible tan line. The nail on my left big toe had turned yellow, a minor flaw, but it made me think: Lauren might be twenty-eight, thirty. She might even be younger.

She gave me twenty minutes. Maybe. She rang the bell before I even got myself dried off. I buzzed her in and pulled on a pair of jeans and a turtleneck from the night before and slipped my mocassins on. I went out on the landing and watched her climb the stairs. She wore her hair in a braid. With it pulled back like that, I could see her long ears, her gold earrings. She wore a short suede jacket, tight Levi's, sandals. Her toenails were as pink as coral.

She stood looking out my window, the sun full on her face. "So last night. Why didn't you knock?"

"Not my style."

She looked at me. "You wanted to scare me?"

That's what I wanted.

"More than you wanted to sleep with me?"

My studio overlooks a neighborhood of white-frame houses; the shingled roofs shimmered like fish scales. I said, "It was more like fifty-fifty."

"Take it or leave it, huh?"

"Something like that."

When I asked her why she called me, she smiled, and I noticed her teeth turned in slightly, a cove of a mouth. She'd found an apartment on Oxford. "Do you know where that is? On the northside?"

I knew.

And she wanted my opinion. She didn't want to take it until she got my approval. She was moving to Berkeley for her book about Gloria and she couldn't do it without me. There was no sense in her taking an apartment if I wouldn't help her with her book. "Just come see the place, all right?"

I couldn't tell her no. I didn't want to let her go and leave me alone. Besides, how could I give her apartment advice sight unseen?

We drove down Alcatraz to Shattuck past Flint's Barbecue and the pink motel, past the auto lots where the new cars sat in the sun, bright as toys. Lauren loved Berkeley, loved being back. Santa Cruz, she said, was wasted on her. The taste of saltwater made her sick. The whole bright beach scene depressed her, especially on weekends when it was crowded with people trying hard to have fun. The boardwalk was awful. Rides and games. If that wasn't trying, she didn't know what was. When she was twelve she rode the Tilt-a-Whirl with her fat Aunt Joan at the Sacramento County Fair. She spun around in the heat. It must've been a hundred and three degrees, the sun as big as the sky. Her aunt slammed into her so hard her collarbone snapped. She heard it crack. She said she'd never forget that sound. She screamed but the machine kept whirling, tilting, everyone screaming with pleasure. No one knew she was screaming with pain. Finally the ride wound down. At the doctor's office she learned a new word: clavicle.

"Here." She took one hand off the wheel and opened her collar, traced the ridge of bone with her fingers. "Feel."

I reached across the car and touched her. Skin and bone: a smooth, true curve. Then I felt the break. "Does it hurt?"

"No, I just think it's weird you can still feel it."

The apartment manager was a gaunt guy in glasses who wore a T-shirt, sweatpants, and red rubber thongs. Lauren called him Campbell. They seemed relaxed together, like old pals. He unlocked the door for us and told us to take our time and then flapped back to the elevator.

The place smelled like paint. (It still smelled like that three months later when I moved in.) All the walls were painted white as milk. Even the radiators were white. Steam heat. Lauren remembered the first time she slept in a house with steam heat. Her first Berkeley boyfriend's place. "All night I thought someone was knocking on the radiator with a hammer. My mom or God or somebody. In the morning I felt like I woke up with a mouth full of ashes."

The floors were the color of honey. The sun poured in.

"Don't you just love this light? I could really work in a room with this kind of light."

She showed me the bedroom, its view of the city, its walk-in closet.

"When I first moved to Santa Cruz, I had to write in a closet."

Here she planned to use the dining room as an office. She loved the doors to the dining room. French doors. With all that glass, she could have her privacy and her light.

"Campbell said I can have a cat." Someone she knew in Santa Cruz had kittens.

No shower, but she liked baths better. She said there was nothing better than a bath and a book.

"Half my books are warped from being read in the bath. I stay in for hours. You should see me, I wrinkle up like a prune."

The tub was as white as the walls. Sky-blue tile. I imagined her tall body curled there, her glistening knees. A pretty picture. As we turned to leave the room, I glimpsed my gray beard behind Lauren's profile in the mirrored medicine chest.

We finished our tour in the kitchen. She showed me the stove.

She said, "Gas is best, don't you think?"

She turned the knob; the blue flame circled and flared.

"The kitchen I grew up in was all electric. You know, those glowing red coils?"

I turned off the fire. I agreed, "Gas is good."

She showed me where a table could fit beside the refrigerator. "I won't need the dining room. In here is big enough to eat in."

She loved the round, smooth shape of the fridge, which was shorter than she was, and white, an antique.

"They used to make things to last. This thing must weigh a ton."

She opened it and showed me the cute little egg-shaped places on the shelf on the inside of the door. I found myself examining that shelf as though I'd never seen one before, as though it were something rare and strange and beautiful. Lauren had suddenly transformed something I'd seen every day of my life into an object of wonder.

"You missed your calling," I said.

She raised her dark eyebrows, gave me a what-do-you-mean? look.

"You should sell real estate."

"So." She smiled. "Have I sold you?"

"I'm not in the market," I said, stalling.

"You know what I mean, Stone."

I stood at the sink, worked the spigot. The water came out rusty. I said, "The place is fine."

"The light is really something," she said.

I held my hand under the tap until the water came out clean, until I felt the cool water warm.

"What do you think?" She was leaning against the refrigerator door, watching me closely.

"I think your pipes are rusted."

"Stone."

I turned the water off and dried my hands on my pants. "You can write in the dining room?"

She nodded slowly, biting the corner of her lip.

"All right," I said. "Then I think you should take it."

Lauren asked me if she could borrow the restaurant van to haul her things from Santa Cruz, but I couldn't let her take it by herself, so I told her I'd help her move on Monday, when StoneS was closed. Sunday night I asked Herbie to clean the van: sweep out the rotten lettuce leaves, hose it down. When I got to the lot in the morning, Lauren was there, waiting in her car. She crawled out and stretched. Her hair looked slept in, her face swollen. She carried a sack and a red thermos; she waved at me, calling, "Coffee!"

In my van, she struggled with her seatbelt, which was tangled and buckled behind the seat and all out of adjustment. When I asked if I could help, she looked at my belly.

"You can do your own," she said. "We're getting on the wicked freeway."

Through Oakland, the freeway was crowded with dusty trucks. Lauren turned in her seat, inspected the cargo area. It looked big enough to her. One trip would do it. All she had was a mattress and desk and books, some clothes and a bicycle. She'd inherited some furniture from her grandmother but it was at her parents' house in Sacramento. Some day, she said, she might go get it, but it depressed her. Sacramento was hot all summer, foggy the rest of the time. She grew up in a development called River Gardens where all was new under the sun. She rode her bike on the graded lots, played house in the half-built houses.

"We had to be careful of nails. You know, you step on a nail, you get lockjaw, you die."

Her mom taught third grade. Lauren couldn't remember a time when her mom's class's picture wasn't stuck on the refrigerator with a magnet. At the change of every season, she helped her mom redecorate the classroom bulletin boards. She remembered how quickly the construction paper faded in the sun.

Her father was an entomologist who worked for the state, an aphid expert. But his passion was fly-fishing. He knew flies. He tied his own in the evenings on a TV tray while he watched Huntley and Brinkley. He wore horn-rimmed glasses low on his nose. He smoked a pipe.

Lauren had a passion for fishing, too, in her past life. (That's what she called her childhood, like part of her had died.) Saturday mornings she drove with her dad to the

Feather or the Yuba or the Rubicon. Predawn drives. The smell of pipesmoke. She poured him coffee, let it cool in her lap. She had her own waders she inherited from her older brother; she caught her share.

Her brother, Ken, never much liked to fish. He took up guitar and quit, and so Lauren inherited his Ovation along with his waders. When he finally found he had a talent for drums, their parents built him a soundproof room behind the garage where he practiced after school with his band of long-haired skinny boys. They smoked Marlboros, listened to records, drank beer. Coors was their brew of choice. Girls with waist-length straight hair and halter-tops came to watch them play.

"I could feel the throbbing come up through the floor of my room, and I thought mysterious things must be going on down there. Ken and his friends had a kind of glamour, if you know what I mean. Rock and roll. I thought my brother was the greatest thing this side of Mick Jagger. And there was this kid, the singer, who was called Paul Sharpe with an "e," which I thought was a really cool name, who looked like John Lennon, you know that long nose, those glasses. He smoked his cigarette like a joint."

Lauren showed me. Her thumb and forefinger touching, she touched them to her lips.

I had the impression all this talk was Lauren's way of avoiding any mention of my sister. But Lisbeth couldn't have been any more present if she were sitting between us in the van.

I drove. Sun bright traffic. Where were we?

"Fremont," Lauren said. She took a donut box out of a sack at her feet. A roll of paper towels. She opened the glove box and laid a towel over it and broke a donut into bite-sized pieces.

"Open up." She popped a piece of donut in my mouth.

I said, "What kind of mysterious things?"

"You know." She poured coffee and I reached for the red cup. "It's hot. Wait."

"No," I said, "I don't know. Tell me."

She held the cup in her lap, letting it cool.

"All right. I'll tell you. I lost my so-called virginity in that soundproof room. To that Sharpe character."

She remembered the acoustic tiles on the ceiling, like at school, the random pattern of holes, constellations.

"Van Morrison was playing on the stereo. 'Brown Eyed Girl,' as I recall."

She even remembered what she had for dinner that night: meatloaf.

"God, it's embarrassing to think about. Anyway, I made an appointment at Kaiser to get birth control. No big deal. No trauma. I got my pills on a summer afternoon and went fishing with my dad the next morning."

Her dad fished one pool above her, and she stood knee deep in the stream, watching him. The slippery stones, the pull of the current. He wore a yellow Cal Berkeley cap with flies hooked into it.

"He's as tall as you are," she said, "but thinner. And his casts were smooth, fluid, graceful as tai chi."

She cast her arm slowly toward my windshield, broke her wrist.

"I fished, knowing Sharpe was at home with Ken and the rest of the boys, rehearsing, waiting for me."

The river roared; the sun shined down.

I said, "So what's so depressing?"

"That it's all so ordinary," she said, "and that it's all over."

All Lauren's talk loosened me up, so I decided to tell her about Donna. I said, "I was married. But we broke up a couple years ago."

"I thought so," Lauren said. "You have that look."

"What look?"

"I don't know. Sort of bereft." She seemed to like the sound of that word. She said it again. "Bereft."

She was right. That's how I felt. I said, "I have a boy named Daniel." I unbuckled my seatbelt and wrestled my wallet out of my pocket and handed it to her. "He's five."

"Cute," Lauren said. "But he doesn't look like you."

"They say boys favor their mothers," I said.

"Do you see him much?"

"Not enough. No."

"She's pretty," Lauren said.

I glanced over at her. She was looking at a picture of Donna holding Daniel in her lap. I nodded.

"Mind if I ask you something?" she said.

"What?"

"It's pretty personal."

"It's all right," I said. "Ask."

"Well, I was wondering, why did you break up?"

I didn't want to tell Lauren about Barbara, so I told her only part of the truth. I said, "Because she believed Tunney."

Lauren looked surprised. "Why?"

I told Lauren what Donna told me. "She said, a woman who could leave her baby behind, could do anything, even what Tunney said she did."

Lauren found my picture of Lisbeth posing beside one of Earl's new cars. She stared at it for a long time. Then she closed my wallet and tossed it on the dashboard.

She sipped her coffee, looked out the windshield, squinting. She said, "I think I know how you feel about your sister."

I doubted that, but I was curious to hear how she thought I felt.

"My brother, Ken."

"The drummer," I said.

"Uh huh. He's what you might call a missing person. I mean, I know where he is, but we're out of touch."

"Where is he?"

"Somewhere between here and Hawaii, probably. He gave up the drums a long time ago." Her hands flew up and made a swift flurry of drumming motions. "Pa da pa, Pow," she said. "Now he sails when he can, as a free-lance sailor on yachts, schooners, whatever they're called. I don't know much about it, except that he hangs around San Diego waiting until some rich guy wants to take his boat to Maui or Mexico or someplace."

"Sounds like the good life," I said.

"But when he isn't sailing, which is at least half the time, he works in a liquor store for four dollars an hour. He lives in a hotel room. It's really depressing."

I wondered what she thought of me after seeing my studio.

"Something happened to him. He did a lot of drugs, and that could be it. I miss the old Ken, though, I really do."

"He can't be too bad off," I said, "if he can sail. It takes some skill, right?"

"Sure. But I'll tell you what kind of guy my brother is. He cuts his own hair with a pair of scissors. He washes it with a bar of soap. You can imagine what he looks like. But that's Kenny. That sums him up."

Santa Cruz. The overgrown yard of a Victorian house. On the porch, Lauren introduced me to Sonia, a woman about my age who wore her straight gray-blond hair to her shoulders.

"This is Marvin Stone. Gloria's brother." Lauren's nervous hand gestured toward the driveway. "But you can call him Stone, like his van says."

Sonia grinned at me. Her teeth looked like ice cubes, white at the center and translucent at the edges. She escorted us in and asked me to excuse the mess. The hall was crowded with bundled newspapers, potted plants. Two bright bicycles leaned against the wall.

I followed Lauren upstairs while she talked to me over her shoulder. "Sonia's great. But a bit wacky. She believes in everything. Astrology, numerology, the I Ching. You name it. She's seen flying saucers. She thinks the Mafia shot Kennedy. Both Kennedys. It's like everything's a conspiracy to her. Everything's connected."

In Lauren's room, everything was packed. A down parka and a camel coat lay over a stack of cardboard boxes. Two suitcases sat next to a stripped mattress. Her desk—a door complete with a brass knob—was bare. The filing cabinets were open and empty.

Lauren said, "She even believes Tunney. If we can convince Sonia, we can convince anyone."

I closed the door behind us. "Lauren," I said. "Don't ever do that again."

She looked at me.

I told her, "Don't give me that what-do-you-mean? look. You know what I mean. Don't ever call me Gloria's brother."

"Lisbeth."

"Lisbeth, Gloria, I don't care. It's just nobody's business. It's our private business. Between you and me." Ever since my sister was murdered and the whole Gloria story was in the news, I'd kept my relationship to her a secret. Even though I knew she was innocent, I didn't want anyone to know I was her brother. The situation seemed too complicated to explain to anyone, so I avoided the subject of Lisbeth as best I could, but now that I think about it, it's not so complicated at all. I was ashamed of how I handled the whole thing; I felt as though I was somehow responsible for the way things turned out. And only a few days after meeting Lauren, I wasn't ready for her to broadcast my business to Sonia or anyone else.

Lauren sat down on a box, ran her fingers through her hair. "Stone. I know. Come here."

I walked over to her and she took my hands, looked up at me. Brown-eyed girl. She squeezed my fingers.

"This is our thing," she said. "You're right. It's just between us."

When we finished loading the van, Sonia served us cold chicken and mineral water in her kitchen. She kept staring at me. After I ate, she stood behind my chair and put her hand on my head and then raised it, held it in the air. She said she could see my spirit escaping out of me like steam.

We got out of there late in the afternoon, after stopping at a motel near the boardwalk to pick up a kitten. I waited for Lauren in the van and watched a boy clean the pool, skim leaves off the surface with a net. I was thinking about things. Lauren's stuff had all been packed before she even came to Berkeley. She knew she'd be moving, she knew I'd say yes.

When she got in the van with the kitten, I said, "Keep him in your lap." I didn't like the idea of being attacked while I drove. We wound slowly toward the summit in the loaded van, while Lauren stroked the skittish kitten and murmured soft words.

"What's his name?"

"Her, I think. I had trouble catching her. She was flying around the room."

"Call her Bird."

"A cat named Bird?"

"Why not?"

"What do you think of that, Bird?"

The cat's ears lay back, close to her head.

I felt skittish myself. I thought, maybe she planned to move anyway, maybe she didn't like Sonia peering at her spirit anymore than I did. Sonia said she saw my spirit rising out of me; she actually saw it flying away. What exactly did she see?

This is Gloria's brother.

SIX

□

I'm just trying to remember what happened now, trying to enter the rhythm of memory. I double-parked on Oxford. Lauren took Bird upstairs, and I started emptying the van. Then I helped her load the elevator. She rode up alone and I stayed downstairs to stack her stuff in the lobby, to watch for thieves. While I waited with the last load, Campbell appeared in his doorway. He had his glasses in his hands. He said, "Tell her what I'll do is I'll pro-rate her rent and take it out of her deposit and she can pay me first and last on the first."

"Her deposit?"

"Yeah," he said. "Don't worry, she'll get it back. Just minus whatever the rest of the month comes to. I haven't figured it yet."

"She gave you a deposit?"

"Yeah. Friday." He put his glasses on, peered at me. "What's it to you? You paying her rent?"

I told him I wasn't paying her rent, and I promised to tell her she'd get her deposit back minus whatever. I waved my hand like it meant nothing to me. Campbell disappeared behind his door.

The elevator opened. Lauren stood there looking exhausted, her hair sticking to her forehead, her shirttails out. Her hands were red and roped with veins.

She said, "I feel like Sisyphus."

We dragged the filing cabinets and a couple of suitcases and the bicycle in.

"I'm happy," she said.

I rode the elevator up with her, holding the bike by the handlebars, balancing it on its rear wheel. I felt hot and dizzy in that crowded box. Lauren wheeled the bike into her apartment while I lugged the cabinets. Then I went back for the suitcases and let the elevator go.

Her boxes were piled in the middle of the living room; the mattress leaned against the wall. Lauren closed her door and said, "We did it."

I said, "That Campbell guy said he'd pro-rate your rent and take it out of your deposit."

"Did he say how much?"

"He hasn't figured it yet."

"What's the deal? It's not calculus." She made her way between the boxes. "Have you seen my purse?" She looked through the French doors into the dining room where she'd locked the cat. "I'm starving," she said.

"Lauren."

She looked at me.

"Do you think I'm stupid?"

"Of course not. What are you talking about?"

"You think I wouldn't notice your stuff was packed in Santa Cruz?"

"Notice? What do you mean?"

"And you gave Campbell a deposit *Fri*day."

"Yes. I did."

"You told me you wouldn't take an apartment unless I helped you with your book. You already had a deposit down."

"So?"

"So you take me for an idiot. You knew I'd help you."

"I hoped you would. I just hoped."

"You don't pack your stuff, you don't put money down on hope."

"That's all I had to go on, Stone."

I looked out the window. Dusk. Below, my van was still double-parked, shining white under the street lamp, its taillights blinking. I thought, I've got to go downstairs, I've got to move that thing.

"Stone. I thought we understood each other. Listen to me."

I told her I understood everything.

"No, you don't."

I started toward the door; I had to move my van.

"Wait. Listen." She grabbed my arm. "I'm not forcing you. You can talk or not talk."

The apartment had darkened at dusk. I looked at her in the gray light. Did she know how much I wanted to tell her?

She said, "I can't make you do anything. You could tell me everything you remember. Or you could lie. You could make stuff up. You could be wrong."

"I wouldn't lie."

"You can tell me everything or anything or nothing." She backed away from me and leaned against the mattress that leaned against the wall. Her hand flew up; she put her fingers to her forehead. "I'm just going on faith here. I'm at your mercy."

My mercy? What was she talking about? I was the one who was getting ready to lay his whole life open for her inspection.

She said, "All I've got is hope and my belief in Gloria. And I trust you. I like you, Stone."

I stood waist deep in boxes, looking at Lauren. In the darkening room, her face looked pale against the gray mattress. Her eyes shined from tiredness and—I couldn't believe it—she was crying.

My shoulders felt stiff. A buzzing made my head feel light. After squinting into the sun all afternoon, my eyes burned.

She blinked. Tears.

Suddenly my doubts seemed like a small pain I could ignore below the greater ache I had to hold her, to talk to her, to tell her about my sister, my life. I felt free, set loose by her tears and my own fatigue. She pushed herself away from the mattress and she was in my arms. Her back felt frail. I could feel her ribs, the bones of her shoulders. She'd heard her clavicle crack as she spun around in the sun. She was at my mercy. She laid her sweaty head against my chest. Her hands lay flat on my back, still as in sleep.

"You trust me," she said. A level whisper; it wasn't a question. She was telling me.

More than I trusted myself, I told her, and it was true.

"You like me."

Yes, I did. I liked the sleepy smell of her hair, and the way she broke a donut over a paper towel, stroked the cat. Her sandals, her toes, the true, smooth curve of her collarbone. The way she worked the stove in the empty apartment, asked me if gas was good. The way she showed me the egg-shaped places on the shelf inside the refrigerator door. The awful god-like banging of the radiator, her conscience. Her dented Datsun. I liked her memories: her father tying flies, her mother's classroom—construction paper fading in the sun.

Her brother and his drums and his drugs. I could tell that she was deeply disturbed by whatever had happened to him. And I liked the simple things she remembered: meatloaf and Marlboros and Van Morrison. I liked how she wouldn't let me have the coffee until it was cool enough, how she made me wear my seatbelt. Her black turtleneck sweater, her briefcase. I liked the way her hands flew up. But most of all I liked her love for Gloria.

"Yes," I said.

Her hand moved on my back. "We understand each other."

"Yes," I said.

She rubbed her face against my shirt, drying her cheek. She looked up at me and said she was starving. Had I seen her purse?

I told her to forget about her purse, I'd buy us something to eat. I had to move the van anyway. Pizza sounded good to her. And beer. And could I pick up some coffee for the morning and maybe some cat litter? She'd pay me back when she found her purse, it had to be somewhere.

Yes. Yes.

I rode the empty elevator down, landed in the lobby, gave Campbell's door a glance, and walked through the newspaper-strewn vestibule into the dark streets. My van sat there waiting, blinking.

I stopped at the co-op supermarket first and walked the bright aisles, pushing a cart. I picked up some coffee and milk and a box of assorted donuts and a carton of eggs and some mint chocolate chip ice cream and a sixer of Coors and cat litter and a red plastic litter tray. I bought us a mushroom and green pepper pizza at Round Table, and back on Oxford, I laid the grocery bag on its side in the litter tray and, balancing the pizza box on top, carried everything the three blocks from where I parked to Lauren's apartment building. The crazy arrangement grew heavier with every step. But I felt as exhilarated as I do on busy nights, a crowd waiting at the bar, a clipboard full of names in my hand. I counted up the front of the building: two sets of lighted windows, one set dark, the fourth—Lauren's—curtainless, bright. She was waiting for me up there.

While I was gone, she'd set her door up on the filing cabinets, stacked a couple boxes for each of us to sit on. We had a dining table. Her purse had been there all along, she said, lost in the mess. I noticed that her mattresses weren't leaning against the wall anymore; she must have moved them into the bedroom.

Lauren took the groceries to the kitchen. "I'm starving," she said. She flipped the lid of the pizza box and lifted a stringy slice to her mouth. She opened herself a beer and drank from the can, her head thrown back. I watched the smooth slope of her throat.

I remembered something. I said, "I bought you a present." I opened the egg carton and held one up for her to see. Pale and perfect, it felt cool in my fingers. I opened the fridge and set the egg in its place on the shelf and said, "This is where I decided. Right here. When you showed me that shelf like I'd never seen one before, I wanted to trust you, I wanted to talk to you, tell you everything."

She smiled, her small teeth as perfect and darkly white as the eggs. She took the carton out of my hand and set each egg in its place. I closed the door. Lauren came into my arms and kissed me, her tongue flowing into my mouth, soft and sweet with pizza. The warm taste of beer. We leaned against the fridge, pressed against it, kissing. "Come with me," she said.

Her bare mattress lay on the floor. A couple of folded blankets. The bluish city light came in the curtainless window. The room felt cool.

Lauren unbuttoned the top two buttons of her shirt and pulled it over her head, tossed it. After unhooking her bra, she let it slide off down her thin outstretched arms. She pulled at the fly of her Levi's—a familiar soft popping sound—and shimmied out of her pants. Her body looked soft as smoke in the blue light, like the spirit Sonia saw rising out of me. I sat at the edge of the mattress and untied my shoes, while Lauren lay naked behind me, a mystery, like the throbbing coming up through the floor of her room, the first of many mysteries.

"Slow poke," she said.

I bowed down and kissed her. "What's the rush?"

She held my beard in her hands. "I'm Stone-cold," she said.

Her body felt cool. Her quick cool hands on my back. The scratchy blanket lay between us, and as I kissed her, I could feel her tugging at it, giving it a kind of life. A tugging under me, an undertow. I rolled away from her, onto my back, and the blanket slipped away. Lauren rose above me in the bluish gloom, her long body suddenly light—flying away—but she drifted down again, the blanket on her shoulders, a cape. The O shape of her mouth saying my name. We understood each other. Her breath on my neck. The smell of her hair. My hands moved down her back and rested in the hollow above her butt. Lauren moved on me. We warmed each other. I could feel the gentle friction on my thigh, warm, wet. A kiss, sudden shudders, the details adding up to something, something to remember. Everything, anything, nothing. And something to forget. Lauren rolled away from me, was under me, her legs open. I saw the ridges of her hips, shadows. We moved together with the slow motions of memory and gained speed, pushed. Images rose, spirit-like, bright: my sister's face looking down from the third-floor window at the Chateau; Lisbeth sitting behind the wheel of one of Earl's junk cars, the baby on the seat beside her; Gloria's bandaged hand; clues to this mystery rose away and disappeared.

We lay on the bare mattress, our hearts pounding. The cold came back, so I found the last blanket and covered us. Lauren put her head on my chest, her hand on my belly. She kissed my neck, let go a slow moan, and then, when I was just beginning to forget, she named the real reason for our intimacy, whispering, "Tell me about Gloria."

SEVEN

I told Lauren: the first time Lisbeth ran away, she came back by herself. It was just after Earl Jr. was born, in the middle of summer. I already lived in San Lorenzo, so I had to piece the story together from bits I picked up from Brenda, Earl, and Lisbeth herself. Lauren didn't care. She said you have to use a little imagination to get at the truth.

Brenda remembered the heat. She said it was one of those days when the guests gather at the mouth of the cave to feel the cool cave-wind. It must have been even hotter down in Grants Pass where Lisbeth and Earl lived. Lisbeth was home with the six-week-old baby, sweltering, while Earl was off on his dirt-bike climbing hills near Lake Selmac.

Earl didn't have his car lot then, but there were always two or three cars in the yard. Usually, at least one of them would run. At around three o'clock, Lisbeth showed up at The Caves in one of the junk cars. She honked the horn, and Brenda went all the way out into the sun and talked to Lisbeth through the passenger-side window. The baby lay on the hot front seat, dirty, crying. Lisbeth asked Brenda, please, to watch him until suppertime so she could go to town to get her hair done. It didn't make much sense to Brenda for Lisbeth to drive all the way to The Caves to drop the baby just to get her hair done. Two round trips from Grants Pass to The Caves is over eighty miles of driving. But the baby looked so sweet and miserable, Brenda just wanted to get him out of the hot car. She said, "That's all I could think about, Marvin. That poor hot child." By the time she got the baby indoors and changed and cooled down and asleep, she'd convinced herself Lisbeth just needed some time alone. "Besides," she said, "her hair needed fixing pretty bad."

Lisbeth promised to be back by five, five-thirty at the latest.

At six o'clock, no Lisbeth.

Earl phoned Brenda because he was tired and hungry and hot, and he wanted to know if Lisbeth was coming home, or if he should come up to The Caves. Brenda said to come on up and that Lisbeth would be back for the baby any minute. She told him she'd tell Lisbeth to wait and they'd all eat on the deck when it cooled down some.

Brenda, Hank, Earl and my dad ate hamburgers and corn on the cob and watched The Caves Highway. They watched for Lisbeth's car as the cars slowly darkened behind their headlights and kept on watching after the headlights were all they could see in the pitch dark.

Brenda called JoAnn, who runs JoAnn's Beauty Parlor, and asked what time Lisbeth left the shop. JoAnn had never seen Lisbeth at all. Brenda started crying and told Hank to call the police and hospital, while Earl sat outside in the dark drinking beer, sulking. Hank made all the calls Brenda told him to make, but nobody knew anything about Lisbeth.

Brenda put Earl Jr. to bed in her room in a crib Hank had bought for their own baby who had died, and which she kept just in case the Lord let her have another.

Earl took a couple of beers up to the room Lisbeth kept for herself on the third floor of the Chateau. Brenda said he must have slept in his motorcycle riding clothes because the next morning she found the sheets covered with dust.

All this time Lisbeth was in Ashland, watching the people who had come to town to see the Shakespeare plays. She told me later—it was the following summer and we were sitting on a bench by the mouth of the cave after supper—that she'd sat in the park below the theater and watched the people walk up the paths.

"They seemed happy," she said. "All of them."

She was so relieved she felt like a pressure had been let loose from her chest. She watched a mother, all dressed up in a blue summer dress, lift her daughter up to the fountain to drink. It was beautiful, that time of night ("Just like now," she said.) the light going, but lingering on the grass and the fountain. Lisbeth imagined the water tasted like lemons.

She sat there until all the people had walked up through the trees to the theater, and it was dark. She told me it was an old-fashioned theater like they have in England, outdoors. She could hear the voices from the play, but she couldn't understand anything. It was like hearing the television from the other room, she said. But she waited there, eating nuts and drinking Coke, until the people came out. She watched them all stream down the narrow paths beneath the lights that were strung through the trees. She watched them cross the lawn in their summer sweaters, walk to their cars, to restaurants, stop to look in store windows. She felt herself again, seeing them, and so she got back in Earl's car and drove home.

Earl found her the next morning in their bed asleep, but he didn't wake her up. Lisbeth had become as much a mystery to Earl as she had to my dad and Brenda and Hank and me. He'd begun to live his own life with his dirt-bikes and his friends. It was better to let her sleep, he said, than to have her look at him the way she did; as though she had asked him a question and she was waiting for his answer. He put the baby to sleep in the crib beside their bed, took a shower, and went to work at his father's garage.

Brenda said Lisbeth would be all right. "It's from having the baby. It's natural," she said.

My father told me, "She's Earl's problem now."

The next time Lisbeth disappeared Earl went after her. It was during the summer the sawmills closed down and the ridge west of town caught fire and the valley darkened with smoke. Above the dam, planes swept down, skimmed the surface of the river, and rose with a scream back up toward the ridge. I imagine ashes dusting down on the streets of Grants Pass, ashes drifting down as slow as snow.

On the third day, Lisbeth left town. She took a bus to the coast looking for a motel with a swimming pool. Earl called Greyhound and talked to Doris. She told him that Lisbeth had ridden to Brookings on a one-way ticket. Earl took the boy up to The Caves and Brenda said he acted as though she and Lisbeth and Hank and my father and even Doris were all playing some kind of trick on him.

"I'll find her," he said. "You'll see."

In Brookings, Earl searched the motels. He told me, "There must've been a hundred of them." The Ebb Tide, The Mardi Gras, The Sea Shell, Motel 6, The Weeaskuinn, The Holiday Inn, The Typee, The Castle. Late in the day, he found her sitting at the edge of a swimming pool, her feet in the water.

Lisbeth told me she knew Earl would come. When she

heard his car door close, she turned, shading her eyes with her hand. He walked toward her through the little gate. The pool water cast spots of light onto his face, and he stood there, tall and awkward in his work shirt and boots. When he was directly above her, casting a shadow, she lowered her hand and said, "Is the fire out?"

Earl just nodded and walked over to the office to pay Lisbeth's bill.

Lisbeth was his problem now, but Earl could only take so much. The next time she ran away, he didn't chase her; he sent the police. This was after his father died and left him the garage. Earl sold used cars out of there for a couple of years, made good money, and moved his business into town to the old AMC showroom on G Street, and started selling Civics and Accords faster than he could get them delivered. He bought a house out on Rogue River Highway that sat at the end of a long, white rock drive. Wild blackberries grew in the yard, and the house was shaded by fifty-foot pines. He put in a swimming pool and cleared a road down to the river.

The afternoon Lisbeth left, Earl was down on the river road teaching Earl Jr. how to ride a motorcycle. Lisbeth told me that the miniature dirt-bike sounded like a chainsaw. From the kitchen window, she could see the blue smoke hovering over the road.

She didn't pack anything. She went to the bedroom and hunted through Earl's dresser. Now that he had money he liked to keep some close by so he could see it. Lisbeth found what she was looking for among his socks. A thousand dollars. While the minibike revved down by the river, Lisbeth escaped up the drive in one of Earl's Accords and turned south toward California.

This time, Earl had no choice. He called the police and reported a stolen car. He told my father that it belonged to the bank. It was not his to give her. The police stopped Lisbeth just outside Medford and brought her home before dark.

For the next three months she lived at The Caves. Brenda said Lisbeth spent most of her time up in her room, but when she came down, she seemed all right. On weekends, Earl brought Junior to visit his mother, and Brenda said she saw them sitting out on the benches in the shade with all the other families. But there was a kind of stillness around them that made them seem different than the others. Sometimes Junior would slip away and come in and watch television with Brenda behind the front desk. Earl and Lisbeth could sit out there for as long as an hour without a word passing between them. Brenda said she felt sorry for Earl for having to drive all that way for nothing. She could tell he wanted her to go home with him. Sometimes Earl and the boy stayed for dinner at the Chateau in the hopes that Lisbeth would change her mind and go with them, but she never did.

Days they didn't come to visit, Lisbeth sat in the lobby reading magazines. She wrote postcards to Earl Jr. Late afternoons, she shared a slice of apple pie with Tommy. She sat in the bar until midnight, but Brenda said the bartender claimed she hardly drank anything. He thought she just came down to listen to the music, to be with people. He said her ice often melted before she finished her drink and he had to toss it and make her a fresh one. It got to be a joke after a while, he said.

After Labor Day, the summer crew left, and during the first rains of October, Lisbeth went back to Earl.

EIGHT

We met at Moe's Books at noon as usual, and after Lauren paid for her paperbacks, we ducked into the cool gloom of a coffee shop on Telegraph Avenue. A room full of voices.

One was Lauren's, saying, "That feeling Lisbeth told you about, that pressure in her chest. I've felt like that. It's like dread and panic and sadness all mixed up."

I knew the feeling, too; I'd felt the aching weight of it since my sister died. But talking to Lauren about Lisbeth was one of the few things I'd found to ease that ache.

Lauren made it easy to talk. During that first month, she never took a note, she rarely pressed for details. Eventually, she became a devil for details, deducing that the first time

Lisbeth ran away was July 14, 1972 based on the fact that the baby was six months old and Earl's one day off from his father's garage was Sunday. She found out that the high temperature in Grants Pass that day was ninety-seven degrees. But during that first month we talked about Lisbeth the way we would have talked about a friend who introduced us and then moved to another state, a friend we both loved and missed.

When I asked Lauren about the pressure in her chest, her hand flew up. She waved my question away. "It just comes and goes," she said.

She seemed more nervous than usual. Her mysteries lay on the table between us, and she sat there fiddling with the books, rifling the pages. I guessed she hadn't slept much that night. That's what the mysteries were for; they put her to sleep sometimes, she said. But from what I saw, most nights they didn't. She rarely slept well. The night after I helped her move, the first time we slept together, we talked about my sister for a while. I dozed. When I woke up, Lauren wasn't in bed. I found her in the living room unpacking. It must have been three or four in the morning and she was up and dressed in her jeans and a T-shirt, padding around the place in her bare feet. We ate some cold pizza standing in the kitchen, and at dawn I drove home. Later, when I lived with her, she wrote most of the night or read or watched TV. When I begged her to come to bed, she'd say, "My nerves are working tonight." She complained of small pains: a crink in her neck, aching ankles, an itching sensation on her skin.

I worried about her at first, but then I noticed that she seemed almost comfortable with her discomforts. I thought that if she could learn to live with them, so could I. Actually, Lauren's insomnia helped her fit into the rhythm of my life. She slept from dawn until late in the morning, which is when I usually woke up. At about five or six in the afternoon, she tried again, and if she was lucky she'd sleep until almost closing time. Then she'd drive down to StoneS to meet me and we'd walk down to Brennan's for a drink and some talk, and finally I'd follow her taillights up to her apartment. We'd make love and I'd leave.

I remember driving home through the empty early morning Berkeley streets and the exhaustion I felt after talking about my sister, after loving Lauren.

After a couple of cups of coffee, we went for a drive in the Berkeley hills. This was another of our rituals. Lauren liked to drive, so we took her car. We snaked up Ascot under the acacia trees. The tiny yellow flowers collected under the windshield wipers and fluttered there like insect wings.

As we drove along Skyline, toward Asilomar Road, I watched her face closely, looking for some sign—a twitch, a glance—to show she knew that Gloria and the girls had been buried a half mile down that road. I didn't catch a clue. We swept past and drove on toward Tilden Park. But Lauren had to know. She'd driven me past that place a dozen times, and every time we approached Asilomar, I waited for her to slow and turn and take me to the ditches where they found my sister. Each time she drove past without a glance, I was grateful. My affection for her deepened. We both knew. We both kept quiet.

There was something intimate about passing Asilomar without a word. Gloria was our shared secret.

But that day, Lauren's silence seemed weighted, as though she drove with that aching pressure in her chest.

We parked at Skyline Gate, near the Big Trees Trails, our usual haunt. Lauren found her jacket in the back seat and got out of the car without even looking at me. A gray-haired woman and her muddy-muzzled beagle emerged from the trails. She recognized us and grinned hello. We often crossed paths with her on our afternoon walks and sometimes Lauren stopped to chat, but that day she barely nodded at the lady and walked on ahead of me, holding her jacket closed with crossed arms.

I said, "What's wrong with you?"

She kept walking. "It's nothing, Stone. I'm just thinking."

That's why she doesn't sleep, I thought, she thinks too much. My problem was that I didn't know her well enough to know what she was thinking about. Sometimes she seemed to carry the weight of Gloria's mystery as heavily as I did. Other times, I sensed something else bothering her. But what that was, I didn't know.

I wanted to stop her and hug her and somehow start our walk all over again, but I kept my hands in my coat pockets and waited. A high, cool sun cast shadows across the trail. It had rained the night before and the medicinal smell of eucalyptus hung in the air. I waited for Lauren to say something.

She kept me waiting for about a quarter mile before she said, "Last night I couldn't stop thinking about what your father said. That she was Earl's problem."

"She was Earl's wife," I said.

"But it's a strange way to put it, don't you think? To call your own daughter someone else's problem. What kind of problem was he talking about?"

"He was just frustrated," I said. "Like the rest of us."

"The rest of you guys weren't much better. Earl just letting her sleep. And Brenda blaming the whole thing on postpartum depression."

"Just at first," I said. "Brenda got really worried after a while."

"But it's like everybody just ignored her. It really upsets me to think about it. How they treated her."

"Nobody ignored her. We respected her privacy is all. What would you have us do?"

"Talk to her. Ask what was wrong."

"We did. We talked to her. But between times she was pretty normal."

"Between times." She said the words slowly, like she was thinking about those times—the every single day of Lisbeth's life—for the first time.

"Yes. Between times we thought, Okay, she's back, let's leave her alone. To me, her running away was like saying, leave me alone. So I did. We all did. Nobody wanted to bother her. It was like pressure was the last thing she needed. We hoped she was all right, that's all. We thought too many questions might make her run off again."

"But she talked to you, right?"

"Sure."

"She told you about Ashland. And waiting for Earl at that motel. The boy's minibike—how'd she put it?—like a chainsaw?—down by the river. It sounds to me like she wanted to talk to somebody."

"Sometimes. Sure. Sometimes, if she was in a certain mood, she'd say something, and you'd wait, thinking maybe this is it, maybe she'll say something to make everything make sense. But she'd get vague. It was like she'd get to a certain point and stop."

"She left her baby behind. Didn't that set off any alarms for you people?"

"Sure. We were worried."

"But nobody came right out and asked her what was wrong?"

"I'm sure Earl asked her."

"What did she tell him?"

"It was hot. Or the smoke choked her, hurt her eyes. Or the sound of the minibike made her nervous."

"In other words, she didn't tell him anything."

"Right," I said. "And he gave up."

"And you never asked her, 'Lisbeth, what's wrong?'"

"No," I said. "No, I never asked her."

"You didn't want to know."

"I did," I said. "It's just I never got the chance to ask."

"You were scared to ask her."

I said, "No. I wanted to ask her. But in the end, I didn't find her."

The old lie. Here, the first time Lauren pressed me, I told her my usual story. A reflex. I'd denied finding Lisbeth so often it almost felt true.

I went ahead and told Lauren about Ruth Haywood's call from Crescent City, how I drove up there to get Lisbeth's box. "She left a bunch of personal stuff there. In the Women's Room. But she was gone."

"Where?"

"I don't know. She was gone. All she left behind was this box. Ruth said Lisbeth asked for a job, but there wasn't a job open, I guess, so she left and Ruth thought that was the end of it until she found the box in the restroom and called me and I went up and got it."

"I see."

We walked without talking for a while. I remember the muddy trail, the sky-colored puddles.

"I hoped she'd come home on her own," I said. I felt like I was talking to myself.

"Yes," Lauren said.

"I mean we couldn't keep chasing her all over the place."

"No."

"She wasn't our prisoner or anything."

"No," Lauren said, "she wasn't."

We cut our walk short. Lauren said she wanted to go home. She didn't explain why or make any attempt to hide her disappointment at my not finding Lisbeth. Lauren walked back to her car enveloped in silence, while overhead the wind made a familiar moaning whisper sound in the trees.

We descended toward town, swept past Asilomar Road. On

Ascot, under the acacias, Lauren asked, "Have you ever been there?"

I knew where she meant. "No," I said. I'd seen the place on television, followed the quick panning of the camera from Tunney's son's outstretched arms to the exposed root of the oak. I'd seen men standing at the edge of the ditch with their heads bowed while other men struggled under the dead weight of a body bag. I'd glimpsed the place over a reporter's shoulder. But I hadn't been there. No.

"I have," she said.

She told me that before she came to see me, she drove up there. She felt drawn to the place, to Gloria. On Asilomar, the houses surprised her. On television, the place looked remote, deserted. The camera's tunnel vision and her own imagination had convinced her that Tunney had buried the girls miles from nowhere. She didn't recognize the place. When the road dead-ended, she turned around and drove back and parked in the most likely spot, a relatively deserted curving stretch about fifty yards from the nearest house. She'd studied the news footage until she saw it in her sleep, but nothing looked familiar. She got out of her car and walked up and down the side of the road. A ditch. Earth and water and trees. Shade. Sky. No different than a million other places in the world. She waited for some feeling to tell her, this is where they found Gloria. Here and only here. But nothing happened. No horror. No grief. Nothing. She just got in her car and drove back to the motel.

The next morning in the shower, she had a revelation: it doesn't matter where Gloria ended up, she thought, it just matters how she got there.

"That's how I found the courage to come see you," she said. When she met me, she felt what she expected to feel on Asilomar. She felt close to Gloria. She felt the awful hollow sense of loss. My loss.

She said, "When you talk about your sister, you talk about

Lisbeth. But there's a whole other level. There's Gloria. After talking to you, I feel like we've lost her again. I just wish you'd found her that last time. You might've found Gloria."

It was slow at StoneS that night. All evening I missed the relief I usually felt after talking about Lisbeth. I regretted lying to Lauren. I'd lied to Donna and lost her. During the years Lisbeth was lost, living as Gloria, the lie came between Donna and me. At the time, I didn't make the direct connection. I blamed the late nights at the restaurant. I blamed Barbara. But when Gloria was murdered and then accused of murder, I knew the lie was at the heart of everything. And I knew it was too late. The truth was too terrible to tell.

I lost my sister. I lost my wife and my son. I didn't want to lose Lauren.

After the short dinner rush, I found time to come to my office and call her.

"Stone?"

"Sorry," I said.

"What?"

"You were sleeping."

"Yes."

"Sorry."

"Don't worry. What's up?"

"I was wondering. Are you coming down tonight?"

"I'm tired. Really."

"Can I come up, do you think?"

"I was going to try and sleep tonight. Tomorrow. Moe's. Noon. All right?"

"I need to talk to you tonight," I said. "Tell you something."

"Tell me now."

"It's slow down here. I can come up now, if you want."

"Stone. What is it?"

"I just wanted to tell you."

"What?"

"I just wanted to tell you I found her."

"What are you talking about?"

"That last time. I found her in Eureka."

"Your sister?"

"Yes."

NINE

□

In the hills above Eureka, I parked in front of a white house and searched the place for signs of Lisbeth. That guy Ruth Haywood told me about—Johnny, at Great Days—hadn't hired her, but he'd taken her name and address and promised to get in touch if a shift opened up. This was the address Lisbeth gave him. The car at the end of the drive was an old blue Impala, not one of Earl's Hondas. A bicycle leaned against the rock foundation, its fenders catching the low sunlight. Beside it, on a ragged patch of grass, a black mound smoldered. Smoke rose, white against a dark stand of cedars, and drifted into the lower branches of the trees.

When I got out of the car, for the first time I felt as though I were in the country. The dry wind smelled of smoke, and high in the trees it made a rushing sound I hadn't heard in a year. A dog barked inside the house, and a high, girlish voice drifted out, "Dixie, please, Dixie!" The woman opened the door before I had a chance to knock. "Hi yah." She had the corn silk hair of a Swede and skin so pale it glowed in the shadows of the porch.

I said, "Does Gloria Simpson live here?" That was only the second time I'd used that name, and the skin under my eyes tingled, like it always does when I lie.

"Who are you?"

The dog kept barking.

I kept on lying. "A friend," I said. "I just want to talk to her."

"What kind of friend? Dixie! Hush!"

"An old friend. Don't worry. She'll talk to me."

The woman led me back across the porch to the side of the house and pointed at a small camper-trailer parked on a patch of concrete just beyond a vegetable garden. "Tell her to let me look at that hand tomorrow. It'll need another bandage."

I looked at her.

"She burned it. This morning. Pretty bad," the girl said.

After Lisbeth opened the door, I still couldn't see her face. The screen remained closed and it caught the light like a thousand tiny silver windows too small to see through.

"How'd you find me?"

"The woman from Crescent City called. It wasn't hard."

"I changed my name," she said.

"Yeah," I said. "I know. Can I come in?"

Lisbeth unlocked the screen and pushed it open.

I sat at the little fold-up table while Lisbeth stood with her back to me making coffee. She poured two cups with her left hand. Her right hand, wrapped in a gauze mitten, was cradled below her breasts. A loud rattling filled the trailer as Lisbeth hunted for spoons in a tin beside the sink.

"What happened?"

"This?" Lisbeth held the bandaged hand up for me to see.

"You burned it?"

"Yeah." She put a cup on the table, then the spoon. "I was burning some things," she said. "I guess I wasn't careful."

"That woman said to let her see it tomorrow."

Lisbeth sat down across from me. "She's been real sweet," she said.

I was surprised how much she'd changed since I'd seen her last. She'd bleached her hair light blond, and now she looked as much like a Swede as the woman up at the house. Her face and neck had grown soft, as though swollen. But it was her mouth that surprised me the most. The buckteeth she had as a girl had seemed to recede when she was a teenager until they just parted her lips. Those days, at first glance, she always looked like she was smiling. But now, the faintly parted lips and the line that ran from her nostrils to the corners of her mouth gave her a pained and distracted expression.

"I've got your stuff in the car," I said.

She nodded. "You can take it to Earl. He might want it."

"I've come to take you home, Lisbeth."

"No," she said. She pulled her lip down over her teeth. "I'm not going back this time."

"You have to, Lisbeth."

"No, I don't. I've changed my name. I've got my own car. They can't make me."

I said, "You can't stay here."

"I'm not staying here." She sat there picking at the edge of her bandage with her fingernail. She looked out the window.

"Come on, Lisbeth, what's wrong?"

"Nothing's wrong now," she said.

"You can just leave him, if you want. You don't have to do all this."

Lisbeth looked at me again. "Earl? Everybody thinks it's Earl. You should hear Brenda. She wanted to know if he hit me."

"Well, does he?"

"No." She kept picking at the ragged fringe of gauze at her wrist. "Earl's all right."

"Then I don't understand," I said.

"It doesn't matter. Nobody understands." She looked at me. "Who sent you?"

"I told you. The lady in Crescent City called."

"But who told you to come? Earl?"

"Nobody told me to come. I wanted to find you."

"Dad didn't send you?"

"He wanted me to find you, sure."

"What did he say?"

"He said to try and find you. He wants you to come home."

She sat there picking at that bandage for a while. Then she said, "When I was staying at The Caves, Brenda asked Reverend Rice to come talk to me. It was kind of cute. He asked me about Earl and I told him Earl was all right. We were sitting in the coffee shop at the counter eating Tommy's pie. I could tell the Reverend didn't believe me about Earl. He had these bushy eyebrows, you know. They went up and down when he talked, and I could tell just what he was thinking. He was thinking that Earl couldn't really be all right or I wouldn't run off all the time. I let him think that. I said to myself, let him think anything he wants. In the end he gave Brenda the name of a psychologist in Medford, but she threw it out. She was shook up for a week thinking I was crazy."

I couldn't look at her anymore. I couldn't stand to see her picking at that bandage, or watch the way her lip moved when she talked, or look at her bleached hair. I looked out the window, listening. The long mountain dusk had set in. The back of the house seemed to glow, and I could see into the lighted kitchen. While Lisbeth talked, I watched for the quick passes of the Swedish woman. Then it was quiet for a long time.

"Well, what the hell do you want us to think?" I said.

"Think what you want."

"I think we've got a problem, is what I think. You've got to let us help. You can't just run off all the time."

"You can't help me."

"Why not? You can stay with Donna and me."

"Nuh uh."

"Lisbeth."

"I'll leave again. And next time you won't find me. What are you going to do? Lock me up?"

"Yeah, maybe."

"Please, Marvin."

"Stay with Donna and me."

"No, Marvin. Just let me go."

So that's what I did. After dark I drove Lisbeth down to the highway and we had supper in a bright diner. We didn't talk much, but she told me she wanted to live in California, near the ocean. I had to ask her how she felt about leaving Earl Jr. behind. I'd been watching Donna with Daniel for a year, and I thought I knew a little about mothers and their boys. Lisbeth told me that Earl Jr. was like his daddy, he could take care of himself. "His daddy made him that way," she said.

On the way back to her place we stopped and bought more gauze and salve for her hand, and coffee and some rolls for the morning. I carried the sack down to her trailer for her. She unlocked the door and took the bag with her good hand. "Thanks, Marvin," she said.

I said, "I don't feel good about this."

"Don't worry."

"I will," I said, "and Brenda will, and Earl and Dad and everybody."

"I don't know what to say, Marvin. I'm just sorry you had to find me."

When Lisbeth was called Sissy, she had a disturbing way of crying. She screamed once as the ball hit her, or the fish hook gouged her hand, or as she rose, stunned, after falling off her bicycle. Then she was silent, inhaling, her face screwed up and red, just like she was screaming out loud. For a minute, I thought she'd never catch her breath. Her silent scream stretched out a heart beat or two longer than seemed possible. And when the real scream came, it was a relief to hear, as it died into sobs.

I remembered this later that night when I was lying on the bed at the motel. I had to call Donna, but I just lay there watching TV. I was thinking. My head and whole body tingled, like the way you feel after having three quick drinks. Lisbeth was too calm, too detached. She was outside herself somewhere, looking at herself, like a woman in a movie hiding in the shadows watching a burglar hunting through her house.

Just before midnight, I called Donna. "Hey," I said.

"Marvin?"

"Yeah, Sweetness. Everything all right?"

"Fine. Yeah. Did you find her?"

"No," I said. "I got her box."

"Where are you?"

"In a motel. In Eureka. I was here looking for her, but she's gone."

"I'm sorry, Marvin."

"Maybe she'll come back by herself," I said.

"Yeah. Marvin? You sound funny. What's wrong?"

"I'm tired, I guess."

"Disappointed?"

"Uh huh. How's Daniel?"

"He's fine. He's asleep. He misses you."

"How can you tell?"

"I can tell. I wish I were with you, Marvin."

"Yeah," I said. "I wish you were, too."

In the morning I drove east over to I-5 and took the freeway toward Grants Pass. I got off at Whitebridge. There's a real bridge there, painted white. It crosses the Rogue about eight miles south of town, and when I was a kid, returning from vacations with Dad and my mother and Lisbeth, crossing Whitebridge meant we were home. And later, going back to San Lorenzo, I'd drive south beside the river, past the dam and the power station, and then I'd come to Whitebridge. After I passed it, I wasn't home anymore. That morning, I crossed it again, and drove past the familiar fruit stands and motels and restaurants, and on toward Earl's place.

Nobody answered the door. I followed the sound of a motorcycle down to the river road, where I found Earl Jr. He was all dressed up in knee-high leather boots and a bright red jersey that matched the paint on his gas tank. He told me his father was in town at the car lot. I thought he might ask me about his mother, but he didn't. When I said thanks, he just nodded and revved off toward the river, his front wheel in the air.

I carried Lisbeth's box through the bright lights and new car smell of Earl's showroom, into his office. I laid it on his desk.

"Why didn't you call me?" I said.

Earl stood up. Even in his three-piece suit and his blow-dried hair, he still looked like a cave guide, like he was just getting used to the light. With a salesman's reflexes, he offered me his big right hand, and said, "Marvin."

I shook his hand and waited.

"I knew what you were calling about," he said, finally. He looked at the box. "Did you find her?"

"No," I said. "The lady at the restaurant found this stuff."

"Brenda told me something about that."

"You talked to her?"

He nodded. "She said you went looking for her. I told her, fine. I said I hoped you found her. For her sake and your father's. But, to tell you the truth, Marvin, I gave up. After I had to send the police after her, I said, that's it. Next time, she can just go."

I could understand how he felt. As a matter of fact, I was counting on him feeling that way.

I said, "I saw Junior."

"What did he say?"

"Nothing. I mean, nothing about his mother."

"He wouldn't, I don't guess. He never was too close to her, you know. Even when he was a little kid, first, second grade, he used to come here after school. Almost never went home on the bus with the other kids."

Earl asked me to sit down. "You want some coffee or something?"

I sat down, but I said, "No, I want to go up to The Caves pretty quick."

He lifted the box off his desk and put it on the floor behind him. "It feels like she's been gone a long time already. I couldn't talk to her anymore, Marvin. When I first met her, when I was driving for your dad, I used to pick her up in Grants Pass. It was my favorite part of my job, I'll tell you. All those miles of winding road, I felt like I was the luckiest guy in the world to have her in that truck with me. She smelled good. That's what I remember. How the whole cab used to fill up with her smell. And she was so pretty and lively. She really loved to laugh. Do you remember?"

I remembered.

"And she was interested in everything. I used to test her on the names of cars and motorcycles. It got so she could tell the size of a bike by the sound of its engine. And she could sing. She used to make me laugh singing along to the radio. But she could really sing, if she tried. When she was riding with me, I never wanted to get to The Caves. But she changed after Junior was born."

He stopped talking and looked out the glass wall at his showroom. He shook his head. "No. It was even before, when she was pregnant. She got quiet. It was gradual. One day she was all right. The next day she was a little quieter than normal. I didn't notice at the time. I didn't know what was happening. Maybe it was before she was pregnant. I don't know. I wasn't paying attention and she drifted away."

We talked some more, but not about Lisbeth. Earl told me business was good, as usual. A lot of people were coming all the way from California to avoid the sales tax. He sent his best to Donna and Daniel, and he thanked me for looking for his wife.

I spent the night at The Caves. When I told Brenda that I hadn't found Lisbeth, she didn't cry or even fret too much. But she didn't feel like eating with us. She said she was tired, and early in the evening, she and Hank went up to their rooms above the gift shop.

Dad said, "Brenda's been sick over this thing. Worse than ever." My father is completely bald. When he's distracted he rubs the top of his head. He was sitting at his desk, holding his head as though it ached.

"She might come home on her own," I said.

He looked at me, surprised. I could tell what he was thinking. His wife checked out of the Chateau. Every summer his young lovers left him. Now Lisbeth was gone again. He said, "Hank tells her that. I tell her that myself, Marvin. But this time. I don't know. This time I don't believe it."

But I believed it. I had to hope she'd come home. It was the only way I could justify lying to everybody. And I believed it right up to the night Gloria was on the news.

TEN

They didn't want you to find her."

That's what Lauren told me. She was sitting at her desk wearing the jeans and V-neck sweater she'd thrown on after my phone call. Her hair was wild from trying to sleep, but her face was calm, thoughtful.

She said, "If Earl wanted Lisbeth back, he would've gone after her himself. Same with your father."

Her voice sounded tentative, whispery; it was the voice she used when she was thinking. "Brenda would've sent Hank if she thought bringing Lisbeth back would do any good."

"But I found her," I said. "I let her go."

"You just did what they all wanted to do. They all wanted to let her go. But none of them could admit it. Just say, let's let

Lisbeth go. You knew that would never happen. You knew it would've been better for everybody if you didn't find her. So you lied. For Gloria. And for them."

"And for myself," I said, still full of the urge to confess.

Lauren shrugged. "Sure. For yourself most of all."

I wanted to be forgiven. Even more, I wanted Lauren to forgive me, but I'd felt too guilty for too long for her to just shrug it off. Her conclusions seemed too easy. It was like she was only thinking about her book, like she was just trying to make sense of something that didn't make any sense. She had no idea how I felt living with this all the time, and I couldn't explain it to her. It was like my mind refused to think too deeply about Lisbeth, so I was in a constant state of confusion. Lauren might have understood if I'd told her that remembering Lisbeth made me feel like I was in the cave. Summer nights when I was a kid, some of the guides and I would go spelunking far from the trails we led the tourists through. We moved around slowly, led by the beams of our flashlights. I could sense the huge cavern around me, but all I could see lay in the narrow strip of light at my feet. That's how I felt talking about my sister to Lauren.

Suddenly, I knew something: it was closing time. Slouched in Lauren's low overstuffed reading chair, I could smell my restaurant. The odors clung to me: smoke and the aroma of garlic; the tangy sweetness of tomatoes. I thought of Ronson closing alone. When I'd left early, all agitated and distracted, he'd given me a wary ironical look that meant, Be careful.

Until I told Lauren, Ronson was the only living soul who knew I let Lisbeth go. I told him just after my sister died, during that crazy time when I was still sleeping with Barbara. It was the night his lady friend, Peaches, showed up at the restaurant with a knife. She waited for Ronson in the parking lot. In the light from the street and from headlights swinging in smooth and random arcs, I could see her leaning against the restaurant wall, one hand buried deep in her purse, the strap tight on her shoulder. I watched Ronson walk straight up to her. He reached in his front pocket and pulled out a roll of bills and dropped it in her hand without even looking at it. He just watched her face, the pout on her lips, in her eyes. I'd seen that look before—on Lisbeth. Peaches's eyes said this was more than a matter of money, but her knife hand stayed in her purse. Ronson looked out toward the traffic at the stoplight. A dog barked. I could hear, in the distance, the wailing sound of a siren. Peaches turned on her high heels and made her way between the cars in the parking lot. Ronson watched her go, his face mask-like under the floodlights.

By ten, ten-thirty that night, business died down to a handful of regulars, and the waiters sat together near the kitchen, drinking coffee. I started drinking early, sharing beers with Ronson, and we kept on drinking after closing time when the waiters were finished cleaning up and the boys from the kitchen came out to join the fun. I turned the tape player up: Lester Young playing "All of Me." Ronson knew the words and sang along. After the song was over, he kept saying, "Take my lips, I'll never use them." The guys all laughed. It was almost one o'clock before I calmed down and got everybody else calmed down and on their way home so I could close the restaurant. Ronson stayed behind to keep me company. He sat at the bar with his cap on, drinking bourbon now, and watched me wash glasses.

When the phone rang, Ronson grinned at me. Then he began to laugh; even drunk he knew who it was.

"What are you doing?" It was Barbara, using her boss's voice.

"Closing up."

"It's one. It's after one."

"I had a couple beers with the guys."

"Is everything all right?"

"Everything's fine. It was slow is all."

"I see," she said. Then her voice went soft. "Are you coming over?"

Two or three times a week, I'd close the restaurant and drive to the hills to sleep with Barbara. The first time was about a year before, a rainy night, dead-slow. Barbara waited at the bar, sipping vodka, while I went through my whole closing routine: double checked the kitchen, set the alarms, turned on the night-lights, opened the curtains.

Outside, the rain had died to a mist. The surface of the parking lot gleamed under the floodlights. Barbara leaned against me and reached in under my jacket. As we kissed, she pressed me against the door of her car.

"Follow me," she said.

I followed her up the winding roads, listening to the radio, rehearsing my story for Donna. I believed she would believe me, so my story was simple. *I went to Brennan's with a couple of guys.* After lying to her about Lisbeth, a small lie like that didn't seem to matter.

In Barbara's yard, rainwater dripped, crackling, through the magnolia leaves. In bed, I told her I'd wanted to sleep with her forever, as her eyes closed beneath me, and she whispered, "Oh yes, oh yes, oh yes, oh yes."

No, I told Barbara. I wasn't coming up; it was too late.

Ronson and I locked the place and then drove up University to the liquor store, where he jumped out and bought a bottle of Ten High bourbon and more Camels, and then I drove onto the freeway and off again into the dark streets near the factories to a reggae bar called Michael's Place. I sat at the bar watching people dance under the flickering lights while Ronson disappeared into the men's room with a blond, pretty woman who reminded me of my sister. In the quiet moment after the music stopped and before the voices rose up, the woman returned to the bar. And then Ronson appeared with the cocaine, happy at last.

In my kitchen, he leaned back in a straight-backed chair with his head against the blue-flowered wallpaper. He talked and I listened. His voice seemed to sing with the cocaine and bourbon, deep and rhythmic. I heard with a rare clarity, as though the words hadn't traveled through air, but had risen to my ears along the flesh of my neck.

He said the preachers were right and the world was going to burn in the end like Hiroshima and that he had a woman in New Orleans who was rich and long-legged, who had seen flying saucers off the Gulf Coast disturbing the water like a storm. He said that women knew things that men would never know because they were tied into the cycles of the moon, like the sea itself. Women were a curse, like the Bible said, and even a white woman he lived with once in Chicago was crazy and couldn't stcp crying for more than ten minutes at a time. The Chicago Seven were betrayed by a woman who worked for the FBI. Every great man was ruined by a woman. Look at Huey Newton. Look at the way Peaches was acting in front of strangers. Look at the restaurant. Run by a woman and doomed to fail because women are blind in a man's world and only feel the way the world moves with some kind of sense they have in their center, their womb, that fills them with fear and makes them cry like that woman he knew in Chicago. But cocaine was something wonderful and as long as it was around he didn't care what women cried about, or if Peaches thought she could come down to the restaurant he worked in and act crazy. Preachers will be right in the end no matter what happens and women know it more than men ever will. That's why they do stuff like Peaches did. It's all tied to this thing called hysteria, he said. Only women get it and most men don't understand it, except preachers, because they're like women being close to God and all. But white guys never even get a clue, he said, and I sure was lucky to have him for a friend because wisdom of that kind was hard to come by.

Ronson hardly stopped talking long enough to breathe. He talked even while cutting his lines, leaning over the mirror, using all the harsh kitchen light to see by, still talking away.

I wanted to talk about Lisbeth. After seeing that look on Peaches's face, after watching Ronson watch her walk away, I thought he'd understand.

It was easy to talk. The words rose up, defying gravity. The cocaine shimmered like light in my head and I saw the whole mysterious sequence of events moving like a movie toward its ending. I told Ronson about the House of Haywood, Lisbeth's bandaged hand, her bleached hair. How one summer the heat had seemed to slow her blood, and she was never the same. I told him she changed her name to Gloria. I told him I lied for her. I told him about Tunney. About the girls.

Ronson was still leaning against the wall. His face caught the kitchen light, his cheeks and forehead shining. He looked suddenly sober. He blinked, as though the light hurt his eyes. He couldn't look at me. When he finally spoke, he said, "I bet you I can tell you the time. Exactly."

The clock was on the wall behind him. I looked up at it.

Ronson said, "It's four-forty-five in the morning."

That's how bad it got: all my lies since I'd let Lisbeth go had led me there. To that kitchen in the middle of the night.

Ronson never made me regret my coked-up confession. He never mentioned Gloria again.

I pushed myself out of Lauren's chair. I wanted to get back to StoneS before Ronson finished closing. I wanted to show him that I was in control of myself, that I could count my own money, put my place in order, lock my own doors. I wanted to tell him, *Look, I told her, but everything's all right.*

Lauren said, "Stay."

"It's late."

She rose from her chair and held me, hugged me. "Please."

"I've got to close."

"I want you to stay. Stay. I want you to."

How could I show Ronson I was in control of myself, when I wasn't? I wasn't any more in control than I was the night I told him about Gloria.

I stayed, and Lauren and I made tentative, whispery love. We moved on the bed as though the sheets were the surface of a pool we didn't want to disturb. I felt like I did whenever Lauren and I drove past Asilomar, both of us knowing Gloria had been buried down that road, neither of us saying a word.

Lauren went there looking for something, some feeling. That's why she wanted me to stay: so she could feel something: my horror, my grief. But that night, I felt as though things balanced out. I stayed with Lauren so that I could share my sorrow with her.

I'd told her.

I'd told her, and it was like I'd let Gloria go again. It was like she disappeared again; we didn't know anything. Nothing. How did she meet Tunney? What was her life like as Gloria? The day by day of it? And how did the day by day of it lead to death?

I'd told Lauren everything, and now we knew nothing together. I wanted to hold her and go on holding her until we knew something.

Lauren lay with her head on my chest. She said, "I love the way you smell."

"You're kidding me."

"I do. You smell like a kitchen full of steaming pots. I swear I could eat you."

I pictured my place: the parking lot empty, my sign gone dark, Ronson gone.

"What now?" I said.

"What?"

"I told you everything."

"Yes. I'm glad."

"I mean we don't know anything really. She disappeared. After I let her go, she was gone."

"She wasn't gone," Lauren said. "She was Gloria."

ELEVEN

For the next few weeks, Lauren slept more than ever. Nights I worked late, she called me close to closing time and asked me to come over, but when I got there I found her asleep in the light of her bedside lamp, her mystery under the covers. She woke only to make love and fell asleep so soon afterward that in the morning she said she'd dreamed about me.

During that time she was hungry for Mexican food, movies, and the blues. Almost every other night, I ducked out of my place after the rush and drove up to the U.C. Theater. I pushed my five toward a serious bearded boy who hardly looked up from his book as he slid the dollar and torn ticket back at me. Then I slipped through the lobby and found

Lauren waiting in the last row, saving the aisle seat for me. Most nights I missed most of the movie, but I didn't care. I just liked the idea that she was waiting for me. I liked that first touch of her cool hand in the dark.

She showed up at StoneS one night all hot to go to El Gordo's. Burritos and beer. Afterward, we drove up toward the campus to the Rathskeller and watched the college kids dance beneath the low basement ceiling. Lauren begged me to dance, but I just laughed, so she asked a tall, bushy-headed, half-starved looking guy who she said reminded her of her brother. Dancing, she was suddenly not gawky at all. She closed her eyes and let the blue beat move through her. The longer I watched her, the lighter Lauren seemed. If the ceiling hadn't been so low, she could've risen up and flown around the room. I saw something I'd never seen in Lauren before. Call it grace.

She came back to the table smelling faintly of sweat, took a long swallow of beer, and confessed that her most secret desire was to be Janis Joplin. She leaned across the table and sang to me. "*Take another little piece of my heart now baby.*"

We didn't talk about Gloria that night. Lauren was curious about Donna, but I tried to shy away from questions about her. I was surprised to find that it was harder for me to talk with Lauren about Donna than it was to talk to her about my sister. The plain fact was that I still loved Donna, and I wasn't comfortable with Lauren knowing. It was easier for me to talk about Barbara and my coked-up nights with Ronson. Lauren loved hearing those stories. "She *gave* you the restaurant?" she said. "That's something." She raised her beer bottle and made a mocking toast.

"The place wasn't much back then," I said. "She wasn't giving me much."

"Still. She gave it to you. Nobody ever gave me anything."

Lauren told me about her last lover, a professor in Santa

Cruz, a musicologist, who looked a little like me, she said. "What is it about you gray-beards?" He was married to a scientist of some kind, and he had a deaf daughter. "I saw him for three years. Well, five actually, if you count all the times he tried to call it off and we didn't see each other for a while." He always called again, though. Let's have coffee, he'd say, which meant let's spend the afternoon on the couch in his office making love while Debussey played on the stereo. He told Lauren he wanted to leave his wife and marry her, but he couldn't leave his daughter. Lauren didn't believe him. "He used to say his wife would never let him take his record collection if he left her. I mean he has hundreds of records, this man. Forget the daughter. He didn't want to leave his music, if you ask me." Lauren claimed she didn't care if he ever left his wife; she knew what she was getting into when she started seeing him. "Besides," she said, "I'd never marry a man who cheated on his wife."

I heard her, but I missed her message altogether. I didn't see myself as that kind of guy, despite the fact that I'd just spent an hour talking about Barbara. I'd been swept away by extraordinary circumstances. If my sister hadn't been killed, I don't think I would've had anything to do with Barbara.

Much to this man's surprise, Lauren called it quits with him a few weeks before moving to Berkeley. "I was looking for an excuse to get away from him," she said. "My book worked well, excuse-wise." Sonia had promised not to tell him where Lauren was, but Lauren had gotten an unlisted phone number just in case he tracked her down somehow, just in case he wanted to come to Berkeley for another cup of coffee.

In the morning Lauren asked me to drive her downtown in the restaurant van. I helped her carry seven cardboard boxes full of copies of court documents and police records across Seventh Street. We made a stack of them in the corner of her office that was almost as tall as I am. That afternoon, Lauren wrote a letter to Tunney, a short type-written note on university stationery, saying that she wanted to talk to him about his relationship with Gloria for a paper she was writing. (I looked. I listened. But I never saw or heard the name Lisbeth in any of Lauren's Tunney material.)

Tunney wrote back maybe a month later, saying several people had contacted him about interviews, and he'd turned them all down. He was too tired to talk. He wrote that nothing exhausts a man more than death row. Only someone who had been through what he'd been through would understand just how tired he was of the whole matter. He said he was sorry he couldn't help. He hoped she understood.

Lauren was surprised he wouldn't talk. During his trial he talked to anyone who would listen. She went ahead and wrote her paper without his help, relying on the court papers, police reports, newspaper accounts, magazine articles, and tapes of local news broadcasts. I knew she spent most afternoons working on it, but she didn't mention it much. When I asked her about it, she acted secretive. She said, "It's nothing." When I pressed her, she snapped back, "I don't want to talk about it, all right? Don't worry." She told me to just relax about Gloria.

One afternoon I was over at Lauren's watching a baseball game with the sound turned down while she worked behind the closed French doors. I sat on the couch with Bird on my lap. I kept glancing in there, and I could see her shuffling her papers. Without the sound, I kept losing track of the count, the outs, but I do remember that Lauren was wearing canary yellow socks.

Just when I was beginning to think about heading down to the restaurant, she came out of her office. "Hot off the press," she said, as she handed me her essay. "Sexual Murder as Male Transcendence," it was called. I sat back and read it while Lauren watched the game. There was a short sketch of the facts of the case, but it was mostly philosophy. Man as subject, woman as object—that kind of thing. When I asked her if her book was going to be that dense, she laughed. No, she was just laying down the theoretical groundwork.

She sent a copy of the paper to Tunney along with a note saying she understood how tired he must be, but if he ever changed his mind, he could contact her at the above address.

I thought, if she wanted to develop her theories, fine, but I wanted to get on with our search for Gloria. Be patient, she told me, but I had no patience in me. For years, I hadn't wanted to know, and now that I was ready to know what happened to Gloria, now that Lauren had made me want to know, she was telling me to be patient. I didn't like it.

And I didn't understand it. Why, after weeks of pressing me to help her, was Lauren suddenly so reluctant to talk about Gloria? All I could think of were those days she waited at The Golden Bear Motel gathering the courage to come down to StoneS to talk to me. What was she waiting for?

One night she called the restaurant. "I'm at Brennan's," she said.

My place was packed. "I've got a crowd," I told her.

"When things calm down, can you come?" She used that tentative, whispery voice.

"What's wrong?"

"Nothing. I mean, I just want to talk."

"What happened?"

"Nothing. Don't worry. I'll wait."

I looked at my clipboard. "Maybe an hour," I said.

"I'll wait."

I couldn't go anywhere until I got the people seated. If I'd had a spare bartender, I would have handed the list to Ronson and walked down to Brennan's right away. But the only other guy who could mix drinks was working a full station of tables that I wanted turned as soon as possible. I let him go on working. That was my quickest ticket out of there.

What did she want to talk about that couldn't wait until

midnight? And I didn't like that *I've-been-thinking* tone in her voice, either.

After I got the last party seated, I ducked out the back door and started across my parking lot. A horn tooted. Once. Two times. I stopped and looked around. A couple dozen dark cars. Then headlights flashed on. I could see a hand waving out of the driver's side window. It was Lauren's Datsun.

"Get in," she said.

In the front seat, I said, "What's wrong with Brennan's?"

"Hanging around bars by myself. I don't like it."

"You could've come in."

"And have Ronson glower at me. No thanks."

"So you sit in the car."

"Waiting patiently." She started the engine. "Now I'm taking you for a ride."

She drove up University without a word and turned right at Shattuck; she wasn't going home.

I said, "What's going on?"

"I've been thinking," she said. And that was all she said for several blocks.

"You've been thinking."

"It's been hard, Stone." She squinted hard at the traffic. "With me being busy. You working all the time."

"What do you mean, hard?"

She took Alcatraz, and I knew where she was going. She pulled to a stop under the yellow light of the Winchell's sign. We both sat there looking up at my apartment house.

"I mean it's hard with you sort of lurking around all the time."

"You call me. Are you coming up? you say."

"I know. I want you to come. It's just."

"What am I supposed to do?" I said. "You call me and then nothing's happening. We're supposed to be getting a picture of Gloria. And nothing's happening."

Lauren put both hands at the top of her steering wheel, laid her forehead on her hands.

"It isn't Gloria," she said.

"What isn't?"

"Everything isn't Gloria. I'm not talking about her. I'm talking about *me.* And *you.*"

"I don't lurk," I said.

She pushed herself away from the wheel and looked at me. "I'm talking about us, Stone. I want things to be different. I don't want to have you just hanging around waiting for me to do something. You make me nervous."

"But we don't know anything about her."

"I'm not talking about her!"

"You're talking about me. I make you nervous."

"Yes. Just waiting for me to do something."

"And you want things to be different. How different?"

She ran her hand around the steering wheel. She tapped it a couple of times with her fingernail. "I want you to live with me," she said.

I stared through the windshield at my apartment house. I don't remember what I was thinking. I was too surprised to think. Now, I know what was going on: I'd been pressing her too hard. Lauren must have begun to feel as though my desire to know what happened to my sister was stronger than my desire to be with her, and she didn't like the idea of being used any more than I did.

"I want you to move in," Lauren said. "I want you to get your stuff and bring it to my house and move in."

I looked at her. Her hair shined golden in the glow of the Winchell's sign. Her face was as calm and thoughtful as it was the night I told her about letting Lisbeth go.

"Go," she said. "Just go upstairs and get something. I don't care what. Just something."

"Now? Tonight?"

"Tonight. Yes. Right now. I want to feel like you're living with me. You can get the rest later. Go on, all right? Please?"

I climbed the stairs to my apartment and found a brown paper bag and filled it with my bathroom stuff. My moccasins. A mug. I looked around the room for something else. But what? Nothing I owned seemed worth carrying down the stairs. After Donna asked me to leave, I needed a place to stay; it was supposed to be temporary, but I stayed in that studio for almost three years, living a temporary life.

For the first year, I hoped Donna would take me back. I saw her fairly often. I visited Daniel in the afternoons before work, and on my rare nights off, we—all three of us—went to movies or out for ice cream. Donna and I came close to some kind of understanding. Then Barbara gave me the restaurant, and I started working sixteen hours a day, seven days a week. What the hell was I thinking? I knew that if I wanted Donna to take me back, I would have to tell her the truth, but I couldn't tell her that I'd let Lisbeth go. I didn't believe she would forgive me. I couldn't forgive myself.

I remember waking up one morning—no, it wasn't morning; it was almost two in the afternoon—about six months after Barbara gave me the place. I didn't feel as though I'd slept all night. I lay in a bar of sunlight, my sheets felt hot to the touch. My legs burned, my face felt moist with sweat, and there was a burning sensation in my chest, like an urge to weep. I looked out the window at the smooth, cream-colored wall across the way. I wanted to take a shower, to get the stink off, to cool the burning sensation across my shoulders, but I just lay there for an hour watching the wall next door, thinking about Donna and Daniel. I hadn't seen either of them in weeks.

After my shower, I dressed in clean clothes. I wanted everything to be clean and in order. I made my bed. Then I drove to the high school where Donna was teaching geometry. I drove up the long driveway past the blue and white buses. Down the hill, kids were finding seats in the grandstand, and the lights above the football field were shining darkly against a stone-blue sky. I walked through the crowd of kids rushing toward the grandstand and buses. Near the buildings there were fewer students. In the quiet halls, I could hear my footsteps echoing.

I wanted Donna back. I wanted to be with my boy, and I didn't care what I had to do or say. I was even willing to tell her the truth.

But Donna's classroom was empty. For a moment, I hoped I was in the wrong room, but I wasn't. I stood in the doorway, studying the blackboard. It was covered with geometry—triangles, circles, cubes, numbers. It was all a confusion to me. The only thing I understood were the two words written in Donna's schoolteacher handwriting: Given and Thus.

About a month later, a man came in the restaurant at opening time, laid the divorce papers on the bar, and walked out. Six months after the thing was final, Donna married a teacher, a man named Nicholini, and moved to New Mexico.

Standing there in the middle of my studio, I promised myself that I would try to always, always tell Lauren the truth. I looked around at my cheap furniture: a table and chairs from the restaurant, a rickety TV stand, the dresser I'd begun to strip and never finished, the tightly made twin bed. I felt like I was just taking a last glance around a motel room to see if I'd left anything behind. I was checking out.

Like Lisbeth. The last time she left, she looked around Earl's place for something to take and found Junior's pictures, his report cards, various documents. Maybe she had to take something with her to feel like she was leaving for good, like Lauren needed me to bring something to her place so she could feel like I was really moving in. By the time Lisbeth was safely away in California, her box had served its purpose, and she left it at the House of Haywood.

I remembered that box, set on Ruth Haywood's table, and her bitten-lip look as she took up Earl Jr.'s pictures. Everything in that box pointed back to Lisbeth's life in Oregon; her name was all over everything. Even Ruth Haywood knew that Lisbeth wanted somebody to find her.

I hit the light, locked the door. I was gone.

As I descended the stairs, my sack of stuff under my arm, I thought, But they didn't want me to find her.

It suddenly made sense: Lauren was right, we all wanted to let Lisbeth go.

Lauren waited for me with her engine running, the radio on. I tossed my sack in the backseat and climbed in and kissed her on the forehead. "You're right," I said.

She put her car in gear. "I know."

I told her she didn't even know what I was talking about.

"Sure I do," she said. "You're talking about your sister."

The next Monday, Herbie and Angel and I moved most of my clothes and some of my furniture to Lauren's place. That night, the boys used the van to haul the rest of the stuff to their houses.

For a week, Lauren and I had a sort of honeymoon, during which Lauren banned the word Gloria from the apartment. It wasn't hard not talking about my sister for a week; I'd had years of practice not talking about her. But I still wasn't ready to believe that Gloria wasn't everything.

Then Lauren got a letter from Tunney. I never saw her more excited. When she finished spinning around the kitchen, she let me read it. It was written on lined paper, in the faintest pencil, like a child's homework. He said he liked her paper, that he respected an intellectual approach that could take several factors into account at once. I doubt he understood the paper any more than I did, but he said he was impressed with Lauren's theories. He wanted to talk with her about them further. He was interviewing the people who wanted to interview him, and he wanted to know if she would visit him at such and such a time on a day about two weeks later. He enclosed a Xerox sheet detailing visiting procedures.

"That clinches it," she said.

"Clinches what?"

"A contract," she said. "A book."

"What do you mean?"

"Don't you see? Tunney was the last piece of the puzzle. Everything's in place now."

I thought, so that was what her hesitation was about; she was waiting for all the pieces to come together. I said, "So what piece was I?"

"Come on, Stone."

I waited for an answer.

"You were the first piece, all right? God, what's wrong with you?"

"I don't like being a part of the same puzzle as Tunney."

"Well, you are, unfortunately. A lot of people are."

"We know his story already," I said. "You've got boxes full of it."

"Listen, Stone. I have to talk to him," she said. "He's the only one who was there."

"He's a liar," I said.

"I know, I know. Believe me, I'll take that into consideration."

The next night, I came home from work and found a list of names tacked on the refrigerator with a magnet, the rest of Lauren's puzzle pieces. Half the names I knew from reading the papers, the other half Lauren must have found in the court documents, police reports. I grabbed a couple of beers and went to her office.

"I saw your list," I said.

Lauren took her beer and leaned back and popped it open. She gave me a tired-eyed look. "You ready?" she said.

I slumped into her low chair. "Let's do it," I said.

She said, "It won't be easy. Some won't want to talk."

I knew that.

"Some'll say things you won't want to hear."

My sister was murdered, then accused of murder. What could be worse than what I'd heard already?

"Details," Lauren said.

The day-by-day of it: I'd thought about that. I said, "You're the one who was dancing around the kitchen yesterday."

She said, "And you're the one who didn't want me to talk to Tunney. You got me worried."

"This was your idea," I said.

"I know, but a lot happened besides three girls getting killed."

"Four," I said.

"Four. I know. But I don't want you to get hurt is all."

"I've been hurt."

"Hurt more, I mean."

I said, "You should've maybe thought about that before."

"I *did.* I spent three days in that motel room. Thinking about a lot of things. That was one of them."

Then she showed up at StoneS, briefcase in hand. She appeared out of nowhere at opening time, during the still moment at the beginning of the night.

I said, "It didn't stop you."

"I didn't know you then," she said. For a long still moment she looked at me. She said, "I didn't love you then."

TWELVE

Lauren's list stayed on our refrigerator door for months; I know it by heart. I watched it evolve from a neatly typed document into a mysterious collection of question marks and telephone numbers and interlocking circular coffee stains pierced by arrows and cross-outs and insertions. Scribbled addresses. Times of day. Strange spiraling doodles circled names and seemed to send them spinning off the page.

I remember those names now as faces, voices. Small things come back to me, like the shock of white hair of Gloria's Oakland housemate, Kim Whiteman's widow's peak. And how Craig Atterbury, a man who once loved Gloria, spoke to us in embarrassed low tones while holding his wife's hand. I held Lauren's hand in the back seat of Scott Carter's Mercedes Benz as he drove us around the Montclair district showing us the houses Tunney left unsold. The manager of LaSalle Market, Alphie McCord, took us upstairs and pointed down through the smoky window at the check-out counter where Gloria had worked. Paul, Tunney's son, missed three straight meetings before showing up at StoneS drunk, his voice slurred by bourbon. But the voice I remember most vividly is Tunney's. Lauren played his tapes over and over as she transcribed them, and the relentless, seductive rhythm of his voice drifted through our apartment for hours at a time.

And I remember the parents of the murdered girls: Lynn Jacobs, mother of Lena; Emerson Cage, father of Carolyn; and Dolores Schiller, mother of Rose: shades of grief.

But the strange thing is, I don't remember Gloria. I mean, I don't remember getting a vivid impression of her from anybody we talked to that summer. Whispers and sighs are all I remember. People shrugged, shook their heads, looked away. Some mumbled, others rambled on about themselves. Lauren and I listened to long stories about their own lives, waiting for some short glimpse of Gloria. We listened to dreams. We collected all kinds of information. There were the verifiable events: Gloria moved to Oakland, got a job at LaSalle Market, met Tunney, moved in with him, she disappeared for days at a time, a girl disappeared, Gloria returned, vanished, reappeared, girls turned up missing, Gloria was murdered, Tunney confessed. Lauren found dates and times and weather data pertaining to these events. She drew a time-line on butcher paper and taped it to the wall of her office.

Beneath these events were other layers. Impressions and details and random facts: Gloria often wore red; she was never late to work; her ears were pierced, but she rarely wore earrings; she sang country songs, clowning; she liked to lie in the sun; her hair went frizzy when it rained. But at first, the facts didn't add up to a person in my mind. Sometimes I recognized Lisbeth, sometimes I saw someone else. I listened, but it was like there was a limit to what people could say with words, a limit to what I could hear. Lauren told me to be patient, to look for a deeper level of detail. Listen and remember and imagine, she told me. She told me to write down my dreams about Gloria, but I didn't. What good would my dreams do me? I wanted to know the truth, what happened, and why. I wanted to know Gloria, but for most of the summer, she stayed a stranger to me, a deeper shade of grief.

If Gloria was a shadow, Lauren was light. She loved me. Windows down, radio playing, we drove through the sunstruck Berkeley traffic. The world was alive with light; I remember everything. We were on the winding, tree-lined stretch of Ashby Avenue by the Claremont Hotel. Lauren's hair whipped across her face. Freckles dotted her forehead. Her lips were chapped and she kept licking them as she drove. The wind whirled through the car. Her pocket-sized spiral notebook flapped on the dashboard. Everything made me think, I'm in love with her.

By that time, I'd given myself over to Lauren completely; it was the only way I could go on with my search of Gloria. My desire to know what happened to my sister fed my love for Lauren the way a man's desire to be drunk feeds his thirst for bourbon.

We were going to Oakland to see Kim Whiteman. Like everyone else in California, Lauren and I remembered Kim from television. She was the dazed, dark-eyed woman they stopped in the courthouse hall during Tunney's trial. For two days running, they played the tape of Kim saying, "I don't believe it," then breaking down, crying. The cameras stayed on her crying face, her quivering shoulders, and it tore my heart out, watching her. Everybody else in the world seemed eager to believe Tunney at the time.

We sipped tea in Kim's kitchen. A prism hung in the window above the sink, casting a patch of color on the floor. Joni Mitchell sang on the stereo. I watched Lauren's hands caress her tea cup. She was leaning toward Kim, listening to a story about a lost job, a lover, something about money, Mexico. I couldn't concentrate. I kept having to remind myself: Gloria lived here. I looked into the living room, into the dusty sunlight. Shelves swayed under the weight of Kim's records. The leaves of the plants were bright as knives.

I heard the word Gloria. Kim was telling Lauren how she remembered Gloria's arrival: her blue car "battered as a taxi cab," her "too-blond" hair, her bandaged hand. These things worried Kim at first, but there was a calm about Gloria that Kim found soothing. Gloria moved slowly, talked softly.

"She sat right there," Kim said, looking at Lauren. She said that when Gloria sipped her tea, she kept her bandaged hand in her lap, giving her a formal presence, and that she used her good hand—stirring, lifting her cup—with the controlled grace of someone performing a ritual. Kim thought Gloria might be into meditation or Zen. There was an other-worldly aura about her.

I watched Lauren put one hand in her lap and then slowly lift her cup to her lips with the other.

Who was I looking at, Lauren or Gloria? I saw Gloria in Lauren's slow, controlled sip, and I saw Lauren take on some of Gloria's formal sorrow. For a long time, I thought Lauren distracted me, that I loved her too much. I thought I was too obsessed with Lauren to concentrate on my sister's story, but it was more complicated than that. I couldn't separate them; it was like Gloria was Lauren's shadow.

I remember sitting with Lauren in the sun on Craig Atterbury's patio, watching his boy splash in a shallow pool.

The child was about the same age Daniel was when Donna asked me to leave. Craig was saying, "We went out. Yes." He was holding his wife's hand. She had long black hair piled loosely off her neck, gypsy-style. (Donna wore her hair like that sometimes.) She squinted at us. It was quiet except for the ocean-like roar of the freeway and the motorboat noises the kid was making.

Craig had lived in an apartment across the courtyard from Kim's during the time my sister stayed with her. Lauren found him living in El Cerrito, teaching high school history. He wasn't sure he wanted to talk to us, but finally, reluctantly, he agreed to tell us what he could. I understood his reluctance. He'd loved Gloria for a short time, a long time before. But he'd held her and kissed her and talked with her through the night. He'd lost her to Tunney, who murdered her. Craig had been that close to tragedy, and he'd come away clean. Now he had a wife and a child and a salmon-colored Spanish-style stucco house almost out of the roar of the freeway. He had all summer off and his wife was growing an herb garden and his son was learning to talk. I knew how tenuous that kind of family happiness could be.

"Off and on for six months maybe," Craig said. He was a blond guy with small, fine hands; I imagined them dusted with chalk.

Lauren looked hot in the sun. I watched her hand fly up and wave a yellow jacket away from her face. Her neck shined with sweat.

"But we never got that close," he said. "And then she met that guy. Tunney."

The verifiable events: that day we left it at that.

Lauren left Craig's house disturbed by the whole scene: the wary wife; the neat rows of herbs beside the patio; the plastic toys on the lawn; the folding furniture; the yellow jackets; Craig's careful story. Ordinary was the word she used to describe him. She could see why he and Gloria never got very close. Lauren didn't want to get close to him, either. She asked me to find the deeper detail about Craig and Gloria. "It's a man to man thing," she said.

Lauren liked having me around to talk to people like Kim and Craig, who were sympathetic to my sister. She introduced me as Gloria's brother, but it didn't bother me anymore. I trusted Lauren. If she thought someone would open up more knowing who I was, she was free to tell them. I wanted them to talk as much as she did.

But the closer she got to Tunney's people, the less she wanted them to know about me. To Tunney's boss, Scott Carter of Carter & Milhous Realty, I was simply Stone, owner of StoneS in Berkeley. Mr. Carter said he'd seen my sign from the freeway, but he'd never been in for dinner. We were in the back seat of his car, taking a tour through the Oakland hills, Tunney's territory. Another agent, Lisa Bianche, rode in the front seat beside him. She had dark eyebrows and jade-green eyes and skin as smooth as butterscotch. She was telling us about the week Tunney called her at two in the morning four nights in a row.

Lauren said, "What did he say?"

"Nothing," Lisa said. "Not a word. That's what was so weird."

"How'd you know it was him?"

"Because," she said, "I didn't know any other creeps."

Scott Carter pointed at a mock-Tudor manor house that Tunney had listed and never sold. I squeezed Lauren's hand. "How much does a house like that sell for?" I said.

"Now or then?" Scott wanted to know.

I told him, Now. Business at the restaurant had been steady for a while, and I had some money in the bank. I thought Lauren and I might want a house of our own when she finished her book.

"Five hundred, give or take," Scott said.

Business wasn't that steady. It was just about steady enough for me to afford something in Craig Atterbury's neighborhood, but that would have been too ordinary for Lauren.

Some people weren't so eager to tell us stories about Tunney. His ex-wife, Pat Wells, wanted ten thousand dollars to talk, but her son, Paul, talked her into talking to us for nothing. Tunney's father said he'd never say a word about his son, and never did, though Tunney's mother met Lauren for lunch as often as three times a week. The old man gave Alphie McCord and everyone else at LaSalle Market strict orders not to talk to anyone about Tunney or Gloria or the other girls.

So we were surprised when Alphie said, "I've been waiting for you folks."

We followed him through the door at the back of the market and up a narrow staircase to his office. He rocked in his chair, his hands clasped over his belly. He told us that during the trial and afterward, he'd turned a lot of reporters away, and he regretted it. He wanted to talk now, even though he understood why the old man laid down a law against it. If Tunney were his son, he wouldn't want anybody talking about him, either.

"But you folks aren't here about him. You're here about Gloria. And the old man has no say about her." Alphie looked down through the smoky window at a row of registers. "I used to watch her work," he said. "Something about her made me want to watch her. She always looked serious working."

When Alphie heard that Gloria had moved in with Tunney, he called her up to his office. "I sat her down right there," he said, looking at Lauren. "I said, what's going on? She just looked at me, wouldn't say a word. I knew the guy was no good, so I told her, don't be fooled by his fancy talk. And as calm as ever, she just looked at me and said, I'm not fooled."

Alphie turned out to be one of Lauren's most forthcoming

informants. He was an important character in long stretches of *Quick Blood,* a distinction that cost him his job as soon as Tunney's father saw the book.

To these people—Pat Wells and Paul, Tunney's mother, and even Alphie—I wasn't Gloria's brother. As far as they knew, Gloria didn't have a brother. Lauren introduced me as her friend or associate, and sometimes she didn't introduce me at all.

Until *Quick Blood* came out, I don't think Tunney knew I existed. Lauren refused to take me to San Quentin with her because I was too emotionally involved. She thought I'd intimidate Tunney. I told her she didn't have to tell him who I was, but that didn't matter to Lauren. She knew who I was. "You'll intimidate *me,*" she said.

Lauren let me listen to Tunney's tapes, though. I remember lying on the couch during one of those long, light September afternoons, listening to the first one. Lauren's voice was too faint to make out; she had the microphone too close to Tunney, I think, but his voice came through loud and clear. Near the end of their talk, he said, "I want to know something, though. I want to know, like, why are you interested in me?"

Lauren's reply was lost, but I imagined I could hear the low tone of the word Gloria.

Tunney said, "What about her and me?"

Lauren must have whispered; I could only hear the hiss of the tape.

"That's not what I mean," Tunney said. "I mean you've got to have some deep-down reason. You maybe don't even know what it is, but you have one."

I hit the stop button, then rewind, play, looking for the place where Tunney asked, "Why?" I turned the machine up as loud as it would go.

"I told him exactly what he wanted to hear," Lauren said.

She stood at the French doors, a mug of coffee in her hand. "I said, if what you say about Gloria is true. I said *if.*"

But that wasn't what I was listening for. I was listening to Tunney's question. Why did she want to know? It was my question, too.

All summer, a picture of Gloria had been taking shape in my mind. Slowly, the events and the random facts and the deep detail began to form a story. I began to trust my imagination. I even dreamed about Gloria. But something about Lauren eluded me. The more I loved her, the more I felt I didn't know her. And I didn't even realize what I didn't know until I heard Tunney's question.

Why?

At that moment, I didn't care what Lauren told him. I was listening for what she didn't tell him. I hoped to hear, in the inarticulate rhythms on the tape, some answer. Why? Somewhere in those lost, low tones was the deep-down reason why she wanted to know about Gloria.

THIRTEEN

□

Let me tell you what I did know.

Gloria left Eureka while I was still at The Caves. She didn't believe I'd lie for her. What was obvious to Lauren, Gloria couldn't see: I wanted to let her go.

While I slept in a third-floor room at the Chateau, Gloria coasted her car under the Swedish woman's windows and glided onto the road. Her car drifted, dark and silent as a rowboat, around the first turn. Then her headlights flashed on. Her Chevy V-8 roared through the trees. She wound down toward the highway through the predawn fog. Empty logging trucks passed her, rattling their chains. She turned south on the coast highway as the sky began to lighten over the mountains. All morning she drove. The fog rose through the trees and disappeared. Her wide hood swept through the shadows, swept south through Fortuna and Scotia and Garberville.

When she stopped for gas, she pumped it herself, using her good hand to unscrew the cap, lift the hose, throw the lever. She leaned against her fender and watched the numbers tumble. The attendant hovered around the pumps, glancing at her out of the corner of his eye. Gloria gave him a what-are-you-looking-at? look, which wasn't only rhetorical. She wondered if he wanted to help her, or if he was afraid she'd drive away without paying, or if he was just giving her the eye. She was used to men looking at her, but that morning she was dressed in jeans and a red plaid shirt, and her hair hung down around her face, unbrushed. So what was he looking at? Could he tell from her Oregon plates and the pattern of splattered bugs on her windshield that she'd been driving for hours? When she bought several Cokes and a fistful of candy, did he know she had hours of driving ahead? Did he recognize a woman on the run when he saw one? She paid him with a fifty-dollar bill and didn't bother to count her change, just stuffed it, coins and all, into the breast pocket of her Pendleton. In the restroom, she wet her face and ran her hand through her hair. She whispered her new name at the mirror.

In the car, her hand smelled of gasoline. She liked the smell; it made her feel light-headed. It was the odor of flight, freedom.

Through the heat of the afternoon, she drove with her windows down. The sack of rolls I'd bought for her breakfast lay torn open on the seat beside her. An empty Coke can rolled on the floor. Her burned hand lay in her lap, gently throbbing.

She followed the flow of the traffic through the brown hills, past oil refineries and tracts of new homes, past long low warehouses, over bridges. She followed trucks through San

Rafael to Richmond. She could see the gray-green bay through a chainlink fence. San Francisco shimmered in the distance.

But she chose Oakland. She knew I lived in San Lorenzo, worked in Berkeley. I believe she wanted to be close to me, so that someday she could slip into a phone booth and call me with a quarter.

For three nights she stayed in a motel on West MacArthur, without incident, but during the fourth night, a man was shot dead in the parking lot below her window. The shots woke her. Sirens and searchlights kept her awake for an hour. The screams of the woman who loved the dead man disturbed her sleep for the rest of the night. Later, she told Kim that the woman was so hysterical, two men had to carry her to an ambulance and drive her away under flashing red lights.

In the morning, Gloria sat at the counter at Bif's on Broadway, eating apple pie, drinking coffee. She read the roommate-wanted column in a free weekly called the East Bay Express. Female wanted to share sunny furn. apt. with same, Kim's ad said. Gloria circled it, and when she finished her pie, she found a phone booth and called. Kim gave her directions to Park Boulevard. "An ugly Spanish place," she said. "I call it the Alamo."

Gloria thought the place looked beautiful. She liked everything about it: the overgrown courtyard, the dusty smell of the stairway, the way the light streamed through the windows. She liked the peppermint tea Kim served and the record she played on the stereo. Kim asked the same questions Gloria had answered for Ruth Haywood and Johnny at Great Days and the woman in Eureka, simple questions with easy lies for answers. What was her name? And where was she from? And did she plan to stay long? Like Ruth and Johnny and the Swedish woman, Kim seemed to believe her when she said her name was Gloria Rose Simpson and she was from Seattle and she planned to stay for a year at least. Kim didn't ask why she'd bleached her hair or how she'd burned her hand. Kim didn't believe in probing into personal areas, like why a twenty-six-year-old woman didn't own any furniture or a TV set or even a shoe box full of cassette tapes. (Kim told Lauren, "I advertised a furnished room. I sure didn't want to see a moving van pull up.") She showed Gloria a small bedroom (twin bed, dresser, nightstand, lamp) overlooking the courtyard. Yes, Gloria said. Perfect. She thought the room looked like an easy place to leave when that time came. For first and last month's rent, she gave Kim six crisp one-hundred-dollar bills, nearly the last of the money she'd taken from Earl's drawer.

The next day Gloria drove farther up Park Boulevard to Montclair to look for a job. I doubt she was impressed by the fine cars parked on LaSalle Avenue or by the tanned ladies strolling down the street in tennis dresses. If these things made any impression on Gloria at all, it was because they were new to her. For the last few years, the only way she could relieve the aching pressure in her chest was to feel some new sensation. The smallest new thing: the smell of gasoline on her hand, the prism in Kim's kitchen, the shape of the antique lampposts along LaSalle Avenue, even a photo of a home for sale in a realty office window, was like a drug for Gloria.

She stood in the shade of an awning, studying color photos of a modern-style redwood and glass house.

"Pretty," a man said.

Gloria turned to see a tall man in a suit peering over her shoulder at the picture. He had a cinnamon-colored mustache and the palest blue eyes she'd ever seen.

"But overpriced," he said.

Gloria side-stepped away from him and started walking down the street. She wanted to see everything. Every storefront was new to her, and each one seemed to shimmer with possibility. Color wheels at Raimondi's paints. Fresh flowers in the window at Blossoms. She passed See's Candies and Coast to Coast and Kenny's Hair Salon. She looked at the well-dressed dummies at McGuire's Men's Wear. At Northern California Savings, she turned the corner. A shoe store. A pizza parlor. Cy's Seafood Restaurant. She didn't see any Help Wanted signs, but that didn't matter. Her spirits were rising, and she felt like she could work up the nerve to walk in and ask for a job when she found the right place. She turned another corner and saw a sign for a shop called The Ice House, which she imagined would be cool and white inside. She headed for it, thinking she might have found her place. When she let the door go behind her, the man who had spoken to her at the real estate office caught it before it closed.

Gloria was disappointed that it was as warm in The Ice House as it was on the street. She thought about leaving, but the blue-eyed man stood between her and the door, gazing up at the list of flavors on the wall.

"Swiss Milk Chocolate," he said. "Have you ever had it?"

Gloria gave him a long quiet-eyed look, meaning, Are you talking to me?

He said, "Swiss Milk Chocolate?"

"No," Gloria said.

"If you like malt. Oh, boy." He smacked his lips. "Do you? Like malt?"

"No," Gloria said.

"Ah. Well. Then Swiss Milk Chocolate is not for you. Strawberry Crush you'd like, I think."

Gloria took a step toward the door. "I'm not hungry," she said.

"Since when do you have to be hungry for ice cream?"

"I made a mistake," she said. "I don't want anything." She brushed past him.

"Wait," he said. "I've never seen you before."

She ignored him and pushed the door open and stepped outside. She looked up and down the street, her head light with sudden panic; she couldn't remember where she'd parked her car.

He followed her out of The Ice House. He said, "You're new around here."

Hearing his voice, Gloria felt a little better, which surprised her. At least he wasn't standing between her and the door anymore.

She said, "You've seen everybody?"

"Around here," he said.

She didn't know which way to walk to her car, so she just stood there watching his face. His pale eyes made him look almost feminine. He was smiling at her, and she could see a neat row of teeth under his mustache.

"I grew up around here. Worked in there in high school," he said, cocking his head at The Ice House. "I didn't mean to bother you. I just wanted to make a suggestion. Old habit."

Gloria scanned the street looking for the blue shape of her Impala.

"You parked in front of my office," he said. "Sixty-eight Chevy, somewhat worse for wear, I'd say. Oregon plates. When I saw you get out of it, I said to myself, beauty and the beast."

"You knew I was from out of state."

"But I also knew I'd never seen you around here before. This way," he said. He led her back past Cy's and the shoe store and headed up La Salle toward C&M Realty. After he found her car for her, he produced a card from the inside pocket of his suit jacket. He held it out to her between two fingers. Gloria took it and read it in the glare of the sun. A. James Tunney. Carter and Milhous Realty.

She said, "I'm not looking for a house."

"I didn't think so, to tell the truth. No. My guess is you're looking for a job."

Gloria looked up from his card.

"My father owns LaSalle Market. They might need somebody. Talk to Mr. McCord. If that doesn't work try Skyline Market and Piedmont Market. My father owns those, too. Tell them you're a friend of A.J.'s."

Gloria nodded and opened her car door and slid behind the wheel. Tunney grabbed her door before she could close it. "Hey, what's your name?"

"Gloria," she said.

"Gloria what?"

"Gloria . . ." She thought about saying, Simpson, but she just shrugged.

"All right, Gloria Gloria." He let her door go and she closed it.

I think running into Tunney bothered my sister a lot. In ten minutes, he knew more about her than she wanted anyone to know. When she told him her name, she felt like a liar for the first time since she stopped being Lisbeth. The lie was easy with the others, but his blue eyes spooked her. It was as though he saw beyond Gloria, beyond Lisbeth even. He saw Liz and Betty and Sissy. He mocked her: *Gloria Gloria.*

Driving home, she decided she was rushing things looking for a job right away. She wasn't ready. At the Alamo, she rifled all her pockets and found almost fifty dollars worth of coins and crumpled singles and fives. She could make that last a week at least.

While Kim was away at work, Gloria played records and stood at the window and watched the way the shadows passed over the narrow courtyard. When the patio was suddenly shadowless, she found some scissors and cut a pair of Levi's off at the thigh. Then she slipped into a red tank top, turned the stereo up, flung open the windows. She went downstairs and sat in the sun on the steps. While Jackson Browne's voice floated overhead, she closed her eyes and felt her lids grow warm.

Someone was watching her. She felt it as a high, fine vibration along her spine. Her eyes opened, and the full force of the sun blinded her. She raised her bandaged hand for shade and scanned the windows, waiting. Nothing moved but a bird swooping from ledge to ledge through the light.

"Jamaica Say You Will" was one of Craig Atterbury's favorite songs. When he heard it coming out of Kim's apartment, he went to his window and looked down to see a strange woman sitting on the steps, her pale face raised toward the sun. He told me that his first urge was to go down and say hello and tell her that he was a Jackson Browne fan, too, but something stopped him. As he watched her, she suddenly raised a gloved—no—a bandaged hand toward her face and glared up at him. Her look was so sudden and fierce, he stepped away from his window. The gesture (at Brennan's Craig raised his arm to show me) and the bandage made her look like she was warding off a blow. "And she was so pale," he said, "she looked like she just came out of the hospital or something." He decided to leave her alone.

Craig didn't remember the record Gloria played the next day, but she played it loudly enough to draw him to his window. And there she was: sitting in the sun in a folding chair, her hair brushed back, her legs bright with oil. A magazine lay open in her lap. She was sipping Coke from a can.

Craig opened his window and went back to his desk and listened. As long as the music played he knew she was out there. All week, he waited for the hour when the sun crossed the patio, then he went to his window to observe the gradual changes in Gloria.

She saw a man step out of the shadows by the door: a young guy with a three-day beard and a shy smile. He looked up at Kim's windows. "I've been listening," he said. Then he looked over at his own windows. "All week."

"Nobody complained," Gloria said.

Craig squinted at the windows around the courtyard. "People mostly work in the daytime except me and Mrs. Edgar and she's deaf. I like it, though. Hearing the music. It makes me feel less all alone here."

Gloria looked him over. He wore a wrinkled white dress shirt, untucked, his sleeves rolled to the elbow, baggy tan pants, no socks, loafers.

"You're like clockwork," he said. "I could set my watch by you." He tapped his wrist, but he wasn't wearing a watch.

Gloria said, "You don't work?"

"At night. I work for this catering place. I go to school is the main thing."

Gloria sipped her Coke.

"You live with Kim?" he said.

She nodded.

He said, "I'm Craig Atterbury. I know Kim. I mean, she knows who I am. We say hi."

"Hi," Gloria said. "I'm Gloria."

Craig smiled. "Like the song," he said.

She squinted at him.

"You know. Van Morrison's 'Gloria.' "

She shook her head.

Craig looked at her in disbelief. "Gee el Oh are Eye aye. You never heard it?"

"I don't know," she said.

"And your name's Gloria?"

"Maybe I heard it," she said. "I don't remember."

"No, if your name's Gloria," he said, "you wouldn't forget."

I don't think it mattered to Gloria whether he believed her or not. By that time, she believed herself. All week, as her skin grew taut under her tan, she'd felt more like Gloria. The day she took her bandage off and saw her white hand and wrist, her scar, she thought, that's all that's left of Lisbeth. Now her hand was as dark as the rest of her, and she felt well and healed and whole.

FOURTEEN

□

I have one of Tunney's business cards. When Lauren and I visited the real estate office, Scott Carter found a small box full of them and slid it across his desk at us. He told us to take some as souvenirs. Lauren grabbed a half dozen of them and handed one to me. I read it and flipped it over and back and read it again. Then, because I didn't know what else to do with it, I took out my wallet and slipped it in with all the cards I've collected from liquor salesmen and linen services and coffee companies. It's been there ever since.

The card Tunney gave Gloria is lost. All I know is that she didn't show it to Alphie McCord when she went to LaSalle Market looking for a job. She didn't mention Tunney's name. Alphie told us that he wished she had, because if he knew

Tunney had sent her, he wouldn't have hired her, and he might have spared a lot of people a lot of grief.

Lauren and I disagreed about why Gloria went to work at the supermarket. I let her go so she could be free, not so she could get tied up with a guy like Tunney. I wanted to think she forgot all about his job offer, that she went back to Montclair and walked the streets until she found herself standing under LaSalle's long awning. Something inside caught her eye: a closed check-out counter, a bag boy's red apron, a bright pyramid of stacked coffee cans. She stepped on the black mat and the door swung open for her. She walked the aisles until she found Alphie and asked for a job. I told Lauren that it was as simple as that.

No, Lauren said, Gloria remembered Tunney's offer all right. Lauren believed that Gloria thought about nothing much but Tunney that whole week she sat in the sun. In *Quick Blood,* she wrote that my sister "tested her sense of herself as Gloria against her memory of Tunney's cold blue gaze." According to Lauren, she went to LaSalle Market so she could prove to herself and to Tunney that she really was Gloria.

Maybe. I don't know. I don't like to think Tunney had so much influence over her so early on. If she had something to prove to him, why didn't she show Alphie his card? Why didn't she use his name? My sense of my sister tells me she didn't want to owe anybody anything. No connections. No commitments. Why else would she run away from everybody who loved her?

What impressed Kim most during the first few weeks Gloria worked at LaSalle was that she never complained about work. Kim never heard a word about rude customers or a slave-driving boss or boredom. Most workdays Gloria came home from LaSalle with a sack full of treats—ice cream, beer, steaks, enough fruit to fill a basket—acting as though she'd just run out to the market on an errand.

One evening during those early weeks, Craig showed up at their door with the Van Morrison record in hand. He told Kim there was a song on it that he wanted to play for Gloria. It didn't take a genius to figure out what song he was talking about. Kim told Lauren that she thought it was a silly way to get in the door, but she didn't have the heart to turn him away. From the polished look of his face, she could tell he'd just shaved, and he was wearing a sweater, and his pants looked pressed. She'd never seen him look so sharp, even when he was hurrying down the stairs late for a catering job.

She asked him in and offered him a beer, while Gloria drifted into the kitchen looking like she'd been dozing on the couch. She didn't seem to recognize Craig until he handed her the record. She flashed it at Kim. "There's a song called 'Gloria' on here."

"I know," Kim said. "Where have you been hiding?"

"She'll remember as soon as she hears it," Craig said.

They took their beers into the living room where Kim put the album on at the beginning to give Craig time to get acquainted. She thought he looked cute perched on the couch next to Gloria, holding onto his beer bottle with both hands. Kim liked that kind of shy blond guy, the sensitive type, and she felt a little jealous that he looked so anxious around Gloria. For two years she'd lived across the courtyard from him and he'd never found an old song to come play for her. What was worse was that Gloria didn't seem to appreciate what was going on. She acted aloof; she didn't even look at Craig. She just sipped her beer and gazed at the stereo speaker waiting for her song to start. "All she cared about was that song," Kim said. "It was like if he'd brought her a bouquet of roses, she would have thought it was a botany lesson."

Craig recognized the beginning of the song before anybody else. He held his bottle up: "Here, listen." Kim noticed that Craig watched Gloria's face the whole time the song played.

What was he looking at? Watching Craig watch Gloria, Kim realized that she'd never appreciated Gloria's beauty before. The day Gloria arrived at the Alamo, Kim thought she had a mystical grace about her, but she looked too pained and pale to be called pretty. But now she could see why Craig had come: relaxed and tanned, Gloria was beautiful beyond envy.

While the song played, Gloria watched the record spin, listening with the solemn concentration of someone looking in a mirror.

When it was over, she said, "I'm five-foot-four."

"From your head down to the ground," Craig said.

Kim admitted she'd forgotten the words. All she'd remembered about the song was Van's chant. She asked Gloria, "You never heard it?"

Gloria thought she might have heard it somewhere. (I know exactly where she heard it. It was one of the songs the guys in the guideshack liked to turn up after a long day in the cave. We could hear their radio down in the Chateau until Hank or my father walked up there and told them to turn it down.) "I forgot about it," she said.

Kim was amazed at Gloria's powers of forgetfulness. She told Lauren, "If there was a song called 'Kim,' I sure wouldn't forget about it."

After Craig and then Kim told us about the record, Lauren and I tried to remember the lyrics, but we couldn't come up with more than a couple of lines. ("She makes me feel so good Lord," Lauren sang in her best Janis Joplin voice. "Makes me feel alright.") So we drove over to Telegraph Avenue and found a scratched up copy at Rasputin's Records. During the next couple of weeks, Lauren played that song over and over until we could both recite it like a prayer.

Alphie always watched his new checkers work. For the first couple of weeks, he liked to keep an eye on them to make sure they were learning the prices and were polite and didn't have a tendency to panic under pressure. Watching Gloria, he liked what he saw. She didn't smile a lot, true, but somehow she managed to look pleasant. She worked her register as though every item that passed before her was worthy of her full attention. And even after Alphie was sure she'd work out all right, he found himself drawn to watching her. Something about the way her hands moved over the keys, the way she brushed her hair off her forehead, the way she sometimes bit her lip, fascinated him.

He was also in the habit of watching Tunney, who often came in the store late in the afternoon and cruised the aisles in an aimless way that made Alphie nervous. Tunney loved to waste time. And Alphie told us that he couldn't trust anyone who didn't respect the fact that time is the most precious thing we've got in this world. Here was a grown man who seemed to have nothing better to do than meander through the streets of Montclair. When Tunney wasn't wandering on foot, he was driving. You could always spot him in his white turtle-shaped Saab. It was uncanny, Alphie said, almost every time he got in his car, he saw the Saab passing him or turning a corner or sitting turtle-still at a stoplight. Tunney was supposed to be selling houses in the hills, but Alphie told me he would've been surprised if Tunney ever sold anything. The only reason he had the job at all was that Mr. Carter was doing his old man a favor. Alphie felt sorry for the boss for having a son who was nothing but a time-waster and a thief.

Every time Tunney came in the store, he pocketed something, which was absurd because he got all his groceries for free. All he had to do was follow the simple procedure of taking his basket to a register and letting a cashier ring his stuff up and circle the total on the tape and mark it AJT. Tunney just had to sign for it. It wasn't like he was under some kind of budget restriction or anything—the whole procedure was simply an accounting matter—but he liked to steal one small thing every time he came in the store. Who did he think he was fooling? Not Alphie McCord. If Tunney got his kicks shoplifting in his own father's supermarket, it was all right with Alphie. But he watched Tunney with a close eye, and if he saw him take so much as a pack of Lifesavers, he made a note of it and added it to Tunney's account.

A couple of weeks after Gloria came to work, Alphie saw Tunney pushing a cart down the soups and sauces aisle. The first odd thing about that was that Tunney never used a cart. What he didn't pocket he carried in a basket. The other odd thing was that he tossed six or eight cans of Campbell's in the cart without seeming to read a label. On the breads and cereals aisle, he did the same thing: in went four loaves and several boxes of raisin bran. Up and down the aisles, he grabbed whatever was handy until his cart looked like it belonged to someone doing a week's worth of shopping for a family of six.

"It took him ten minutes, tops," Alphie said. "Quite a feat for a man who was allergic to hurrying."

This was strange enough behavior to get Alphie up from his desk and downstairs to take a closer look. By the time he was on the floor, Tunney was at Gloria's counter.

Alphie heard him say, "Don't tell me you don't remember me."

Gloria didn't look at him. She was reading the price on a jar of jam. But, as much as I don't want to think so, Gloria must have remembered Tunney. (I concede that much to Lauren.) If he came in as often as Alphie said he did, she'd probably seen him several times since she'd started work. So far, he'd avoided her register, but she'd felt him watching her, which made her concentrate even harder on the task at hand. That's what she was trying to do now.

"I remember *you,* Gloria Gloria."

"It's just Gloria," she said. She turned to show him her name tag.

"Yes," he said. "Gloria Rose. It's a pretty name. You couldn't make up a prettier name if you tried."

How did he know about Rose? She felt penned in by the counter, Tunney's cart, the register, a partition behind her. She couldn't help looking at him.

He was smiling at her. "I'm not psychic, if that's what you're thinking. But I am on friendly terms with the woman who writes your check. She let me look at your application."

A familiar calm came over her; it was the calm of feeling sheltered by a lie. She'd described Gloria on that application, and now she was standing there in an apron with Gloria's name tag pinned to it. (When Alphie showed her application to me, I didn't recognize Lisbeth at all; even her birthdate was changed. I had a sudden moment of hope, thinking maybe there had been some mistake, maybe this woman wasn't my sister at all. When the moment passed, I felt like I knew Gloria better than ever.)

"You know everything about me, then," she said.

"You're from Seattle?"

She nodded. She was looking at the shopping cart. There was ten minutes worth of work in there.

"It rains a lot there, they tell me."

"Yeah."

"Depressing, I guess."

"You get used to it," Gloria said.

"Not me. I like the sunshine. Let there be light, I say."

"Uh huh." She worked as quickly as she could; she wanted to get him away from her.

"But I thought you were from Oregon."

She looked at him again.

"Your plates. On your car."

"Oh."

"What happened? You bought it in Oregon?"

"No," Gloria said. The Impala was a trade-in Earl was thinking about junking. She took it because she didn't think it would be missed.

She said, "I stole it. In Portland. It was parked behind the Greyhound station. The keys were in it and I was tired of the bus. So I stole it."

Tunney wasn't surprised. He said, "Anything's better than the bus. But I might've found something a little more reliable."

"It got me here."

"I see that. But you know something?"

"What?"

"I don't believe you."

"What do you mean?"

"I mean you didn't steal any car."

"I did."

"If you stole it, you wouldn't tell me, now would you?"

"I'm not ashamed," Gloria said.

"You know we don't let car thieves work the registers around here."

Finally, she smiled. "If you're going to be hard-nosed about it, all right. I didn't steal my car. I bought it from an old lady who moved up from Oregon to live with her son who happened to be my landlord in Seattle. I paid eight-hundred-fifty for it. Bargained them down from a thousand."

"You were robbed."

Gloria shrugged. "So maybe I should've stole it."

While she finished ringing up his cartload of groceries, Tunney told Gloria other things he'd learned from her application. She was five-foot-four, though she looked taller than that to him. A hundred twenty-five pounds seemed about right, though. Hair: blond. He teased her, telling her that that made two lies he'd caught her at. Brown eyes, true.

Born: August 24, 1951, which made her almost twenty-six years old. She was an American citizen, never convicted of a felony. She'd attended something called Cascade Community College, never graduated. Worked at Safeway in Seattle and at Tempest Motors as a bookkeeper. Married: no. Children: none. Which was great news as far as Tunney was concerned. He also knew that she presently lived on Park Boulevard in a grand Spanish villa of an apartment house with an overgrown courtyard complete with bicycles chained to the wrought-iron banisters and newspapers strewn on the steps.

"You've been there?"

"I drove by a couple times."

"What for?"

"Professional curiosity. I like to keep my eyes open for income properties."

"Liar," Gloria said. "You were spying on me."

Tunney laughed. "All right. I wanted to see if I could see you. Anything wrong with that?"

"That makes us even," she said, "lie for lie."

When she finished ringing everything up, Tunney told her how his procedure worked, coming around the counter to show her how to advance the register tape so that his total appeared in the opening so she could circle it. He found the black binder and signed for his groceries while she loaded the sacks into the cart.

"From now on," he said, "it's God's truth between us. All right?"

Gloria nodded and watched him walk away pushing his cart through the opening automatic doors and into the bright sunlight.

After work she found six sacks of groceries piled on the backseat of her car. Confused, she moved around the car slowly, looking at the bags from all angles. All her doors were locked. She looked for a note under the windshield wipers.

Nothing. She turned in a tight circle, scanned the parking lot for movement. No one. She opened the back door and wrestled the bags around to see if he'd written anything there, but he hadn't.

She didn't want all his stupid food. She thought about taking it back in the store, but what would she tell Alphie? It was too weird. She got in the car and drove home faster than was safe, half-expecting Tunney to pop up out of the backseat any second.

As she tried to sleep that night, the thought of Tunney kept rising up in her mind. An aching pressure rose in her chest and made her blood run quick.

You know something? I don't believe you.

She had a sudden urge to get up from bed and get dressed, find her car keys and leave. She wanted to drive all night. She closed her eyes and imagined it and saw herself pumping gas in a strange town at daybreak. The vision relaxed her almost to the point of dozing.

Then she heard Tunney's voice: *You couldn't make up a prettier name if you tried.* Gloria Gloria.

Gee el Oh are Eye aye.

As she chanted it to herself she began to feel better. How did it go?

Something about his baby, how she used to come by. Just five-foot-four from her feet up to her eyes.

She'd felt Craig watching her while the song played. What was he looking at?

He was looking at Gloria. Yes. He believed her. From her bed she looked out her window across the courtyard. His light was on.

Around midnight. Something about midnight and she was walking down the street. Gloria imagined a woman walking down the middle of a rain-slick road alone.

She got out of bed wearing only the tank-top she slept in,

pulled on a pair of jeans, and barefoot, moved through the dark apartment. She found herself in the hall, her eyes aching in the light.

She could feel the rhythm of the song, as though it were in her blood. It made her feel like Gloria. She couldn't remember the words exactly, just something about a house, a door, a room, an inevitable progression. She had to follow it.

Craig would take her in, no questions asked. She didn't have to run from Tunney; Craig would hold her still. She'd feel his weight on her. She didn't have to run to leave Lisbeth behind, because Craig would whisper in her ear, Gloria, and slow her quick blood. *Makes me feel so good, Lord, makes me feel alright.*

Makes me feel so good, Lord, makes me feel alright.

FIFTEEN

Sometime in late September, Lauren started spending her Thursdays at San Quentin, talking to Tunney, and the rest of her mornings listening to his tapes. I remember waking up alone in the tangled sheets, into the smell of the cat box and coffee and the sound of Tunney's voice drifting out of her office. The sunlight made my eyes ache as I made my way to the bathroom and turned on the water in the tub to drown his voice. I remember feeling pretty useless sitting there in the water. After she started talking with Tunney, Lauren didn't ask me much about my sister. Whenever I wanted to talk about her, Lauren would hold up her hand and say, "Please, Stone. Save it." She said she was overdosing on

Gloria stories, but my impression was she was overdosing on Tunney. When I told her so, she accused me of being jealous of him. I was, and I admitted it. "That's absurd," she said. "The man's a murderer, a monster, scum." She told me she took no pleasure in talking to him, but she didn't make me feel much better.

One morning, wet-headed, I wandered into the kitchen, and poured myself some coffee. When I went for the milk in the fridge, I noticed Craig's phone number on Lauren's list, and while Tunney's voice droned through the apartment, I copied it down to take to work with me. But when I got to the restaurant, I didn't make the call. I sat at my desk for almost an hour, fiddling with the waiters' schedules. Why did I hesitate? I loved talking to Lauren about my sister. It felt intimate, our own private business. And driving around with her, meeting people, I felt close to her; we were partners. But this was different. This was between me and Craig. Ever since I'd seen him with his family, I'd been thinking about Donna and Daniel and everything I'd lost. I wanted to know something from him that was separate from what Lauren wanted to know. I remembered how quiet he was that day on his patio. I sensed he wanted to talk and that something stopped him besides the fact that his wife was sitting there holding his hand. I had a feeling he knew something about my sister that wouldn't be much easier to listen to than what I'd been hearing coming out of Lauren's office. Lauren was right: a lot happened.

When I finally picked up the phone, I dialed Donna's number in Santa Fe.

"It's me," I said.

"Marvin?"

"Uh huh. I don't mean to bother you."

"Danny's out with his friends. You just missed him."

"That's too bad. But I really wanted to talk to you. Do you have a minute?"

"Sure," she said. "I have a minute."

"It's about Lisbeth."

"What about her?"

"I'm trying to figure out what happened," I said. I told her about Lauren's book. "I'm helping her with some stuff about Lisbeth."

"What do you want me to say, Marvin?"

"I think I have to do this."

"You probably do."

"I mean to figure out what happened to us and everything."

"I hope you're not doing this for me. I know what happened."

"I've been thinking about you a lot since I started this. You and Daniel and everything. That's all. I just wanted to tell you I've been thinking about you."

"All right. I'll tell Danny. But listen, Marvin. Don't you think?"

"What?"

"Nothing. Never mind."

"No. What were you going to say?"

"Marvin. It's over. Don't get yourself all upset again. She's not worth a second thought."

Then why couldn't I stop thinking about her? I said, "I have to do this, Donna."

"I know, I know. You'll do what you want."

"I have to."

"Yeah. All right."

"I miss you," I said.

"All right. I'll tell Danny you called."

When I hung up, it was almost opening time. If I wanted to talk to Craig, I had to call him quickly or I wouldn't have a chance until after the rush. I picked up the phone, dialed. Craig's wife answered. Her flat tone of voice reminded me of Donna and made me doubt she'd give him my message, but she did. Craig called back about an hour after I opened and said he would meet me at Brennan's later that night.

We met at the bar and carried our drinks to a quieter table and talked. He was a shy guy, but after a couple of beers he loosened up, and by the time he got to the part about Gloria showing up at his apartment in the middle of the night, I could see that he was almost as haunted by her as I was.

Something happened to Kim. That was the first thing Craig thought when he saw Gloria standing at his door. But she didn't say anything about Kim. She didn't say anything at all. She glanced down the corridor toward the stairway. When she looked back at him, she smiled. Embarrassed, Craig thought. The way she stood there hugging herself made her look cold, so he stepped back and opened the door wider and she slipped in.

"I saw your light," she said.

He'd worked late, he told her; he'd just come home.

"I thought you might want some company. I hope it's all right."

Sure. It was all right. He never could sleep right after work anyway.

Craig lived in a studio, and his twin bed doubled as a couch in the daytime, if it was made. When Gloria showed up, it wasn't, so she sat in his desk chair while he went into the kitchen to wash a couple of glasses and get the half-empty bottle of wine he'd scavenged on the job he'd worked that night.

He wondered what was going on. The evening he took the record over to Kim's, Gloria had hardly looked at him, and when she had, it was with such total indifference he'd felt invisible. When he came out of his kitchen, she wasn't looking at him like that. How could he explain it? She had a look on her face like she didn't know what was going to happen the next second. An expectant look, he called it.

Craig was busy being careful; he didn't want to do anything to spook her. The sudden, fierce look she'd flashed at him the first time he saw her sunbathing had left an impression on him. He set the glasses on his desk. He poured the wine and handed a glass to Gloria. He asked her if she wanted to hear a record. She nodded. Any request? he wanted to know. She shrugged. He didn't remember what he played, but he turned it down low and then sat on the edge of his bed. They talked about something: Kim, school, his job, hers, but they didn't have what Craig would call a long conversation. He didn't think Gloria finished the half-glass of wine he'd poured for her before she came over and sat next to him.

"Then," he said.

He sipped his beer.

"You know."

He couldn't look at me.

I was embarrassed, but I don't think I was as embarrassed as he was. I took some things for granted, and this business wasn't what I was afraid of hearing; I was afraid of something else, something deeper than just sleeping together.

After a few seconds, he said, "Nothing like that ever happened to me before."

He knew that Gloria's coming to him was too good to be true, but that night he didn't want to question it, even in his own mind. He just let it happen. He told himself the simplest explanation he could think of and tried to believe it: she liked him, and she was too shy to show it in front of Kim. Of course, coming to a guy's room in the middle of the night wasn't exactly a shy thing to do, but he got the impression she'd never done anything like that before.

"She was serious," he said. He'd never slept with a woman who seemed so serious. "Especially when I said her name. That's what I remember. When we were in bed, if I said her name, she got very, very serious."

She stayed all night, entwined with him on the twin bed. In

the morning she made him promise not to tell anyone about what had happened. Gloria didn't have to go into it; Craig understood. She'd only lived with Kim for a few weeks, and Kim might have interpreted Gloria's visit as sort of sluttish behavior. How could she know how serious Gloria was?

She told Craig, "If you tell anybody, I'll know."

He believed her. He promised he wouldn't tell a soul. The idea of sharing a secret with Gloria excited him. She never said so, but he understood that if he kept quiet, she'd come again.

She didn't return that night or the next, but the third night she arrived less than a half hour after he got home from work. She brought him a sack full of grapes and a quart of orange juice. After they made love, he lay on his bed and watched her while she explored his apartment. She wore his robe. Its sleeves covered her hands and made her look like a kid. She sat under the glow of his desk lamp and studied a photo of his brothers for so long he thought she might say she recognized them. As she flipped through his record collection, she sang snatches of songs from the records she knew. She went to his window and looked down at the courtyard. "I could feel you watching me," she said. "Like a vibration. It was weird."

A pattern developed. Every two or three days, at around midnight, Gloria knocked on his door. She usually had some kind of treat: ice cream, beer. The only personal item she brought was a toothbrush that she left in his medicine cabinet stored in the plastic container it came in. She always stayed all night, but most mornings she woke early and slipped out while Craig slept. At first, he didn't question this arrangement. She worked all day. He had his classes, long hours of study, a night job. All he could do was keep her secret and hope that she would keep coming back.

Their secret changed his life. Not knowing when Gloria would come again kept Craig in a constant state of anticipation. He shaved every day. He made his bed, tried to keep his bathroom clean. The light of day grew brighter. He could hear the articulate sounds of traffic for miles around him. Time slowed down; it speeded up. On campus people walked with the herky-jerky motion of old movies. In class, he couldn't concentrate, but he had more energy for his catering jobs than ever. One night while he worked a retirement party, a middle-aged woman stood up and sang an off-key rendition of "Unforgettable" that almost moved him to tears. Gloria's mysterious midnight visits made him more sensitive to the beauty and terror of life. Anything could happen!

A month passed. Six weeks. Time found its natural rhythm.

"But I got uncomfortable," Craig told me. He began to wait for Gloria every night, sitting at his window watching her dark apartment. If she didn't come, his disappointment was unbearable. He couldn't sleep. He started drinking his scavenged half-bottles of wine by himself and slept until noon and fell behind at school and had to drop two classes.

He told Gloria, "You know, we can't keep this a secret forever. Kim might even know already."

"Kim?"

"She probably knows."

"Nobody knows anything," she said.

"But if she does, it looks worse."

"It doesn't matter."

"So let's go out. Let's get out of here for once."

"I like it here."

"Let me take you to a movie."

"I like it just me and you."

"Don't you want to go to a movie or something?"

"I don't care," Gloria said.

"You don't want to go out?"

"Sure. I don't know. I never thought of it."

Craig said, "When?"

"You don't like me coming over?"

"Of course I like you coming over."

"I was worried maybe you didn't."

"I'm not working Friday night, if you want."

"Friday?" she asked.

"I'm totally free," Craig said.

The night after he asked her to the movies, she didn't come over. She didn't come the next night. Or the next. Friday came and Craig didn't hear from her. He called Kim's when he got back from campus, but no one answered the phone. He went to their apartment and knocked on the door. He pounded on it. Around midnight, he was sitting at his window when Gloria and Kim passed through the courtyard with a flurry of whispers and dropped keys and laughter. He watched the lights come on in Kim's apartment. He waited an hour at least, as one by one the lights went out again, and Gloria's room went dark.

He slept most of Saturday. Between dozing, he told himself, just let her go. Forget about her. For a few minutes the idea of being free of her soothed him, let him sleep, but an hour later he woke in a panic, disturbed by half-remembered fragments of dreams about Gloria. Fear, sorrow, confusion followed him out of his sleep. He was more convinced than ever that he needed her. But why? She gave him all of herself and none of herself. He felt like everything was out of balance, and the only way he could restore equilibrium to his life was to get closer to her.

He remembered the first time he saw her, her bandaged arm raised to her face. He remembered stepping away from his window. He knew he had to be careful, but the slow changes the sun made in her gave him hope. He thought that if he was patient and gentle, he might be able to work some kind of change on Gloria, too. If she ever came back again, he wouldn't say a word about the movies or dinner or anything.

He'd let things fall back into the old pattern, and he'd be satisfied with that.

Sunday night she arrived with a package of popcorn and a liter of Coke. Craig let her in. As he locked his door, he noticed that his hand was shaking. He felt strung out. He was so nervous that when the first kernel of popcorn went off, he flinched.

Her first touch calmed him. She pulled him down on top of her, held him still. He let his full weight press her into the bed. They didn't move for a long time, until Craig put his lips near her ear and whispered her name.

The old pattern never developed again. Her visits became utterly random. She'd come two nights in a row, then disappear for almost a week. His anticipation turned to apprehension; he never knew if she'd ever come back. In order to live from one of Gloria's visits to another, he relied on ritual. It happened gradually. The morning after a visit, he found himself repeating the things he'd done the day before. Soon he was leaving the house at the same time every morning, wearing his lucky leather jacket. He drove to Berkeley along a ritual route and always parked on the same block. The closer he got to the place he'd parked the last time she'd come to him, the greater the chance she'd come that night. His whole day became ordered and patterned and precise. And for a while, he felt fine. He passed the classes he'd kept. He made a living with his catering company. If he wanted to go to a movie or to hear some music, he went with a friend from school or by himself. He never told a soul about Gloria.

She didn't want to go out, Craig knew that much. He thought that maybe if he knew more about her, he could figure out what she did want. The first night she came to his room, he didn't let himself ask any questions. Now he had nothing but questions.

One night he decided to ask. He could feel her beginning to breathe like she was asleep. He shook her gently. "Gloria?"

"What?"

"Are you awake?"

"Uh huh."

"I can't sleep," he said. "Why don't you talk to me for a while?"

"What do you want to talk about?"

"I don't know. What about your family? Your mother. Your father."

"My father?"

"What does he do?"

"Do?"

"For a living."

"He was a smoke jumper. He jumped out of airplanes into the burning forest." (I know where this came from: there was a smoke-jumper's camp a few miles from The Caves. The guys used to come up every summer to meet the waitresses and girl-guides.) "But he got hurt. Smoke in the lungs. He had to quit."

"Your mom work?"

"No, she's the stay-at-home kind. She'll die with her apron on."

"Do you have brothers or sisters?"

"I have a sister."

"Older or younger?"

"She's older than I am."

"What does she do?"

"Her name's Lisbeth."

"Is she married?"

"She's a housekeeper at a hotel. She makes beds for a living."

"In Seattle?"

"No. She was married once."

"Where?"

"She has a little boy."

"Your nephew," Craig said.

Gloria rolled away from him. She said, "In Oregon."

Three nights, four nights later, she still hadn't come back. The evenings he didn't work, he could see the light on in her room until around eleven. He waited until midnight, one o'clock, but she never knocked on his door.

"I went kind of crazy," he told me. He wandered the halls of the apartment house trying to resist the temptation to knock on her door. He sat on the stairway and held his head. He felt himself rocking.

Would she let him in?

No. She'd look at him like she did the night he took the record to her.

He felt dizzy; everything was out of balance.

He wanted to call Kim and tell her everything, every detail. But when he tried to think of everything he knew about Gloria, he couldn't think of much. He could talk to Kim for hours about what he didn't know about Gloria, though.

She was a name, a knock at the door.

Where did she come from?

Why all the secrecy?

Her comings and goings had some secret motive, some design he couldn't decipher.

What was she hiding?

What did she want?

He saw himself standing in the courtyard calling, Gloria! Gloria! Gloria! until every light in the building came on and she opened her window and looked down at him. He heard himself yelling, What do you want from me?

Craig didn't call Kim or go to Gloria's door or call her to her window. He wasn't quite ready to ruin everything. He relied on his rituals. He waited another night. He waited three days. The fourth morning he left his apartment at the usual hour, but instead of following his route to Berkeley, he drove up

Park Boulevard to Montclair and parked across the street from La Salle Market. He could see Gloria through the plate-glass window. He propped a book on his steering wheel and tried to read, but most of the time he just watched her work. He didn't know how long he sat there. What he was doing exactly, he didn't know. He just felt like he was doing the only thing he could do.

The door swung open. Gloria stepped into the sunlight brushing her hair. A tall man in a three-piece suit followed her. As they walked through the parking lot, Craig noticed that the man was slightly pigeon-toed, like a tennis pro. He watched the guy open the passenger side door of a white Saab. Gloria got in.

Craig tailed them up the winding roads. It wasn't easy keeping up; the guy drove the snake-like streets as though he knew every curve as well as Craig knew his ritual route from the Alamo to Berkeley. The turns were so tight, Craig lost sight of them for minutes at a time, caught in a series of maze-like switchbacks. Then he glimpsed the white car flashing through the trees. He wound through an S-shaped bend and suddenly swept past their car parked on the side of the road. He drove ahead until he found a safe place to turn around and circled back, but the Saab was gone. He pulled over and studied the place for some clue to tell him why they'd stopped there. Across the street, a redwood and glass house sat half-hidden in the trees. Beside the mailbox stood a sky blue diamond-shaped sign: Carter and Milhous Realty. Craig coasted down the hill hoping to see the Saab again. He didn't, but he counted four more diamond-shaped signs.

At home he set his desk chair near the window, put his feet up on the sill, and rocked, waiting for Gloria. Around midnight, he saw her light go out. No more than three minutes later, she knocked.

Like every other night Gloria came, they listened to music. They made love. But for the first time in weeks Craig didn't feel like he was sleeping with a shadow. He held a flesh and blood woman in his arms. The fine, dark hair near her neck smelled dusty with baby powder. Her breath tasted like metal and mint. Her feet were cold.

She lay beneath him, waiting for him to whisper her name, to set everything in motion. But Craig couldn't say it. He just wanted to hold her still, to get a good long look at her, to have something to remember. For a long time he'd believed that her name was all he knew for sure. Now he didn't know what to believe. He let his full weight press her into the bed. He hoarded every detail: her bitten fingernails; her flame-shaped scar. The shape of her ear; the tiny dimple on the lobe. The curve of her eyebrow and the waxy look of her closed eyelids. These things were all he'd ever really know about Gloria.

When he closed his eyes, he saw a white car flashing through the trees and felt a deep fearful sorrow he'd only known in his dreams.

SIXTEEN

□

Lauren was driving us up Ascot toward Skyline. The road cut back and forth. Sweeping curves. Blind turns. She was quiet for a while, brooding. I'd just told her Craig's story over coffee at the Mediterranean. I felt dry-mouthed and heavy headed after all the beers I'd drunk with him the night before, and I wanted to go back to bed, but Lauren didn't want to go home. She was in one of her driving moods. We passed a Carter and Milhous sign, but I didn't say anything; Lauren must have seen it.

"He was telling you about his baby," she said. "That's what he was doing. Don't you see? He still thinks he's the guy in that song."

I reminded Lauren that Gloria went to Craig's apartment

in the middle of the night, like one of my father's girlfriends.

Lauren said, "But Craig watched her from his window, right? What was he thinking? She was beautiful. He wanted her. He went down there and what was the first thing he said? She went, 'My name's Gloria,' and he went, 'Like the song.' That's how he saw her from the start. She didn't even remember the song."

I said, "He played it for her. It gave her ideas."

"That's right. That's exactly right. He knew what that song was all about. On some level, anyway. I'm not saying he thought, 'I'll play this record for her and she'll come knocking.' I'm just saying there's complicity here."

"He didn't even know what she wanted."

"Well, he figured it out fast enough. Then he started being very careful. He wanted her there. He made that clear to her."

"Why are you straining to lay the blame on Craig?"

She said, "You think he's totally innocent?"

"Innocent of what?"

"Of making her fit his own fantasies. It's something men like to do. Especially with someone like Gloria."

"Why make it so complicated?"

"It's not complicated," Lauren said. "It's the simplest, truest thing in the world. It's about control. She was his dream come true. He didn't care who she was and where she came from and what she wanted until she stopped showing up."

"She came and went," I said. "That's all I know."

I didn't like hearing Craig's story any more than Lauren did, but it made sense to me. I didn't know what all it meant, all I knew was that the woman he described sounded too much like my sister. The whole time I listened to him, I kept remembering how I felt while I sat with her in that trailer in Eureka. I remembered why I let her go.

The night before, after Brennan's closed, I walked Craig across the almost empty parking lot to his car. Neither of us said anything; we were all talked out and tired and more than half-drunk. I could tell he was relieved after talking to me. He seemed suddenly younger, lighter on his feet, despite the beers and the time of night. When we got to his van, he told me it had been a long time since he'd closed down a bar. He felt like he did in his college days, getting off from a catering job in the middle of the night, going home to Gloria. He told me he hadn't talked to anyone about her since he heard about her murder on the news. She had made him promise not to tell a soul, and after she died, he thought that keeping her secret was the least he could do. That's one reason he didn't want to talk to Lauren and me in his yard that day, but after we left his house, he couldn't stop thinking about Gloria. It all came back to him, the obsession, the confusion, and he felt like he had to tell somebody or he'd go crazy. He thanked me for listening to him. When I reached out to shake his hand, he pulled me to him and hugged me, slapped my back.

And driving home to Lauren's, I'd realized that he'd told me the truth. I'd heard what I'd been afraid of hearing. Memories came flooding back, and I was too tired and drunk to keep them at bay.

The summer our father found his first waitress, that girl named Gail, my sister started calling herself Liz, after our mother. It was a summer of distant forest fires, sudden thunder, smoke and lightning, and driving rain. Record numbers of tourists toured The Caves. Our father's voice called out tour number eighteen or twenty or twenty-three until almost dark. We were shorthanded and everybody was working overtime and nobody was too very happy. The hotel was running close to the edge of out of control. Crises, major and minor, plagued us all summer: freezers broke down, and meat spoiled, and pipes burst and flooded the kitchen, and some kind of creature died under the floor of the employee dining room, and its odor grew more intense every day. During the Fourth of July weekend, Tommy set his sheets on fire sleeping off a drunk and was saved by Big Jim, who vowed to quit drinking while the smell of the smoke was still in his clothes, but he got so mean three waitresses quit before the August rush got started, so in the best interest of the Chateau, he bought a case of Seagrams 7 and split it down the middle with Tommy.

Brenda's baby had been dead since the fall, but Hank still wasn't talking too much. When he drove the truck, he moved a toothpick around in his mouth with the tip of his tongue, a skill I spent hours practicing, but I could never quite do it with his solemn concentration.

I was sixteen that summer, and I had a furtive, burning crush on two of the college girls, buddies from Brooklyn named Gina and Sarah. They didn't couple up with any of the guides or waiters; they seemed content to taunt me with their exotic accents and ankle bracelets and deep tans. I had a girlfriend, though, a freckled-faced believing Baptist named Steph, who I'd known since the third grade. Twice or three times a week, I'd ride down the mountain in the truck with Hank and we'd pick her up in the parking lot of her parents' bowling alley and drive to the tennis courts in Riverside Park in Grants Pass. She could beat me if she tried, but most of the time she played half-heartedly, saving her passion for afterward when we lay in the shade of the bridge and kissed and groped and worked ourselves into a frenzy of frustration. Steph let me touch her breasts, if she was sure no one was watching us, but if my hand ever drifted below her belly button, she stopped it with a practiced gentle slap. I dreamed about Sarah and Gina every minute I was with Steph, the sassy way they popped their gum and the way their waitress uniforms hugged their butts and their big-city voices sounding tired and tough after a long shift behind the counter. In my mind, Gina and Sarah were interchangeable, and because they were untouchable, I never thought about choosing one of them over the other. When summer ended, and they got back on the bus to Brooklyn, I felt twice as heartbroken as I would have over any single girl.

Then school started and the rains came. Hank drove Liz and me home from Grants Pass, working his toothpick around in his mouth, while Liz leaned against me through the switchback turns. I could smell her wet hair, her parka. Her red hands lay in her lap. Halfway home she sometimes fell asleep on my shoulder. I was surprised how much I liked the feeling of her snuggling against me. She made me relax. I put my head against the cool glass of the window and closed my eyes and imagined she was someone else: Gina or Sarah or even Steph.

We arrived at the Chateau at dusk, the rain glittering in the beams of the headlights. The gabled Chateau was tall and dark except for a glowing row of first-floor windows: the coffee shop. Liz and I went down there and asked Big Jim to fix us burgers and served ourselves soup and milk. Liz twirled on the counter stool next to me while we ate ice cream and pie for dessert.

That was my junior year in high school, the year I stopped studying altogether. When the school year started, I didn't have much energy after that frantic summer, so I didn't do much work. When I realized nobody noticed, I kept on doing nothing out of habit and inclination. After dinner, instead of doing homework, I usually went to the front desk and found an old paperback among the books guests left behind in the rooms. Sometimes I stayed in the lobby for an hour or so, if there weren't many people there, then I'd take the book up to my room and stretch out on the bed to read. More often than not Liz would knock and come in and flop on my floor amid a pile of magazines she'd brought up from the lobby. She liked to show me pictures of pretty women. Did I like that dress, those shoes, that purse? I didn't really care about any of that stuff, but I liked having Liz's company, which surprised me. I remember looking up from my book and seeing her lying on her stomach, resting on her elbows, her feet raised and crossed at the ankle, her butt round in her jeans, the dip in her back, her hair over her high shoulders. I was pleased that she wanted to be with me in my room, flattered that she bothered to ask what I thought.

This was all new since our mother had left. We were both lonely that winter, I guess. It was a low time for everybody. Brenda was still mourning her baby, and our father seemed to become even more of a shadowy figure after Gail left. (In the winter, he didn't call out tour numbers over the intercom, but we could hear him move through the hotel by the sound of his keys jangling on his belt.) Tommy was gone, and even though Big Jim would never admit it, I think he missed Tommy when he was away over the winter—no one to get drunk with. I could hear Jim's radio—those old croners, Sinatra, Mel Torme, Tony Bennett—coming from his room late at night. The songs reminded me of our mother because they were often playing in the bar where we'd find her for our goodnight kisses when we were kids.

Liz liked to talk about our mother, but I didn't. Flipping through the magazines, she'd say, Where do you think Mom is now?

California, I'd say.

But where? At the beach or in a house with a view or riding in a car?

How would I know?

Liz wanted to imagine her in detail. Was she wearing a dress and stockings? Or slacks and a sweater? Earrings? She imagined our mother at the beauty parlor under a dome dryer, getting her fingernails painted red. She saw her smoking Pall Mall cigarettes, the red package on a coffee table. She described our mother sitting on a couch, her legs crossed, picking a bit of tobacco from her lip with a painted nail. She showed me how our mother's tongue flicked out to snatch the tobacco.

Liz's pantomimes got me down. One night I said, if you know so much, when is she coming home?

She said, No. She's never coming back. Why would she come back?

Even when Liz wasn't trying to imitate her, I saw our mother in her: when she licked her finger to turn a glossy magazine page or when she patted her hair behind her ear or pressed the corners of her mouth with her thumb and forefinger. She wore eye makeup and lipstick and stopped biting her nails long enough to let them grow so she could paint them. She smoked cigarettes she stole from behind the front desk counter. Pall Malls. She even smoked in front of our father. And when he didn't try to stop her, I learned a lot about how he felt after our mother left. Two years before, he'd caught me smoking with some of the guides in the shack and called me into his office and made me confess and promise never to smoke again. He told me that if he caught me hanging around the shack with those guys any more he'd cut my ears off. But Liz, he let smoke all she wanted. It was like he didn't care about anything anymore.

Liz even started to walk like our mother—a slow sort of gliding walk, as though she were going nowhere in particular, but just moving through the halls on some kind of current. I'd also noticed a slight deepening of her voice and a change in the way she looked at me. She seemed to be searching for something or waiting or wanting to say something to me. I had my own secret inner life, inhabited by Gina and Sarah and the characters in the books I was reading. Liz must have had one of her own.

I remember falling asleep on my bed with my book and waking up surprised to see her still lying on the floor. I told her to turn the light out when she left, then I lay there thinking about Sarah's tight uniform, tan legs, Gina's dark hair in a loose braid on her back, and Liz leaning against me in the truck, breathing evenly, dozing, and the musty smell of her hair drying in the truck's close heat and the rain drumming on the roof while Hank's toothpick made its slow circle around his mouth. I saw Liz spinning on her counter stool.

I couldn't sleep. I lay in bed reading a loose paged paperback of *The Valley of the Dolls.* Some sexy scene. Instead of thinking about Sarah or Gina or even Steph, I thought about Liz up in our mother's old room. I knew it was wrong to want my sister, but laying there that night, I felt so close to her that wanting her seemed to make some kind of sense. I knew how she felt, how she smelled, I knew every freckle, every curve and muscle of her body. I wanted to touch her—the dip in her back, the curve of her narrow shoulders.

I thought I could smell cigarette smoke and I imagined a small girl on a wide double bed, surrounded by pale hotel furniture exactly like the furniture in my room. I lay there wide awake thinking about being upstairs with her. Was Liz as lonely as I was? Yes. That's what she was trying to tell me with that look she gave me. I knew that if I knocked on her door, she would let me in. All fall she'd been trying to tell me that she wanted me to come up and see her to talk about our mother and the people we missed from the summer and the boredom of the long dark winter. I wouldn't have to say anything. She would close the door. All alone on the empty third floor, it would be our secret.

I got up from bed and dressed in my jeans. No shirt, no socks. I told myself I was just going to go see what the halls were like in the middle of the night. They were cold, quiet, and dark. First, I went downstairs to the lobby to make sure nobody was up. I took a package of M&M's and listened hard to the nighttime silence in the hotel. I started up the stairs again, past the second floor where I slept and then climbed halfway up to the third. On the landing, I stopped and listened, wondering, should I knock or just open the door? My mind was racing, remembering why it was wrong to want her.

She was my sister, my sister, my sister.

But something was drawing me up the stairs. My desire felt natural, right, inevitable, as I stood on that landing. I don't think I ever felt closer to anyone than I did with Liz that winter, not Donna or Barbara or Lauren.

But she was my sister. My sister.

Then I heard a door close down on the first floor. The sound of it filled the stairwell like a crack of thunder. The creak of the stairs. In my panic, I could feel the hotel around me, sense every room and corridor and closet by the sound of that echo. In my mind I was navigating through the hotel like a bat. Then I heard the rattle of keys and knew it had to be my father. I could see him coming up the steps in my mind's eye: his bald head, his white shirt and green guide's pants, a cluster of keys on his belt.

I went on up the stairs and hurried past Liz's door to the rear stairway and circled back to my room. My father must have heard me. Back in bed I lay very still and listened to the rain shaping the huge hotel and to my heart and my exhausted breathing, as slowly I came back to my senses and realized how close I'd come to catastrophe. I listened for my father's footsteps outside my door, but there was only stillness and the slow calming of my heart, then sleep.

Lauren turned down Asilomar Drive and pulled to a stop near the ditch where they found Gloria. I didn't feel very well. Driving the winding roads for the last half-hour hadn't helped my hangover much at all.

"Looks different doesn't it?" Lauren said. She meant different from TV.

We were parked on a deserted curving stretch of road

overhung with trees. I could see houses in the distance, hear an occasional car hissing past on Skyline. The high side of the road was on our right: a steep wall of clay as pale as flesh. The other side dropped off into a ferny ditch lined with oak and eucalyptus, some pines. It was late September. The ditch was dry.

"Yeah," I said.

I don't think I would have driven there by myself. If I had known Lauren was going there, I would have asked her to turn around. I was beginning to feel much worse than I'd felt all morning.

"What if Craig's telling the truth?" she said.

"He is," I said. I told her what she'd told me: a lot happened. But I didn't tell her about that winter when I was sixteen. She would have wanted to know too much, more than I could tell her. Suddenly, I had another secret to keep.

She said, "Just be careful. If you buy Craig's story, the next thing you know, you're paying for Tunney's."

That was a big jump. All I was saying was that Craig's story fit a pattern. That's all.

"Have you listened to Tunney's tapes?" she asked.

"I've heard some things, sure. It's a small apartment."

"Do me a favor and give them a close listen. I want to know what you think."

"I can tell you what I think right now. Whatever pattern comes clear, it doesn't lead where Tunney says it does."

"No," Lauren said. She turned away from me and looked out her side window at the ditch. Crisscrossed with tree shadows, it looked darker and deeper than it did on TV. It cut into the canyon like a wound, a gash. When Lauren went there the first time, she said she didn't feel anything: no sorrow, no anger, but, as I looked into that dry ditch, I felt like I was looking into the mouth of hell.

Lauren gave me one of her long looks. "But it does lead here," she said.

SEVENTEEN

Listen to Tunney: "It's a matter of record in this state that I never lied about what happened to those girls. Or about my life with Gloria. And I'm not going to start making up stuff now. This is the truth, all right?"

All right. That was their deal. As long as Lauren pretended to believe him, he pretended to tell the truth.

I made no deal with Tunney. So why did I listen to him? He knew something about my sister; there had to be some kind of truth buried beneath his distortions, his evasions. Even liars don't lie all the time.

But it wasn't easy listening to his story. I remember lying on the couch with the cat on my chest. Lauren was in her room writing something or reading or dozing in her low overstuffed chair. Light poured in through the dusty windows, as Tunney's voice lulled me into a daze. I felt hot and sleepy and I couldn't concentrate. He talked in circles, contradicted himself, rambled, speculated. He never stayed on a train of thought too long. He claimed he couldn't remember long stretches of time, and then he'd describe some event like it was a movie he'd seen over and over. Sometimes he sounded like one of my waiters calling in sick on a Saturday night: too much detail and a please-believe-me tone in his voice. Other times he sounded like one of those guys who sit at my bar and collar the fellow on the next stool and recite long stories about desire and betrayal and revenge. I kept asking myself, what was I hearing? A rehearsed story or a memory worn smooth by rumination?

Listen to him: "I was obsessed with her. I admit it. I saw her every day for months, and every time I said hello, she looked at me like she didn't recognize me. When I reminded her of something we'd talked about, she blinked, frowned, like she didn't remember. That drove me nuts. That's why I kept putting groceries in her car: to say to her, 'I'm here. Don't forget me.'"

(When Lauren left me, she took Tunney's tapes, but I found copies of the transcripts in one of the boxes she left behind. I don't need the tapes. When I read his words, I hear his voice as clearly as if he were in this room with me.)

I think Gloria remembered him more than she let on. He passed through her line at least once a day to tell her a dim-witted disc-jockey's joke or report on the weather or give her a news flash he'd heard on his car radio. She heard herself called Gloria Gloria so often she got used to it. She decided she kind of liked the sound of it: Gloria Gloria. Every few days, she found stuff on the front seat of her car: a magazine, a six pack of beer, a watermelon, a rose, and she knew where it all came from. Tunney was a presence, like the

Musak, like Alphie's voice over the intercom. Stories about him were in the air: his father had gotten him out of some secret serious trouble in Los Angeles and brought him back home. His ex-wife often called the market making wild accusations, deadly threats, even though Tunney Sr. sent her a payroll check every other week. One day, as he walked out of the automatic doors, the checker next to Gloria pressed one nostril closed with a finger and sniffed loudly. Gloria heard him called a thief, a liar, and a fool, and she believed everything she heard. She collected Tunney-stories and brought them home to tell Kim, believing that the more she knew, the less of a threat he was to her.

Listen: "Things got out of control in L.A., all right? You probably heard about some of the stuff I was doing. Cocaine, all right? Everybody was doing it, but I liked it more than most people, I guess. The stuff made me feel great, made me want everything, every woman I saw, every house, car, clothes in store windows. I wanted to feel like that all the time. After work, I'd do a line or two and start driving home and I'd keep on driving. I wanted to see everything. I wanted to take it all in, but I was never satisfied. I drove through endless streets of low ranch-style houses. I saw glimpses inside. Televisions. A man passing a window in his undershirt. I heard music. Shouts. Dogs barked. Boys rode up and down the streets on bicycles. When it was getting dark and the windows of houses started to light up, I felt drawn in. I wanted to be invisible, to sit and watch and not be seen. All my life I sort of felt like I was here and not here at the same time, you know? I had this distance from myself, from people, a distance that I liked. Sometimes it was like I was watching myself. Around that time, I watched myself slip a kitchen knife and this pair of handcuffs I bought at a flea market under the seat of my car. I didn't even know what I wanted to do with them. I liked them as things, objects. I felt good knowing they were under there. I felt like, prepared, but for what, I didn't know."

Tunney was right: Lauren knew some things about his life in Los Angeles. She knew about his shoplifting and the cocaine and the huge debt he owed his dealer. The police had been to his house three times for domestic disturbances. And once he was caught inside a neighbor's house in the middle of the afternoon, but talked his way out of there by claiming he'd seen a burglar breaking in. But the last and worst story she found actually made the newspapers. A fourteen-year-old girl accused Tunney of making her take her pants off at knifepoint in the backseat of his car.

Listen: "You want to know about that? All right. She came to me. I was getting in my car in a parking lot at the Sunset Mall and she appeared out of thin air, it seemed like. She looked sixteen, at least, to me. She was wearing a man's sweater three times too big for her and jeans and scuffed tennis shoes, but she definitely had a sixteen-year-old face. She asked for a ride and told me a story about how she'd snuck out of her house to come down to the mall and how she was desperate to get back home before somebody missed her. I said, fine. Hop in. Then I drove, following her directions home, until I came to a side street that turned up into the hills. I took it, not saying anything. I was watching myself, like from a distance. She started getting nervous and said to stop, so I did. I watched myself pull the knife out from under the seat and show it to her. You'd be surprised at the calming affect that knife had. On me and on her. I told her to get in the backseat. I remember everything. Her belly, when she pulled her sweater off, looked as pale as paper. Her eyes were wide open with fear, and she was breathing shallow, fast. She moved with quick, jerky motions doing what I asked her. When I handcuffed her, she was sweating and I could smell her. It sort of made me dizzy to smell her, but I wasn't nervous. In that backseat, I had control, and nothing else mattered in the world. I didn't even want to touch her. I sat there looking at her for, I don't know, it seemed like a half hour, then I slipped the knife back under the seat and told her to get dressed."

He let her out of the car and drove away. On the next lonely stretch of road, he tossed the knife and cuffs out the window. He'd left the girl a long way from anywhere she wanted to go, so Tunney was fairly confident he wouldn't get caught. But she knew who he was. That's why she asked him for a ride; she'd seen him at the shopping center with his wife and son. She provided the police with a good description of him, and he was arrested one morning when he opened his garage door before going to work and saw three police cars blocking his driveway. When the cops questioned him, he admitted he'd asked the girl to get in the backseat, but he denied ever owning a pair of handcuffs or having "brandished a knife." The handcuffs, the knife, were never found, and the girl conceded that he'd never touched her, so the police didn't have much to go on. The girl's father wanted to press charges anyway, but Tunney Sr. talked to him and made a few promises. One of the conditions of the deal was that Tunney had to leave the L.A. area, which was all right with him, he told Lauren. His wife, Pat, decided to stay behind after the humiliation of his arrest, and after his father promised to send her money for their son, Paul. "She might tell you different, now," Tunney said, "but staying was her idea." A few weeks later, he moved back to his parents' house and started working at Carter & Milhous Realty.

Listen: "I was good at selling houses when I was into it, but after a while it was like, who cares? I went out with the buyers with the attitude: Buy it or don't buy it, I don't care. Either it was the house for them, or it wasn't. I was more interested in this woman, Lisa. Lisa Bianche, she was an agent there. Very professional, but stuck up about it, like she was better than everybody else just because she sold a house or two. I asked her out three or four times, but she wouldn't have anything to do with me. Every morning she'd go around the office with her cup of coffee in her hand and perch on people's desks for a few minutes to talk about something like what was on TV the night before or where she went over the weekend or something, but she wouldn't stop at my desk. She acted like I wasn't there, which made me restless. I couldn't stay in the office for more than an hour at a time. Then I met Gloria, and Lisa vanished from my mind. All I could think about was Gloria."

That winter, Pat was on the phone once a week threatening to send Paul to Oakland, and Tunney's mother was pressuring him to let the kid come. She wanted Tunney to sever all emotional ties with Pat. Tunney saw a chance to get his own house, so he agreed to take the boy if his mother would talk the old man into making an offer on a house he had his eye on. The day the offer was accepted, he asked Gloria to go for a ride with him.

I figure Gloria needed a good reason to go for a ride with Tunney, and when she saw Craig's car parked across the street from the market, she suddenly had a very good reason. Earl had come for her at that motel in Brookings; I'd found her in Eureka. She knew it was only a matter of time before Craig would follow her to work. She hadn't been to his room since the night she almost told him about her life in Oregon, the night she found out that Lisbeth was just under her skin. She couldn't go back to him. From her bed, she could see his light. She could see him sitting at his window, rocking, waiting for her. All week, she watched for him between customers, turning toward the tall front windows, squinting at the traffic. Then she saw it: the tan Volkswagen fastback, and Craig's shadow behind the bright glass of his windshield. She felt hot, dizzy; the whole morning was a blur of bright boxes and fruit by the pound and bills as smooth as skin.

Then she looked up from her register and there was Tunney. She wasn't surprised to see him; he always seemed to be around. He came to her counter empty handed, wanting all of her attention. He hooked the chain across the aisle behind him and closed her down.

"What are you doing?"

"It's lunchtime," he said.

"You can't do that."

He looked at his watch. "The schedule says you break at one. It's almost ten after."

She felt as though she'd just been shaken awake.

"I want to show you something," he said.

"What?"

"Something nice."

"Show me."

"I can't here. I have to drive you there."

"Where?"

"It's a surprise."

Gloria glanced out the window and saw Craig's car parked beneath the blue Ice House sign. She said, "All right."

The automatic doors swung open. Gloria made her way across the parking lot, walking as slowly as she could. She wanted to give Craig a good long look at her, to give him something to think about. In her mind, it was better for him to think she was seeing another man than for him to think he was getting too close to Lisbeth.

Everything seemed to happen slowly: Tunney opening her door; her awkward ducking into the bucket seat; Tunney making his way around the front of the car, his door swinging open. She had time to remember Mr. Spenser and his blue convertible, our mother's freckled arms in the sun, our father's voice blaring out of the loudspeakers. Once the car was moving, a calm came over her, like the calm she felt the first time she drove away from the Chateau without her baby, like the world outside was rushing past her, and she was sitting perfectly still. She closed her eyes. Then she felt a fine vibration running up her spine; she could feel Craig following her.

"Faster," she said.

Tunney downshifted and gunned the gas through a sweeping uphill curve. He took her for a wild ride, cutting across the center line to slice the arc of the turns, whipping into short shady straight-aways, passing blind. When he reached the summit of Snake Road, he slowed and stopped. They were sitting in front of a boxy modern-style house surrounded by trees. Its windows reflected the branches as darkly as still water.

"Look familiar?" Tunney said.

Gloria shook her head.

"You remember."

"I've never been here."

"You saw the pictures. You were looking at them the first time I saw you. You looked like you were in love with it."

"Oh."

"What does that mean? Oh?"

"I kind of remember."

"I hope so," he said, "because I bought it for you."

Gloria gave him a look. "Sure."

"In other words, I bought it because you liked it."

"Oh."

"Come on. I'll give you the grand tour."

Gloria shook her head. She wanted to keep moving.

A few days after that first ride, Tunney found a note under his windshield wiper.

> Dear AJT:
>
> Thanks for all the stuff you put in my car. Your house looks great. Someday you'll have to give me that grand tour.
>
> Gloria Gloria

Listen to him: "Her note took me by surprise. It was my first clue that she was aware I existed outside her aisle.

During the day sometimes I reached into my pocket just to touch that note."

He took it home and tacked it up on the wall beside his bed. He lay there eating chicken, watching a basketball game on TV, the sound turned off, while the Allman Brothers played on the stereo. He was thinking about Gloria, how she looked with her eyes closed in his car, the sunlight on her face. When he finished the chicken, he rolled off his bed and opened another beer and stood at the sliding glass door, looking out. The pool was spotted with rain, and rust-colored pine needles littered the bottom. He imagined Gloria on his bed, her scarred arm across her belly. He imagined running his finger down the length of her scar.

The next clear morning he cleaned his pool. Barefoot on the warm concrete as he swept storms of dust up from the bottom. He described the silt drifting down toward the silver filter vent in a slow whirl. Music poured out of his house. He skimmed the surface—leaves, pine needles, waterbugs—slapped the scoop against the retaining wall and left it all clinging there.

The afternoons stretched out, and he grew even more restless in the office. He started taking Gloria for hour-long lunchtime rides several times a week. I don't think she liked Tunney as much as she liked getting out of the market, being in the front seat of his car, feeling the swift back and forth of the twisting roads.

The days he didn't go for lunchtime rides with Gloria, Tunney went for solo dazed drives in the hills, trying to stay away from the market until close to Gloria's quitting time. Often, he found himself on some winding back road north of Berkeley after blanking out for miles. Then he'd turn around and find his slow way down the winding streets toward Montclair.

One day he arrived at the market during the hour when the sun slanted through the front windows. Gloria was bare legged. She wore her hair in a loose braid. She wasn't wearing any makeup and her eyes looked swollen, sleepy.

He set his basket on her counter. "So do you want to go swimming with me?"

Gloria said, "Swimming?"

"At my place."

She shook her head.

"Come on. Don't you like to swim?"

(My sister loved to swim.)

Gloria rolled the register tape forward and circled Tunney's total. "I don't know."

"Come on. It's getting hot," he said.

She found the black book under the counter and flipped it open.

"How about tomorrow? I'll pick you up."

She stared at the open page of Tunney's book, the long column of his initials: AJT. "All right," she said. "Pick me up here."

Tunney remembered driving Gloria up Snake Road. His naked back stuck to his car seat, the gas pedal felt smooth and cool against his bare foot. He remembered Gloria standing beside his car looking up at his house the way she'd gazed at the photos in his office window. She cradled her towel in her arm. While he gave her the tour, he felt rich watching her run her hand along the shoulder of a leather couch. He followed her through the kitchen. Her sandals flapping, Gloria moved through the bright sunlight that bounced off the white-tile counter. He noticed that her legs were whiter than his, except for the little dark marks near her ankles. Insect bites. Where his skin would have turned red, hers turned brown, like an apple slice left in the air. She pulled the sliding door open and stepped out onto the deck. She looked down at the swimming pool. It sparkled. The sun cast a web of light on the bottom.

"It has a diving board," Gloria said. "Can you dive?"

Tunney dove for Gloria. His first dive landed him among the cool bubbles.

Listen: "I could taste the chlorine in my nose. Under water, looking up, I could see the sky refracted, my diamond. I came to the surface and bobbed there, while Gloria clapped for me. She was sitting at the edge of the pool, kicking the water with her toes. I slipped under again and aimed myself at her feet. They flashed like fish on a line trying to escape. I caught her by the ankles and her feet went still. Her ankles were as thin as my wrists. With one strong pull, I could have pulled her in, but I didn't. I just let her go and rose to the surface. I remember breaking through to the sunlight, and how the red of her tank-top seemed to shatter like glass and then fall back together again. Her laughter dripped down on me. Her feet were in the air and the drops of water that hung from her heels looked as silver and heavy as mercury. 'Hey,' I said, 'you remember that note you gave me?' "

Gloria lay as he'd imagined. (And as I listen to him, half-asleep on that couch, I could imagine her, too.) Her scarred arm was folded like a wing, her legs were drawn up for warmth. Her thin calves scissored. The soles of her feet glowed. He lay down next to her. Her legs, still wet, felt cool, but her shoulders held a warmth, like flagstone after dark. He said, "Hey, Gloria Gloria," and she smiled. He kissed her and she became eager. She squirmed toward him, a sidestroke across the bedspread. Her mouth tasted like wax, a doll's mouth, and when their teeth touched, he felt it in his skull, bone against bone.

Listen: "We were under the covers, Gloria's head on my chest, her arm across my stomach. I held her wrist between my thumb and finger, like this. I could feel the ball of the joint roll in its socket. Then I found the beginning of her scar. I could feel it, raised, smooth. With my finger, I followed it, moving really slow in the dark, up her arm."

Tunney wanted her. And he sensed that if he didn't have

her full time, all the time, completely, he wouldn't have her at all. On their next lunchtime drive, they stopped at his house for a quick swim. While they lay in the sun, drying off, he said, "Wouldn't you like to live here?"

She wouldn't answer him yes or no. She didn't say anything.

He remembered waiting until he felt the full heat of the sun on his dry chest.

Finally she said, "I can't be late. We'd better go."

Tunney waited two weeks for an answer.

June 16. (He remembered the date because it was three days after his thirty-sixth birthday.) Midnight. His doorbell rang. On the tape, you can hear Tunney singing out the notes: Diiiing, Doong. He said he knew who it was. He believed that sooner or later all the things he desired would come to him.

Listen to him: "She was standing under the porch light, and she looked lost. She was wearing a plaid Pendleton shirt, which was weird for June, I thought. Her hair hung down around her face. She was hugging herself. She said her stuff was in her car, and I looked over her shoulder and saw her Impala parked on my driveway. I couldn't let her leave it there. My parents lived ten minutes away, and I didn't want one of them to drive by and see that blue car in front of my house. They'd recognize it, for sure. I wanted to keep Gloria a secret for the time being. Her bleached hair, her scar, her bitten fingernails, the who-cares? look on her face, the battered Impala: they added up to something I didn't really understand. All I knew was that they were just nobody's business."

EIGHTEEN

□

Summertime," Tunney said, "and the living was easy." He was rich and Gloria was good looking. Everything he wanted had come to him: the Saab (a hand-me-down from his father); a job he enjoyed, because he could get out of the office as often as he wanted to; a house in the hills with a swimming pool; Gloria. It all felt especially good after his troubles in Los Angeles.

Those first few weeks Gloria lived with him, they stayed close to home most of the time. "We swam. We screwed. We sat in the sun." But sometimes they drove around and looked at the houses he was trying to sell. Gloria liked the furnished homes best. In the first few houses he showed her, she just wandered from room-to-room and gazed at everything. "It was like she'd never seen the inside of a house before," Tunney said. Then one day he noticed her touching things: a tea pot, a book, a framed photo. Another day, she sat at a kitchen table, lounged on the couch. After a while, she began to open drawers, closets. She tried on women's coats, men's hats. Once she opened an umbrella and twirled around the entry hall, laughing. Finally, she got so bold that she turned on TVs and ran showers until the bathroom mirrors fogged up.

Tunney preferred the empty houses. His favorite was a white stucco place on Asilomar Drive that sprawled out in all directions as though they had built all the rooms onto it one at a time. If he'd known it was on the market, he would have asked his father to buy it for him instead of the house on Snake Road. He loved its view of Oakland, the Bay, San Francisco. He took Gloria there several times after work. They went out on the deck and leaned against the railing and drank wine and looked down at the city all laid out below them. The cars looked the size of insects, the people were invisible. Tunney told Lauren that the view gave him a sensation of well-being that was better than cocaine. He felt like he was the only man in the world and Gloria was the only woman.

Then in early July his son, Paul, flew in from L.A. "An hour flight," Tunney said, "and the kid drags his ass off the plane like a refugee." Tangled surfer hair to his shoulders, a T-shirt, jeans, high-top tennis shoes, untied. His luggage consisted of a skateboard and a boom box. I've seen a few pictures of the boy taken that summer. His eyes were as pale as Tunney's and they gave his face a bewildered expression.

His first words were, "Who are you?"

"Gloria," Gloria said.

She wasn't Tunney's secret anymore. Now that the boy was there, Tunney's mother started coming around the house to drive Paul to the tennis courts, to sailing lessons on Lake Merritt. She arranged for him to work for pocket money on weekend afternoons at Skyline Market.

Even though her husband forbade her to discuss their son with reporters, Virginia Tunney met Lauren at the Ice House in Montclair a couple of times a week. Lauren often arrived to find her sitting up front by the plate-glass window. From her chair, Mrs. Tunney could see the checkers working at LaSalle Market, and they could see her. Lauren said, "It was like she was flaunting her desire to talk."

Lauren came home from their first lunch in awe of the woman. Mrs. Tunney was almost as tall as her son, and she was so deeply tanned her skin had the texture of leather. She wore sunglasses, indoors and out. "And gobs of gold jewelry," Lauren said. Her hair looked stiff with spray; her nails were long and polished, and the whole effect made Lauren think of a suit of armor. While they talked, Mrs. Tunney drank great quantities of black coffee. She chain-smoked, and the ashtray slowly filled with lipstick tinged cigarette filters. Lauren had the impression that Mrs. Tunney wasn't talking to her at all. The woman spoke in a hoarse whisper directly into the tape recorder, which lay on the table between them among crumpled Virginia Slims packs and matchbooks and coffee mugs and Lauren's empty plastic creamer cups.

She said, "The first time I saw Gloria working the register, I said to myself, where did Alphie get this one? She wasn't like the others, the junior college girls and the part-timers, the housewives. I could tell there was something rootless about her, like a drifter, like a man, almost. There was actually something sinister about how unattached she seemed. That's the only word for it: sinister. She didn't talk much, even to the other checkers. And she didn't wear much makeup to speak of, and her clothes looked like they came from the Salvation Army. And that bleached hair, my God! She tied it back with a rubber band, and once I saw her use a paper clip to pin it behind her ear. A paper clip! But she was beautiful in a way, and that was the strangest thing of all. What a waste, I thought. I mean, you had to ask yourself, what's wrong with her? Doesn't she own a mirror?"

Mrs. Tunney went to her husband's office and looked at Gloria's application. She made some phone calls to Gloria's old employers, but got nowhere; Gloria didn't even have the area code for Seattle right. When Mrs. Tunney told her husband, he shrugged. "She's just a checker," he said. "Alphie says she does her job." Mrs. Tunney didn't press him, but she decided to keep an eye on Gloria.

"You can imagine my shock," she said, "when I went by A.J.'s house and found her living there."

No one answered the doorbell, so she used her own key. Inside, she called for Paul, but heard no answer. She made her way through the kitchen, where she noticed the sink full of dirty dishes and the greasy stove-top and the morning's newspaper unfolded on the table. She slid the door open, stepped onto the deck, and looked down to see Paul and Gloria lounging beside the pool. Gloria lay in the sun, shining with oil. Tunney's mother stood there, watching, thinking, no, Gloria didn't belong there; she belonged at the market behind the register in a smock, not beside the pool nearly naked in the sight of her grandson.

When Paul saw his grandmother, he waved and rose from his chair. Mrs. Tunney saw Gloria slowly turn and raise her hand to her face to shade her eyes. Gloria looked up toward the deck, but she didn't say anything. "She stared at me like she didn't know who I was and didn't much care, either." Mrs. Tunney turned and retreated into the house.

The next morning, Tunney got a call from his father at the real estate office. "Your mother's worried Gloria's giving Paul the wrong impression."

"What do you mean?"

"She doesn't like her demeanor around the boy."

"He likes her. They get along fine."

"That's what has your mother worried, I think."

"There's nothing to worry about. Tell her don't worry."

"And she doesn't like the way the girl looks at her."

"Looks at her?"

"Like 'who the hell are you?' "

That night Tunney asked Gloria to try to show his mother a little respect. After all, the woman was paying for the house Gloria was living in and for the groceries they ate and for the kid's clothes and tennis lessons and sail boat rentals. For all practical purposes, his parents owned them both.

He thought he'd gotten through to Gloria, but the next day she didn't show up at work. Tunney returned to his office about midmorning after showing a house and found a message that Alphie had called. Before he could sit down to call him back, the phone rang. It was his father wanting to know where Gloria was. Tunney had no idea. She'd never even been late to work before. He drove home and found her Impala gone. While he was there, his mother called.

"Is Paul there?"

Tunney didn't know. He hunted through the house and out by the pool. "He's not around. No."

"Well, where is he?"

"How would I know?" he said. He hadn't talked to his mother since she'd complained about Gloria. Now with Gloria missing, he felt pretty tense about the whole situation. "I can't keep track of him every second." He was certain that when he found Gloria, he'd find Paul, but he didn't say so to his mother. "He's probably off on his skateboard or something."

"He promised to meet me at The Ice House."

"He forgot. Kids forget," Tunney said. He told his mother he was busy. Houses to show. People to see. If he saw Paul he'd have him call her.

"Don't forget," his mother said.

Driving to an appointment that afternoon, he saw the blue shape of Gloria's car disappear into the tree shadows on Skyline Drive. He drove after her, winding through the hills in a daze.

Listen to him: "I was thinking, what the hell's going on? What were they trying to do to me? I didn't have to put up with that kind of disappearing act. And if my mother didn't like the way Gloria looked at her, what was I supposed to do? I tried to tell Gloria. I mean, I told her, She signs your paycheck. That's who the hell she is!"

He drove from shadow to shadow as the blue car vanished, reappeared. He drove faster. Why couldn't he catch that car? Where was Gloria going? He pulled into Roberts Park and circled the parking lot looking for the Impala, but it wasn't there. He stopped near the pool. Through the chain-link fence, he could see swimmers churning through the bright water. A coach paced in the sunlight. Tunney remembered the whistle in her teeth. He looked at his watch and saw that he'd lost an hour chasing Gloria's shadow.

When he found the house he was supposed to show, nobody was there. He drove down to the office where Scott Carter told him the people had just come by looking for him. Scott had sent Lisa Bianche up with a set of keys to show them around. This was not good. Scott told Lauren and me that there was nothing he hated more than standing up potential buyers; it made the whole agency look bad. He sat Tunney down. Six months, almost seven: where were the sales? Tunney showed Scott an inch of air between his thumb and forefinger; he was that close to selling the Asilomar place. Scott didn't believe in being close. He even had a word for it: horseshoes. Tunney got defensive, said the buyers were watching the interest rates. It wasn't his fault the rates were nineteen-five. Scott told Tunney that he was definitely right about the rates. They sucked big time. And that was exactly why when people wanted to see a house, he had to be there to show it to them.

Tunney left the office and drove up Ascot toward the house Lisa was showing for him, hoping to arrive in time to salvage some goodwill from the buyers. The higher into the hills he climbed the less hope of that he had.

Listen: "I wasn't in any mood to sweet-talk strangers. I thought, let Lisa handle them. If she had to cover for me, she'd have to talk to me about it. I was tired of her ignoring me, making me feel invisible. It was like she looked right through me. But I liked her eyes and the dimple in her chin and her long neck. I always wondered, did she know it was me on the phone those nights? I could hear the fear in her voice: *Hello? Hello?* (Lauren told him that Lisa did know.) Good. I wanted her to think it was me, so that every time she saw me in the office she'd think about lying awake in the middle of the night. I wanted to get her alone sometime in an empty house and remind her of those calls."

He turned down Asilomar and pulled to a stop in front of the white house. He'd lied to Scott about being an inch away from selling it. He didn't even want to sell it. As long as it was empty, it was his. Nobody deserved to own that view but him. He got out of his car and found the key in the lockbox and let himself in. He'd been in a hundred houses during the past year but none of them made him feel like this one did. It was built like a jumble of boxes stacked on the hillside so that most rooms had views from two or three sides. Late in the afternoon, the sun flooded through the curtainless windows. Tunney's footsteps echoed. One room led into another, then another, in a maze-like way that fascinated him.

Listen to him: "I walked from room-to-room, thinking about Lisa. It was weird. As soon as Gloria vanished, Lisa came rushing back into my head. For a while, I stopped thinking about Gloria and Paul and all my problems. I imagined finding Lisa there alone. Maybe she'd be waiting for a buyer, or better, she'd just let a buyer out. She was staying behind to take some notes on the place. I'd find her in one of the smaller bedrooms and stand in the doorway and wait for her to turn around. The look on her face in that instant would tell me if she knew I'd called her those nights. There'd be no way she could ignore me in an empty room."

He went out on the deck into the heat. Jacket off, vest unbuttoned, he leaned on the railing and surveyed the view. It soothed him to stand there with the empty house behind him and the city below. Nobody could bother him there.

So where was Gloria? Paul? It was bad enough that they thought they could disappear, but then they brought all that trouble down on him. A call from his father. His mother's voice on the phone: Don't forget. Seven months, Scott said. They could take everything away from him in an instant. Didn't Gloria see that?

Listen: "Then I remembered Lisa. It calmed me down thinking about being in a room alone with her, in a big empty house. Nobody could hear anything. It would be like it never even happened. It would be like we were the only people in the world. As safe as a phone call in the middle of the night."

How long did he stand there? He couldn't remember. The sun was going down. The fog was rolling in over the bridge. It grew cool enough for him to put his jacket back on, and then he drove home.

Gloria and Paul weren't there. Tunney sat by the pool and drank beer until way after dark. He heard her car pull into the garage around ten, ten-thirty. He met them in the kitchen. Sand in their hair. Barefooted. Sunburned. Tired. Gloria was carrying a life-sized stuffed panda. The kid was lugging his boom box.

"Where the hell?"

Gloria ignored him and dragged her panda into the living room.

Tunney followed her.

"Santa Cruz," Paul said.

"You don't tell anybody?"

The boy said, "The boardwalk."

"You don't call in sick?"

Gloria lay on the couch using the panda as a pillow. She closed her eyes.

"It was last minute," Paul said. "We were driving down to Montclair. She was going to work. But we just kept going."

"Mom called."

"We didn't plan it."

"Where's Paul? she asked me. How was I supposed to know?"

"We're back," Paul said.

"They've been on my case all day."

"We're safe."

Tunney turned on Paul and told him to get out of his sight. He didn't want to look at the kid.

Paul sauntered down the hall, slammed his door.

Gloria opened her eyes.

"You just kept going," Tunney said.

"Uh huh."

"Down to Santa Cruz?"

"He said he missed the beach."

"He's got a pool right out here."

"It's not the same thing. Anyway. He doesn't like pools. He told me he wants to drain it so he can ride his skateboard in it."

"He's crazy."

"I told him I'd ask you."

"You're both crazy."

"I'm tired," she said. She got to her feet. "I can hardly keep my eyes open." She carried her panda back to the bedroom. He watched the door close.

Then he went out to the garage and turned on the light. Her

blue Impala sat there ticking, cooling down. He could smell the thing: the nauseating stench of burned oil. He found his sledge hammer. The smooth handle was in his hands. He walked around the car picking his spots. The headlights shattered easily. Slivers of glass went flying. Tunney closed his eyes and pounded the windshield. It took two, three, four hard baseball-style swings. When he opened his eyes he saw the broken glass piled on the front seat like bright gravel. The taillights: red blasts. The rear window cracked like a jagged web. The passenger-side window exploded. He dented the doors with two huge blows.

Gloria stood in the doorway in her tank-top and panties, watching him. He remembered the fresh sunburn under her eyes and how quiet she was, how still. While she watched, he took a chisel and attacked all four tires. When he was finished the car listed like a sinking ship.

He stood there, breathing deeply. He was sweating. The hammer was heavy in his hands. "The beast is dead," he said. "Out of its misery."

NINETEEN

Now Gloria wasn't going anywhere. The next morning Tunney called a tow truck to come and haul the Impala away. Before the truck arrived he unscrewed the Oregon plates and put them in the backseat of his car. For the rest of the summer, Tunney drove Gloria to work in the morning and picked her up in the evening. During her lunch hour, they continued to go for rides in the Saab. She didn't seem to miss her car at all.

If she did, she didn't say anything to Tunney about it until late September, early October; he couldn't remember exactly when. It was one of the first rainy days of the fall. They drove up to see a house for sale on Thornhill Drive. He remembered the sheen of oil on the wet roads. The house smelled as musty as a wet dog. They took off their shoes in the entry hall, which seemed to make Gloria feel more at home than usual. She looked in the refrigerator as Tunney tossed one of his cards on the kitchen table. She grabbed a Coke and popped the top before Tunney could stop her. "Want a sip?" she said.

No, he didn't want a sip. He picked up his card and put it back in his pocket and followed her into the living room. He opened the drapes and stood at the window while Gloria went exploring down the hall. He couldn't see much of the view through the mist. The sky was as dark and iridescent as the oil-slick roads he'd driven to get there.

Listen to him: "I felt sort of low that day, even though I had most things under control. Paul was in school. My father hadn't called me in a month. My mother hadn't given me a hard time about Gloria since the swimming pool incident. But I hadn't sold a house since I sold the Snake Road place to my father, which didn't look good. Lisa had sold three houses over the summer. Now summer was over. Scott hadn't said anything to me yet, but it was only a matter of time."

He heard Gloria calling him and followed her voice down the hall, glancing in each doorway until he came to the master bedroom. He saw her shoes, her jeans, her sweater on the floor. He couldn't believe it. She was sitting against the headboard of the king-size bed, like she was posing for a picture.

"What are you doing?"

"It's huge," she said.

"Get out of there."

"Why?"

"You'll mess it up."

"I already messed it up." She slid down under the covers. "Come on."

Listen: "That's why I liked her: she was wilder than I was.

Suddenly, I didn't feel so low. Scott, Lisa, neither of them would do something like that, the chicken-shits. I thought about Lisa finding us there."

He shed his suit and slipped in beside her. The bed smelled like strangers. The rain drummed on the skylight.

"We went at it like a couple of teenagers," he said.

When they finished, Gloria was on top of him holding his wrists down like a wrestler. She put her lips near his ear and said, "Don't forget, Mister. You owe me a car."

Tunney told her he didn't owe her anything. "If you want a car," he said, "steal one."

He said it was easy. There were millions of cars out there. If she wanted one badly enough, she'd find one. She didn't have to even think about it; it would make itself available to her, the keys in the ignition, nobody around. He knew she could do it. She just had to be attuned to the opportunity, just had to be brave enough to take it. There were risks, sure, but if she took the risk, she deserved her reward. If she could steal an hour in a stranger's bed, she could steal a car.

He said, "You stole the Impala."

"I told you I lied."

He said, "Make it true, Gloria Gloria."

Before they left, Gloria made the bed. Tunney watched the sheets billow up and come slowly drifting down. He said, "When she was done, it looked as tight and smooth as a bed in a hotel room."

I stopped the tape and listened for a sound—a cough, a radio, the scrape of a chair—to tell me where in the apartment Lauren was. I couldn't hear anything; she must have been asleep. The shadows in the room told me it was almost time to go to the restaurant, but I rewound the tape and played that last part again. ". . . as tight and smooth as a bed in a hotel room." Here was a detail Tunney couldn't have invented. Up to that moment, I'd been listening to him suspiciously, but suddenly his whole story took on a tinge of truth that made me nervous. I didn't want to believe him, but that hotel-smooth bed made me feel differently about everything I'd heard. I couldn't get away from it; the woman he was calling Gloria was the girl I grew up with at the caves.

The second summer our mother was gone, Brenda always had to keep a close eye on Liz when they worked the rooms together. To Brenda, it seemed as though Liz had an unnatural curiosity about the guests. She wanted to know everything about them; where did they come from, and where were they going? Brenda told her it was a sin to look too closely into other people's lives. Their secrets were sacred, between them and God. But Lisbeth went ahead and looked in their luggage and at the labels in their coats hanging in the closets and at the bathroom stuff scattered beside the sink. Brenda let it go as long as Liz didn't touch anything.

I didn't see her a lot that summer. She rarely came to my room. It was light until after nine, so she stayed outside playing volleyball with the guides, then she went up to the Chalet to listen to music. I didn't miss her too much, because I'd found a girlfriend among the waitresses. Her name was Rachel, and she was two or three years older than I was. She came from a small town east of San Diego and had a vaguely Spanish accent. When it didn't rain, we slept beside the stream below the Chateau, our sleeping bags zipped together.

Rachel told me that Liz was a real pest when she visited the girls in the Chalet. She wanted to know everything about them: what was it like to live in, say, New Orleans or Toledo or Brooklyn? She begged the girls to read to her snatches of letters from home. She wanted to know what their boyfriends looked like, and asked to look at wallet photos.

Liz found her own boyfriend that summer, the bellboy, a tall, straight-laced local kid with ambitions to go to the Air Force Academy, as I recall. He wore his hair like a pilot already—so short you could see a pale band of skin around his ears—when most of us had hair to our shoulders. He had to sit around the lobby for long hours between arriving and departing guests and that's where Liz found him during the heat of the day. She flirted with him in front of Brenda and our father and dozens of passing guests. Brenda seemed worried, but my father thought it was innocent as long as they just talked in the lobby.

Then one night, my father caught the guy wandering the Chateau halls in the middle of the night, looking for Liz's room. He fired him on the spot. Hank drove him down to Grants Pass the next morning before the staff was finished with breakfast. I had to take over the guy's bellboy shifts, which I resented because my father constantly passed through the lobby all day. I preferred working out of his sight, guiding tours through the cave.

Liz was furious. She stayed up in her room for almost a week. Sometimes in the afternoon, I could see her looking down at the guides on the benches near the mouth of the cave. Every one of them had gotten the message: stay away from the boss's daughter.

Some evenings, when Rachel was working a late shift in the coffee shop, Liz would come to my room. She asked me all about Rachel. Did she have brothers and sisters? And what did her father do? Was she going to go to college? Liz seemed surprised when I didn't have the answers. She asked, "How are you going to feel when she leaves?"

I hadn't thought about it; they all left in the fall. "I'll get over it," I said.

Around that time, guests started to report things missing from their rooms—a pair of sandals, a book, sunglasses, maps—small things that most of them assumed they'd misplaced. But they told us anyway, in the hope that, if their things turned up somewhere, we would mail them to them. It seemed to me that people were losing a lot more stuff that summer than ever before. Then a radio disappeared, a woman's watch, a bird watcher's binoculars. In mid-August, a man returned from touring the cave to find his Stetson hat missing. When a search of the hotel and Chalet and the guideshack turned up nothing, my father had to pay the man three hundred dollars to replace it. As soon as I had carried the man's luggage out of the lobby, my father found the key to Liz's room and climbed the stairs. Her closet looked like a lost and found locker. He made her haul it all down to the lobby. He sat her at his desk with the guest ledger and told her to find the addresses of every guest who lost anything and to wrap up the stuff and send it back to them. Except for the Stetson hat. He'd paid for it and it fit, so he kept it for himself.

After that incident, Brenda did without Liz's help making beds.

I didn't like it, but I had to believe Tunney when he said that Gloria stole a car. Two weeks before Thanksgiving, a Monday, he closed the deal on the Thornhill house in the morning and took Gloria to lunch at the Claremont Hotel that afternoon. Coming out of the restaurant, walking through the parking lot, Gloria grabbed him by the elbow.

"Keys," she said. An orange Civic station wagon.

Tunney kept walking.

Gloria opened the driver's door and got in and started the car. ("Nonchalant as hell," Tunney told Lauren.)

He followed her up the tree-lined stretch of Ashby onto the Warren Freeway and off again at Moraga Road. No trouble. Up Snake. Into the garage. He had Gloria back at work at La Salle before her lunch break was over. That evening he put the Oregon plates on Gloria's new car.

Tunney believed that everything happened for a reason and that significant events occurred in clusters. (Selling a house, finding a car.) He attributed it to something he called "energy fields," electrical currents that moved through his life in a positive or negative direction, like the poles on a battery. The energy attracted events around points in time. He said, "That's why all the good things happened to me that year, after I came home from Los Angeles. I was attracting a lot of positive energy." He felt like a lightning rod for good fortune, and he wanted to give thanks.

The Wednesday before Thanksgiving he went to the market and loaded a cart with a turkey and yams and boxes of stuffing mix and wheeled it into Gloria's aisle.

"What's that?" she said.

He told her that he'd invited his parents to Thanksgiving dinner to thank them for setting him up with the job, the house.

Gloria didn't say anything. She just added up his groceries and gave him his black book and circled the total on the register. She bagged everything and put it in his cart.

After work she went to Alphie's office and asked for a cash advance to get her through the long weekend. Two hundred dollars was what Alphie gave her. He told Lauren that Gloria didn't look too good to him. Her tan had faded, she'd gained weight, and her fingernails were bitten to the quick. He said she didn't even look like the calm-eyed woman who had come in asking for a job. When she asked for the advance, she could hardly look at him. It was amazing, he said, how much she'd changed since she moved in with Tunney.

Gloria missed Thanksgiving dinner. She missed work on Friday. Nobody saw her between Wednesday at seven P.M. when she left the market until Sunday night around nine when she showed up at Snake Road.

Tunney called his mother Thanksgiving morning and told her that supper was off. He invited his parents to dinner at the Equinox, the best restaurant in Montclair. Mrs. Tunney told Lauren that he hardly talked all evening. She tried to keep things light by talking about her tennis club, but it didn't do much good. Nobody likes Thanksgiving dinner in a restaurant. Paul seemed sullen in a fresh hair cut and shirt with a collar and a cast on his wrist from a skateboard fall. Tunney Sr. kept going outside to smoke between courses, to brood about the disrespect Gloria was showing him. He was her boss, after all, and Tunney's father. Even though they all felt the weight of Gloria's absence, nobody said her name through the whole meal.

Mrs. Tunney was secretly glad about the way things turned out. A holiday dinner at the Snake Road house would have legitimized Gloria in a way she wasn't comfortable with. She hoped that Gloria was gone for good. According to Mrs. Tunney, things had been going great for her son in Oakland until he met Gloria. (She must not have known about his midnight calls to Lisa Bianche or his aimless dazed drives in the hills.) She hated to see Gloria taking advantage of her son's generosity. He must have felt sorry for the girl; that was the only explanation Mrs. Tunney could think of. She pitied Gloria, too. "She seemed like such a lost creature," she said, "but I drew the line at having the girl move in."

Paul wished he could go outside with his grandfather between courses. His collar bothered him, and his arm ached. He'd been purposefully reckless trying a trick off the top of a flight of stairs beside the tennis courts that none of his buddies thought possible. It was so outrageous—a high speed jump down six or eight steps to a short landing and then another jump down more steps—that none of them would even dare him to do it. He'd known he couldn't make it without some kind of fall, but he wanted to make his new friends think he was crazy. He'd learned from his father that there was a certain advantage to making people believe you'd risk anything, a kind of fearful respect.

He picked at restaurant turkey. He couldn't believe that Gloria had left him behind to sit through a long dinner surrounded by angry, silent adults. His trip to Santa Cruz with her had been the best day he'd had since he'd moved to

Oakland. They'd been driving down to Montclair, Gloria had planned to drop him at the Ice House and then go to work. In the car, she'd said, "What's wrong?"

Everything was wrong, but he hadn't had anybody to complain to until she asked, and then it all came spewing out. He missed his friends down south; he missed the beach. And who did his dad think he was fooling walking around in a suit all the time playing Mr. Real Estate Salesman? It was so boring living way the hell up in the hills where the buses didn't run and having to depend on his grandmother to take him everywhere. Who wanted to float around scummy Lake Merritt in an El Toro and hang around the tennis courts all day and bag groceries for two dollars an hour?

Gloria let him talk all the way down to Montclair. Then she kept driving right onto the freeway. Where were they going?

"The beach," Gloria said.

What about his grandmother? What about work?

"What about them?" she said.

All day in Santa Cruz, it was like Oakland didn't exist for her. She seemed to like the beach more than he did. She definitely liked the rides more; she went on the rickety wooden roller coaster three times. With Gloria, Paul felt like anything was possible. For the first time in his life he didn't feel like a kid, constantly having to gauge what the adults wanted from him. He felt like he'd gone out into the wide world.

All through dinner, he kept asking himself: Why did she go without me? And what if she never came back?

Tunney knew she was coming back. His only question was how much humiliation was he going to have to endure before she showed up again.

Listen to him: "She was doing it on purpose, taunting me. She knew my parents owned me and that I was risking everything by having her live with me. She was rubbing my face in the fact that everything I had, including her, could be snatched away at any moment. I had to sit there while my father stood out on the street, smoking. And my mother was so god damned happy Gloria was gone. The kid wouldn't even look me in the eye. Everything was wrong."

He couldn't eat. He drank more than his share of the wine, and during one of his father's walks, he ordered a second bottle and drank most of that himself. He didn't remember driving home.

TWENTY

I know why Tunney still claims that Gloria was with him when he killed Lena Jacobs. In his mind, she *was* there. Gloria's absence was palpable. Didn't he follow the shadow of her Impala for an hour the first time she disappeared, when all the time she was in Santa Cruz with Paul? He said so himself: he was obsessed with her.

But Gloria was gone. Paul was home from school the Friday after Thanksgiving, and he didn't see her or his father. He was sure of it, because he was waiting for Gloria, hoping she'd come home while his father was out, so he could warn her about how angry he was.

And on Saturday afternoon, Kim got a phone call from Gloria. Long distance. A pay phone. Kim remembered the operator's recorded voice, the sound of coins dropping. Clicks, beeps. Gloria said she was sorry for leaving the Alamo without notice. Kim said it was all right, she knew about Craig and assumed Gloria just didn't want to be around him anymore. Kim was surprised that Gloria wanted to keep talking. She kept putting quarters in the phone, a whole roll it sounded like to Kim. When Kim asked Gloria where she was, she said she didn't know the name of the town, but she was in a restaurant near the ocean called Duarte's. Gloria never told anyone exactly where she went. She just said, Down the coast. Nobody really cared at the time.

But listen to Tunney: "I go to work on Friday morning a little hung over and still steamed about Gloria and the next thing I know Lisa Bianche drives up in a brand-new car, this emerald green BMW 320i. She starts taking everybody for rides. Of course, she doesn't even invite me to sit in it, right? When she and Scott Carter take off for a drive, I slip out and drive home. I find Gloria asleep in our bed. I say, Get up Goldie Locks."

Tunney told Lauren that he asked Gloria to go for a ride with him to get some breakfast. They took her car, he said, because Scott and Lisa were out driving around in the BMW and he didn't want them to spot him driving around with Gloria or spot his car parked near the Egg Shop and Apple Press. He told Lauren he wasn't angry, he just wanted an explanation. After breakfast they went for a ride, Tunney said. He remembered it was raining. He didn't want to go back to work; Gloria didn't want to go home.

He said they parked at Roberts Pool. "Have a nice time?" he asked.

Silence. She stared out the window.

Tunney waited. He said he would have sat there for a week if necessary.

Finally, she said, "They didn't want me there anyway. What's the point of pretending?"

"I am the point, understand? I wanted you there."

"That's not enough," Gloria said.

Listen: "I had a tough woman on my hands. Something was wrong with her, and I knew it. That was the power I had over her. She knew that I had her figured out. I might not have known her secrets, but I was satisfied just knowing she had them. I thought, I can deal with this. I didn't have a plan or anything. I had more like a state of mind. That's when I saw that blond girl trying to stay out of the rain."

Where do I start? It's all lies, except for the business about Lisa Bianche's BMW. We have two witnesses who say Gloria was gone. No one told us they saw her with Tunney.

This is what I think happened: like that first time, Tunney drove through the hills in a daze, looking for Gloria. The rain poured down. Serious winds whipped through the trees. He found himself near the entrance to Roberts Park. He turned in and circled the parking lot and stopped and watched the rain fall in the empty pool. He felt as empty inside as the swimming pool. There was negative energy all around him, a low pressure system. He believed that the pull of the negative current carried Gloria away from him and that he had to follow that current in order to find her.

As he drove out of the lot, he saw a young woman standing under the eaves of the closed-up concession stand, waiting out the rain. She was truly blond, but a little less pretty than Gloria, judging from the pictures in *Quick Blood*. Her bicycle leaned against the wall. Tunney stopped and got out of his car and ducked under the eaves with her. He introduced himself, saying he'd come in the park to read a map, turn around. He said he was a real estate agent; he might have handed her his card. Did she want a ride? It didn't look like the rain would let up for a while. He said he was heading back toward Montclair where she could wait it out in a coffee shop or something.

She looked him over. He was a handsome, well-dressed guy with a nice car, but something told her, don't go with this guy. Maybe it was his eyes. They looked too light blue to be true. Or maybe he was right about his negative energy and she sensed the downward pull of that current. She shook her head.

He smiled, said fine, hurried back to his car. He wouldn't press her. He was flowing with a low pressure system, and he saw no sense in going against it. He started his car.

The next second, the young woman was knocking on his window. All right, she said. She looked in the backseat and saw several of the diamond shaped realty signs and decided he was who he said he was. Sure, she told him, she could use a ride. She slipped the front wheel off her bike while Tunney moved his signs to his trunk. They wrestled the bike into the backseat while the rain poured down on their heads.

On Skyline, Tunney asked her if he could make one stop. Did she know where Asilomar Drive was? She didn't know, so Tunney pulled over and made a big show of studying his map. He told her he had to stop at a house and set up a For Sale sign. It wouldn't take more than a minute. When they got to the white house on Asilomar, he played like he was surprised to see one of the signs on the lawn already. That's strange, he said. Did she mind waiting while he went in and looked for one of his colleague's cards? When she hesitated, he said, Or you can come in, it's really some house. If she didn't come in, it wasn't meant to be. But she wanted to come in. He got the key from the lockbox and opened the door.

Inside the house, a calm came over him. He could feel a positive energy in the room which he attributed to the angle of the sun all summer coming in the curtainless windows. The house acted as a trap for positive current. Suddenly he felt balanced. The girl was in there with him. He had control. He wanted the calm to last as long as possible. Like when he was in the backseat of his car with that girl in Los Angeles, he remembered everything. It was cold in there. He could hear the rain outside. Their footsteps echoed. Time slowed down. She was standing at the window. Her wet hair stuck to her neck. The shoulder of her parka was dark with rain. One sock was outside her pant-leg. She had a chipped front tooth, and a light dusting of freckles he hadn't noticed in the car. Her hands were red from the cold. She cupped them near her face and blew into them. She was at his mercy. He didn't know what was going to happen. All he knew was that he didn't want her to ever leave him. He showed her every room in the house.

Tunney's calm deepened the longer they were in there. If she screamed nobody could hear her. Tunney wouldn't even hear her. It would be like she wasn't screaming at all.

He touched the girl on her shoulder and turned her. He wondered why she look so surprised. Didn't she know what was happening?

Lauren's theory was that Tunney wanted to turn Lena Jacobs into Gloria, and, in a leap of logic I couldn't quite grasp, that he felt like he had to kill her in order to bring Gloria back to him.

I told her, Now don't go overboard. I said, The man was crazy, and he had a young woman alone in an empty house. It was a situation he'd been obsessed about. He could have just as easily have wanted to turn her into Lisa Bianche.

Lauren was forced into a certain amount of speculation. Tunney never talked in detail about what he did to the women or why, exactly. She pressed him several times, but he always said he couldn't remember exactly what happened, which seemed unlikely to me, considering the details he remembered leading up to the murders. When Lauren asked him, "Did you strangle them?" he said, "They were strangled, yes." "Did you have sex with them?" He might have nodded, or he might have shaken his head; I couldn't hear anything on the tape. In *Quick Blood,* Lauren says he had sex with them after he strangled them, but I don't know where she got her information or if it's true.

What did he remember? Listen to him: "I felt like I was doing something utterly necessary. There was no choice in the matter; the thing had to be done. It was like I had to satisfy something outside myself, like I was doing it for someone else, I was doing it for Gloria."

He struggled to get her clothes on, then he stuffed her into the closet. He drove home and put the bike in his garage. That night around midnight, he coasted down Asilomar with his headlights out. He carried a shovel down into the ditches where the ground was soft from the rain. He dug a shallow grave, then circled around the back of the house on foot and crawled through the bedroom window and dragged the girl down the hill and buried her.

The next day, Tunney couldn't wake up. Paul remembered his father dozing on the couch all afternoon. The only time he talked to Paul all day was when he gave him the blue bike.

"An early Christmas present," he said. "It's safer than a skateboard. At least it has brakes."

Gloria came home Sunday night. Paul was surprised: his father didn't yell at her or hit her or smash her car. He welcomed her home like she'd just returned from work. He offered her a beer. They sat on the couch and watched the late-night news together.

TWENTY-ONE

□

I left Stones after the rush, drove up University to the U.C. Theater, fed a meter, hurried to the ticket booth. The bearded boy looked up from his book and said, "She's not here."

My five was already in the slot; he thought I didn't hear him.

He said, "That lady you meet. She isn't here yet."

I'd heard him; but he'd surprised me by connecting me with Lauren. I thanked him and pulled the bill back and stood around under the bright lights of the marquee watching the traffic pass for fifteen minutes, maybe half an hour.

That morning, when Lauren had asked me if I wanted to meet her at the movies, I was surprised. She wasn't sleeping much at the time. When she did sleep, she dozed in her reading chair or lay hugging her pillow on her office floor. In the beginning, her insomnia had helped her fit into the rhythm of my life, now it effectively took her out of it. She slept all evening while I worked, and she worked through the night and morning while I slept. We'd only made love once in three weeks when I went into her office one afternoon to wake her to tell her I was leaving for the restaurant. She pulled me to the floor and kissed me, held me. I remember her sleep-stale breath tasted like it was tinged with wine; she'd drunk herself to sleep. That evening she called the restaurant and talked to me for an hour about everything but Gloria. When I got home I saw her office light shining through the French doors. I went and peeked and saw her cardboard boxes open and papers scattered fan-wise across the floor. She was on her hands and knees, a pencil between her teeth, reading something. She didn't even look up at me, so I watched some TV and drank a beer and showered and fell into bed.

I lay there alone thinking, she's drifting away from me. I was losing her. I felt like I did those nights when I was still living with Donna, half-drunk, curled with my back to her, trying to hurry myself to sleep. I'd learned from losing Donna that there was only one way for me to get close to Lauren again. I had to tell her the truth. But how could I tell Lauren that for one whole winter I wanted to sleep with my sister so badly that I haunted the halls of the Chateau some nights until close to dawn? How could I tell her that every time Liz came to my room, or we rode in Hank's truck, or ate together in the coffee shop, I felt a desire to touch her, to hold her and stroke her and kiss her mouth. I was afraid that Liz knew what I wanted. How could she help but know? When I was with her, it was all I thought about. And I was afraid that my desire disturbed her, and that all of her strange behavior since then had been my fault.

How could I tell Lauren that every time Lisbeth ran away, I thought she was running away from me?

I looked up at the marquee: *Lolita—Despair*. Lauren had been excited about those movies, but I assumed she'd gotten engrossed in some trial testimony or police report and forgotten all about them. I drove back to the restaurant and phoned her. No answer.

Maybe I'd gotten our plans mixed up. Maybe she said to meet her at Brennan's. I checked for her car in my parking lot, because she usually parked there when she met me at the bar. No old Datsun, but I wandered down to Brennan's anyway. He wasn't busy yet, so I could see pretty quickly that Lauren wasn't there. I asked Mike, the barman, if he'd seen her. No, he was sure he hadn't seen her, but I waited and watched two or three women go in and out of the Women's Room before I gave up altogether.

I used the pay phone. I let it ring eight, nine, ten times.

She answered.

"Lauren?"

"Stone. Hello."

"You asleep?"

"No. What time is it?"

"I thought we were meeting. That Dirk Bogard movie."

"God. I forgot."

"All right."

"I went for a drive."

"Where?"

"I don't know. The hills."

"It's almost eleven," I said.

"Where are you?"

"Brennan's."

"I want to get out of here. Wait for me."

I waited, watching the side entrance, for almost an hour. I

knew that she'd driven back to Asilomar, that she'd wound down Snake Road in the dark. Her drives got to be a habit that second summer, when she was working hard on her book. When she got an idea, she liked to drive up there to think about it. She liked to test it against something she knew was true: the place itself. If she came home still believing her idea, she wrote it down.

I was working on my third beer when she slipped through the door looking pale and disheveled. Her hair was pulled back in a pony tail. It looked darker than usual, dirty. She wasn't wearing any makeup so her lips looked chalky and she had dark circles under her eyes. She wore a down vest over a white T-shirt. While I brought her her Irish, she sat there playing with her vest's zipper, sliding it up and down.

She looked like she'd driven down the hill believing something that bothered her a lot, which surprised me. I thought we'd cleared up the most troubling question when we looked at the Lena Jacobs murder. Lauren said she had it all figured out: Tunney kept saying Gloria was with him because in his mind Lena was Gloria. It was so obvious to her, she didn't have to drive in the hills to think about it.

But now she was acting as distant and distracted as my sister had in that trailer in Eureka.

I set her drink on the table. "What's wrong?"

She pushed a loose strand of hair behind her ear. "I'm mad I missed the movies is all."

"They'll come back," I said. "They all come back."

"Uh huh." She kept looking around the bar like she was hunting for somebody.

I said, "Lauren? What is it?"

"I keep thinking about my brother," she said. "I heard a song today that he used to do. The Allman Brothers, I think. I started feeling low and I couldn't shake it. I guess all this Gloria stuff depresses me, too. You have no idea."

"Yes, I do," I said.

"I was sitting at my desk, right? And the next thing I knew I was crying and I couldn't stop. I had to get out of the house."

"You had to go to Asilomar."

"Yeah."

"Thinking about what?"

"Between times," she said. "You used to talk about your sister 'between times.' That's where we are now."

We were between Lena Jacobs and Rose Schiller. This was the period Lauren knew least about. On the surface of things, the time between that Thanksgiving and New Year's seemed to be the least eventful period of Gloria and Tunney's life together. But according to Lauren, everything changed after he killed Lena Jacobs: Gloria was living with a murderer.

"She didn't know that," I said.

"Probably she didn't."

"What do you mean?"

"I don't know what she knew. That's what I'm trying to figure out."

"She was gone," I said.

"True."

"A hundred miles away."

"All right. She didn't know. But I know." Lauren knew that when Gloria came home Sunday night, Lena's bike was in the garage. Tunney's shoes were covered with mud from that ditch. Lena's mother was on the news. In Lauren's mind, these facts shadowed everything. Gloria had returned to a world of evil whether she knew it or not.

Lauren was full of questions. What was that phone call to Kim all about? Did Gloria want to go back to the Alamo? Or back to Tunney? What did she leave for? It couldn't have just been the thought of Thanksgiving dinner with the Tunneys. How could Lauren reconcile the Gloria who asked Alphie for an advance, the Gloria who called Kim, with the woman who crawled into a strange bed in a strange house, who stole a car?

She said, "But the big question is, what happened to her? Something must have happened to her way back to really mess her up."

"Our mother left," I said.

"That's not enough."

It felt like enough to me. After my mother left, I never took anything for granted again. Deep-down, I think I expected everyone I loved to one morning get in a car and leave and never come back. Why did she think I let Lisbeth go? Why did I let Donna and Daniel slip out of my life? What else would I have to lose to make Lauren see how much Mr. Spenser took from us when he drove away that morning?

"I mean something harrowing," Lauren said, "something horrible. Everybody I ever read about who goes as far as your sister went had something god-awful happen. Rape, abuse, beatings. We're not talking subtleties, Stone."

"Nothing like that happened," I said.

"Are you sure? What about Hank? What about all those guys who came and went, the guides, the bartenders? She was a pretty girl."

"Hank's born-again," I said.

Lauren shrugged. "Something happened."

"She had boyfriends," I said. "Some of them were guides."

"What was going on with your father's girlfriends? I mean, they were awful young, weren't they? For him."

"That was his business."

"You have to help me, Stone, because something happened to your sister somewhere along the line. I'm sure of it."

I couldn't help her that night. We closed Brennan's down and walked back to my place and found our cars sitting by themselves in the dark parking lot. Lauren was leaning on me, but she wasn't as drunk as she was tired. I followed her up University and over to Oxford. We both circled the block a few times before we found parking places. She found hers first and waited for me in the lobby. Once I circled past the building and saw her standing behind the glass door, gazing out with a kind of inward yearning expression I'd seen on my sister when she looked down from her third-story window at the Chateau.

A couple of weeks later, I looked up from my clipboard in the middle of the rush and there was Lauren at the bar sipping white wine. She'd never come to my bar before; she knew Ronson didn't like her. She was reading a paperback mystery. I went to her and leaned over her shoulder and said, table for one? She shook her head. She said she just wanted to stay at the bar and read and watch me work, which was fine by me. Every once in a while I'd look over there and see her hair shining in the candlelight. I noticed that Ronson stayed at the far end of the bar talking to Eli.

We had a long rush. At ten-thirty or eleven I was still chasing waiters into the kitchen to tell them to drop checks. Ronson followed me through the swinging doors saying, "I think she's had enough. What do you think?"

I looked through the window in the door and I saw her nodding over her book, her eyes half-closed. I went around the bar and leaned over her shoulder again and said, let's go upstairs. I pulled her off her stool and led her up to my office. She sat in my desk chair in the blue light. She swiveled around smiling like a kid on a carousel pony.

"Want to tell you something," she said.

"Let me take you home now."

She shook her head. "Remember Paul Sharpe?"

"Your first boyfriend."

"You remember. We left school during lunch and went to my house. Nobody home. We went to the soundproof room. We were doing it. The music was going and I didn't hear the door open. Neither did Paul. We were doing it. Then I felt something—like that vibration your sister talked about—somebody was watching us. I turned my head, and there was Kenny, watching us. When our eyes met, he didn't move and I didn't stop Paul. I just looked at Kenny. And he looked at me. Seemed like a long time that we looked at each other before I closed my eyes. When I opened them, Kenny was gone. Paul never knew he was there."

"What's the point?" I said.

"I remember. That's what. Some things you can't ever forget."

A knock at the door. It was Ronson carrying a cold cloth and a Coke. When Lauren saw him, she said, "It's not my fault."

"It's all right," I said.

"Can't help it."

"Don't worry."

"If she knew."

"What are you talking about?"

"She had to know. I know she knew."

In the morning I told Lauren I didn't want her getting drunk in my place ever again. Now every waiter, busboy, and cook thought that the woman I lived with was a sloppy drunk.

"That's not what you're mad about," she said. "You didn't like the story I told you. It reminded you of what you're not telling me."

I'd told her my whole life story. What did she want from me?

"I don't know," she said. "Only you know."

I left the apartment and stayed at the restaurant from ten that morning until well after midnight, then I went down to Brennan's with Ronson for a few beers. When I got home, Lauren's office light was on. I leaned in her doorway and said, "What did she know?"

Lauren swiveled toward me in her desk chair.

"Gloria," I said. "What did she know?"

"I was drunk," she said.

"Lauren."

"She knew something. All right? I don't know what exactly. I'm working on it." Lauren asked me—no, it was more like she begged me—to let her work in peace. She needed all her concentration, all her energy for her book.

She never came back to StoneS again. She started writing day and night, getting by on catnaps, with her cat on her lap in her low reading chair. I used to watch her sleeping through the French doors. I could see her time-line winding around the wall of her room. Red for Tunney's story. Black for testimony from other informants. Green for where she thought Gloria was at any given time.

She was on the phone every other day with Kim, having lunch with Mrs. Tunney once or twice a week. She went out to San Quentin every Thursday to talk to Tunney, but she wouldn't talk to me about the case at all anymore. She started listening to his tapes through headphones. I admit that the sound of his voice bothered me, but the headphones bothered me more. It was like watching someone whispering into someone's ear. What was so secret? She claimed nothing was secret; I could listen to the tapes all I wanted, any time I wanted to.

I knew all I wanted to know. Gloria disappeared, Tunney killed the girls, Gloria went back. That mystery was solved, as far as I was concerned.

The more Lauren shut me out, the less I cared about what Tunney told her. Lauren spending her nights in her office bothered me more than the things we were learning about Gloria. Lauren was the mystery that bothered me now.

I felt like I was watching her watching Gloria watching Tunney.

Lauren was weaving her own pattern on her red, green, and black time-line. She was obsessed with "between times."

Details were adding up: Craig's story, Gloria's attraction to Tunney, his secret serious trouble, the stranger's bed, the stolen car, what Lauren called Gloria's "exquisite sensitivity," that tingling in her spine, the pressure in her chest. Lauren believed that Gloria knew something about what Tunney had done, and she stayed with him. That's why she was desperate to find some secret trauma from the past to explain everything. I knew she was beginning to suspect that I had something to do with Lisbeth's problem, but even knowing that, I couldn't tell her the truth. The pattern was spiraling out of control, and Lauren was spinning away from me.

One night, maybe three weeks after she got drunk at my bar, I came home from work and Lauren was gone. The cat was screaming for food and water. Lauren's desk lamp was shining in her office. Her pillow was on the floor. I fed the cat and wandered through the apartment a couple of times in a desperate kind of daze, thinking maybe I missed her sleeping in some strange place. Then I went outside and walked around the block looking for her car until I came to my car and got in it and drove back down to my restaurant. I circled the parking lot and then Brennan's parking lot, and even though I didn't see her car, I stopped just in case and talked to Mike, who hadn't seen her. Then I got back on University for a slow cruise by the dark marquee of the theater, hoping to see her car, but I didn't.

In the morning her call woke me.

"Where are you?"

"Oregon. Grants Pass."

"What's going on?"

"I came to talk to Earl. Brenda and Hank. Maybe your father, if he'll talk."

"You don't tell me where you're going?"

"I'm telling you now."

"That does me a lot of good last night."

"I'm going to The Caves tomorrow."

I didn't say anything.

"Stone?"

"Don't go up there. Don't bother those people."

"I have to."

"You've got no right to go there."

"Something happened up there, Stone. And you're not telling me."

"Nothing happened."

"I won't tell them I talked to you. I promise."

"Don't go, Lauren."

"I'm sorry, Stone. I have to."

When I hung up, I threw the phone across the room. She'd left without telling me and gone to see my people. I felt like this wasn't about my sister anymore, it was about me. She was prying into my life, searching for some secret of mine. What Lauren didn't know, though, was that Hank, Brenda, my father, Earl, none of them would ever talk. They didn't even talk to each other about Lisbeth. The subject was closed. Like me, they felt too responsible, ashamed, tainted.

Lauren came home from Oregon more distant than when she left. My father had refused to even see her. He gave her a free trip through The Caves, which she thought might be valuable for background for her book. She ate dinner at the Chateau. Her car battery went dead because, in her nervousness, she left her lights on, and Hank helped her jump-start it, but that's the only help she got out of him. Brenda told her that Lisbeth was a lost soul. She thanked God for Earl Jr., who was a blessing. He called Brenda on holidays and Earl had her and Hank for dinner every once in a while. He sold them a car at a deep discount. Earl talked to Lauren over the phone from the lot only to tell her he didn't want to have anything to do with her book. He told her not to go by the house. He said, "Don't bother my boy. He doesn't know anything." But Lauren drove by the high school and asked some of the kids who Earl Jr. was, and they pointed him out. Lauren was amazed by how much he looked like pictures of Lisbeth. Much to her credit, she didn't approach him. She drove down Earl's long white rock driveway early one afternoon when she was sure he was at the lot and Junior was at school. She circled past the house and she could see the blue of the pool through a gate. She said there was a Winnebago parked under a carport. A fire engine red Jeep sat in the shade of the pines. The morning Lauren was going to drive back to California, she made a last effort to see Earl at Rogue River Honda, but she was intercepted by a saleswoman who kept her out on the lot for an hour talking about the new Accord. The woman didn't know Earl at all. He was the aloof kind of boss who came in late in the mornings and spent his afternoons in his office looking over paperwork. Mr. Avery, the sales manager, handled most of the business. Would Lauren like to meet Mr. Avery? No, Lauren told her. In the end, she assured the saleswoman that she could get a year or two more out of her Datsun.

Early September. Early evening. I drove home from the restaurant. I'd forgotten something: keys, a telephone number, some checks I'd written; I don't remember. Some kind of van was parked in front of our building. Furniture was stacked on the sidewalk. A mirror caught the sun, threw off light. I circled the block a couple times before I gave up and double parked. A couple of sweaty guys were sitting on boxes in the lobby surrounded by skis and stereo speakers. They were waiting for the elevator, hoping it wasn't broken; they'd been waiting a long time. I told them it hadn't been broken two hours before when I'd ridden it down. We all watched the gray doors, waiting.

They opened. There stood Lauren, hip deep in suitcases, a couple of cardboard boxes. She had her best suede jacket on and her purse over her shoulder.

"What's this?" I said.

She took a step toward me, but the doors started to close on her. I grabbed them and held them open.

She said, "I was going to stop at the restaurant."

The college guys wanted to be helpful, I guess; they started pulling her suitcases out. Whatever was happening, I didn't want to argue with Lauren about it in front of them. I grabbed a couple of suitcases and followed her outside. Her Datsun was parked a half block from the building. She opened her trunk and I threw her stuff in. She stood there with her keys in her hand, rattling them a little, like she was in a hurry or nervous or confused, I couldn't tell.

"I was going to come to the restaurant," she said.

"Yeah?"

"And say good-bye."

"Were you going to tell me where you were going?"

"Los Angeles," she said.

"And when you were coming back?"

"I need to get out of here for a while. I don't know."

"What do you mean, you don't know?"

"I mean I have a lot of work to do I can't do here."

"Why not?"

"There's something you don't want me to know. When I was up in Oregon I could tell: you're all hiding something from me."

"I'm not hiding anything," I said. What did she expect? Was I supposed to tell her every thought I ever had? Every secret desire?

"I don't know, Stone."

I said, "You told me, you said Gloria wasn't everything."

"She's not. But she's part of everything."

I stood on the sidewalk and watched the Datsun disappear

into traffic. Then I walked back to the building where the guys let me ride up with them in a crowded load of boxes, chairs. In our apartment, I looked for a note in the kitchen, our bedroom, but I didn't find one. I saw her pillow on the floor of her office. I went in there and picked it up. It smelled like her. I slumped into her reading chair and held the pillow in my lap. Her desk was bare except for the brass doorknob. The file drawers were open, empty. A few boxes were still stacked in the corner. Bird was curled on Lauren's chair, asleep. Her time-line ran around the wall, a confusion of green and black and red ink. There was the note I was looking for. It was clear that it had everything to do with why she left me, but I didn't want to read it or decipher it or understand its ultimate meaning. I just stared at it from across the room until it got too dark in the apartment to see, then I found whatever it was I'd come home for and went back to work, grateful I had someplace to go.

TWENTY-TWO

It's hot here under the skylight. The fan doesn't do much good. Most of the summer, I leave my office door open to let the air move as much as possible, but today I've got it shut. Since noon, I've been rereading these ledgers. I've filled two of them in six months, coming up here in the afternoon while the cooks prep and delivery trucks come and go. I usually write until the waiters arrive, but sometimes I keep at it while they set the tables and Ronson stocks the bar. There've been days I didn't knock off until opening time. And every once in a while, I come back up here after the rush, if I remember something.

I'm satisfied with my story, as far as it goes. I think I told the truth, anyway. After Lauren left, I tried not to think about her or Gloria or Tunney or the rest of it for a long time. I might have forgotten some things, but I doubt it. When I sat down and started writing, memories came rushing back so thick, it was sometimes hard to keep them straight.

This isn't easy, though. Lauren had me; she had a whole list of people to talk to; she had that tape recorder. I'm on my own here.

I still sleep on the bed we brought up from Santa Cruz. I thought she might come back for her furniture, the rest of her clothes, Bird, but I gave up hope of that almost four years ago. Of course, Lauren's time-line's gone now—I tore it off the wall when I got home from work that night—but I have a half dozen boxes of documents, transcripts, testimony. I've made a hobby out of arranging it all in chronological order, filing it according to categories, making lists, comparisons. By now, I think I have most of the facts straight.

And I have *Quick Blood.* Last night, when I finished writing about Lauren leaving me, I found her book in my desk drawer and brought it home and took it to bed. I read it until I fell asleep, then this morning, I stayed in bed reading until it was time to come to work. I was looking for what Lauren knew about "between times," and for the reasons why she left me. I found what I was looking for.

You went to work the Monday morning after Thanksgiving and waited at your register for your drawer, like every other morning that you worked at La Salle Market. When Alphie saw you, he shook his head, slowly, sadly. No, this morning wasn't like every other morning. He took you upstairs to his office, where you sat across from him and watched him rock in his chair, his hands clasped over his belly. When he asked you what was wrong, you told him nothing was wrong, but he knew you were troubled. Was A.J. the trouble? You told him A.J. was all right, but you were lying.

It broke Alphie's heart to fire you. You were a fine cashier, one of the best he'd ever had. He told me that you were never more than a dollar out of balance the whole time you worked for him. If it were his store, he would have let you off with another warning, but Mr. Tunney had brought your last paycheck by the store personally and told Alphie that you were out for good. Alphie didn't tell Mr. Tunney about the advance he'd given you the week before. When he gave you your pay, he asked you, Why don't you think about going back to Seattle? Why don't you think about going home?

You held the envelope in your hand. You stared at the name written on it: Gloria Simpson. You were quiet for a long time. Alphie worried that you might break down and cry. Were you thinking about all the reasons why you couldn't go home?

All you could say was, You're a nice man, Alphie.

Later that week, Lynn Jacobs went to A.J.'s office and asked Scott Carter if she could put a flier in the window.

MISSING: Lena Marie Jacobs. A blurry graduation photo. Age: seventeen. Five foot four. Blond hair, brown eyes. Last seen November 24, riding a blue Schwinn ten-speed on Skyline Drive.

After work, A.J. found one of the fliers slipped under his windshield wiper. When he got home, he showed it to you and said that he thought she looked like you, but you didn't think so. And you were right.

A.J. said he could see it, someplace in Seattle or somewhere, a flier was fading in a store window: Have you seen Gloria Gloria?

How did he make you feel when he talked like that? Did you feel like running? Driving until dawn? I don't think so. I think his taunting drew you to him, made you want to prove to him that you were Gloria.

Scott Carter told me that he was surprised how hard A.J. worked that winter. Even Lisa Bianche was impressed. Apparently A.J. took no more two hour drives to nowhere. When he wasn't showing a house, he was in the office on the phone drumming up listings, chatting up buyers. When he sold the Surrey Lane house, Mr. Carter thought it was a fluke. Then two weeks later, an offer came in for a beautiful big house on Skyline Drive. A.J. hadn't done a thing all summer long and now suddenly he was outselling everybody in December, the slowest season of the year.

Christmas day, he dragged you and Paul to his parents' house. He'd sold some homes, he had a few thousand dollars in the bank, and he was feeling like a family man. You didn't want to go to the Tunneys' anymore than you wanted to cook Thanksgiving dinner, but A.J. wouldn't let you spoil this holiday. He made you get dressed up in a white blouse and blue wool pants and pair of boots he'd bought for you. He told me that he got you to wear a tasteful amount of makeup for once.

Virginia remembered that Christmas being especially pleasant. It had been a long time since she'd had a child in the house for the holiday. She and Mr. Tunney had bought Paul a stereo and a Raleigh ten-speed, and they were surprised to hear that he already had a bike. Paul told them that he liked the Raleigh better than the Schwinn because it was a better make and it was new. They also promised him a ski trip in February.

They gave you some gloves and a scarf of the finest quality, which you didn't seem to appreciate. The gifts A.J. brought for them were signed: From A.J. and Gloria, but you didn't even know what was in the boxes until they were opened. Virginia didn't remember you saying three words all afternoon. After dinner, you and Paul went into the den and watched It's a Wonderful Life.

Gloria, did you know this? The first week in January, A.J. got a call from his father at the office. He wanted to talk about you, about the fact that you were unemployed. A.J. reminded Mr. Tunney that he'd ordered you fired himself. There was a good reason for that, of course; you'd put Mr. Tunney in an awkward position. He couldn't bend the rules for A.J.'s girlfriends and expect everybody else to come to work on time. This was the problem Mr. Tunney wanted to talk about: he couldn't go on supporting two women for A.J. He was paying the mortgage on the house. Your groceries were coming out of his stores. He asked A.J. which woman he wanted to keep, you or Pat.

A.J. knew what this was all about. His mother wanted you out of the Snake Road house and she was putting pressure on his father. Mr. Tunney thought A.J. wouldn't want to stop paying Pat because Pat knew too much about what went on in Los Angeles. She knew a few things A.J. and his father wanted to protect Virginia from. A.J.'s father thought he could apply this little bit of pressure and the choice would be simple. But now that A.J. had some money of his own in the bank, he felt he could afford to stand up to him. He told his father to go ahead and cut Pat off.

A.J. started sending Pat money out of his own pocket. When she got the first personal check from A.J. she called the Snake Road house.

You answered.

Pat wanted to know if you knew who she was.

You did. She was Paul's mother.

She knew that you were Gloria. Paul had told her about you, how you'd taken him on a whim to Santa Cruz, how you never backed down to Virginia. He said that you acted more like a big sister than a step-mom.

Pat asked you why she was getting a personal check all of a sudden, but you didn't know anything about it. You told her to call C&M Realty and talk to A.J.

"Mind if I ask you a question?" Pat said.

You didn't mind.

"I was nineteen. I was pregnant. And I was stupid. What's your excuse?"

You told her you didn't make any excuses. Then you hung up.

When A.J. came home, you told him that his wife had called asking about the check.

"It's good," A.J. insisted, "if that's what she wants to know."

"Why are you paying her anything?" you asked. "You take care of Paul. What, do you owe her money?"

"I don't want to talk about it," he said.

"Deep dark secrets," you said. "Blackmail. Blood money."

Two could play the teasing game.

You made it through the holidays, but you got bored sitting around the house in January, so you went looking for work in Montclair. You walked the streets, like you did your first day in town, looking for the right place. You passed McGuire's Men's Wear, Coast to Coast, Kenny's Hair Salon. In almost every window, you saw Lena Jacobs' missing *poster. You remembered A.J. taunting you: Have you seen Gloria Gloria? You stopped and studied the poster for a long time.*

Did you remember where you were on November 24th?

In a phone booth in a restaurant called Duarte's. The town was called Pescadero, but you didn't know that.

Did you recognize the blue bike?

Something upset you, I know, because you drove home without asking anybody for a job.

In February, the Tunneys took Paul on the promised ski trip to Tahoe. The weekend of the twelfth, thirteenth and fourteenth. That Sunday afternoon—dusk—A.J. said that you and he were driving up Snake Road, when you saw a young woman walking up the hill.

But you weren't in that car. Where were you, Gloria?

You weren't working, Paul was gone: I can't find anyone who remembers seeing you that weekend.

I could tell that A.J. was lying by the way he talked about that girl. He was describing a private compulsion, not a conspiracy. He said a girl appeared on the side of the road. From the back, she looked just like Lena Jacobs: blond hair to the shoulders of a down parka, jeans, sneakers. The next thing he knew his car had stopped. He didn't know what was going to happen. He said it was like suddenly nothing mattered in the world. He didn't care about anything: whether he ever sold another house, whether his mother liked you, whether you stayed or disappeared. He felt like he was living second to second.

When the girl got in his car, everything became vivid, intense. She was carrying a sack; he could smell the pizza in it. His skin felt sensitive under his shirt. His mouth went dry. He told me how the lift tickets attached to her parka's zipper made a rustling sound as she settled into her seat.

"You should be careful," he said. "You don't want to end up like Lena Jacobs."

"Who?"

"The girl who's missing."

"Oh, her. She ran away. Everybody knows that."

He asked her whether she minded if he stopped on Asilomar for a second? He had to check on something. She said she didn't mind. She recognized the house—she'd known the girl who had lived there, the most stuck-up girl in the world—and she asked him if she might she go in and see it.

Yes, she might.

A.J. followed her from room-to-room as though retracing his steps. He felt as though she were the same girl, and a calm feeling came over him. This was all just a memory; it wasn't really happening at all.

I asked him several times, "Where was Gloria?"

Every time, he told me something different: You were upstairs or right beside him or in the bathroom. But you weren't there, Gloria. Where were you?

You didn't see him take his tie off. You were miles away when he put it around her neck. She fell to her knees in an empty house. Only A.J. heard her struggle.

On Sunday night, A.J. asked you to go for a ride with him after the eleven o'clock news. He said he'd forgotten to replace the key in the lockbox at the Asilomar house. You didn't ask him why he couldn't put it back in the morning, you liked the idea of a midnight ride. On Asilomar, Tunney turned off his lights. He coasted down the drive.

What was that all about? Why did you think he wanted to sneak up on an empty house in the dark?

He told you to wait. You watched him open the front door, watched him go in the house. His flashlight came on. You marked his progress through the house by the sudden movements of faint light through the windows. Then all was darkness.

You rolled your window down and listened to the wind, to a car hissing by on Snake. You didn't like being left alone in a cold car in the middle of the night. There was a sack on the floor at your feet; you opened it—cold pizza—then tossed it out the window.

You watched the dark house, waiting. Did you remember watching Craig's window, knowing he was waiting for you?

You looked at the ignition: no key. If it had been there, you would have driven away. You might have driven all night.

A half-hour, forty minutes passed. The rhythm of your blood slowly quickened. You felt as trapped as you had when you saw Craig's car across from the market. What did you think A.J. was doing in there? Did you think about going to the door? Knocking? Did you want to look in the windows? Call his name? You were too frightened to do any of that. You felt that tingling sensation in your spine. You were too sensitive not to know that something was going on in there.

Here is where it all breaks down, Gloria. You're in that car. A.J. is in the house. You had time to think, remember. You remembered where you were Thanksgiving weekend. You remembered A.J.'s strangely sweet behavior when you returned. You saw a blue bicycle in the garage. She looks like you, he said. Blond hair, brown eyes. Five foot four from her head down to the ground. You opened your door and got out, leaving it open for quiet's sake, and started walking, running. You headed toward Montclair hoping to find refuge in the bright lights of the 7-Eleven store.

When A.J. returned to his car, exhausted after his work down by the ditches and found your door open, saw that you were gone, the fear he'd been fighting off all evening made him dizzy. Killing this girl had been a mistake. While it was happening it felt so familiar that he didn't even have to think, but afterward everything felt different. He didn't even know why he'd done it. He'd gotten away with Lena Jacobs, but he'd promised himself never to do anything like that again. Now he felt out of control. That's why he took you along for the ride, I think, to give himself the illusion of control. If he couldn't control himself, at least he could control you.

He got in his car and drove toward Montclair until he caught you in his headlights. From the back you looked just like the girl he'd stopped for that afternoon.

You saw your long shadow when his headlights hit, you kept walking.

He drove up slowly beside you.

All around you was darkness. Where could you go? For the first time in your life, you felt as though running was more dangerous than standing still. You stopped.

He reached across the car and shoved the passenger side door open. You sank into the seat, slammed the door.

You pretended not to know anything. "What were you doing in there?"

He pretended to lie. "Kids," he said, "I think they're breaking in. Screwing around."

Three days later, you saw a report about another missing girl on the five o'clock news. The reporter said that Rose Schiller had met a friend who was having boyfriend trouble, a teenaged crisis, in Montclair at Round Table Pizza. The friend remembered that Rose had left the restaurant around five-thirty and walked through Montclair to Snake Road. She carried some left-over pizza in a sack. It was already dark that time of year, but Rose often walked up Snake Road after school and in the evenings. She knew a lot of people, parents of friends, friends of her parents, and often someone would stop and give her a ride home. Rose's mother said it was a very rare occasion when she had to walk all the way home. Her mother hoped that Rose had just run away and that she would come home on her own.

You went to your bedroom and ransacked Tunney's drawers for cash. You found a couple of twenty-dollar bills in his nightstand drawer. In Paul's room, you found a crumpled five and a handful of change in his parka. You filled a grocery sack with the warmest clothes you could find. You went from room-to-room, turning on every light in the house, then went to the garage and got in your car and drove away.

Where were you going, Gloria? And why did you ever come back?

TWENTY-THREE

□

I know where she went, Lauren. She called me at the restaurant. "This is Lisbeth," she said.

I couldn't tell you about that phone call, even though I knew that if I kept it a secret, I'd lose you. I was afraid of what you'd make of it. I knew where it fit on your time-line, how it fit your theories. When Lisbeth called me, they were still searching for Rose Schiller in the hills.

Lisbeth was in a phone booth; I could hear traffic in the background. I was behind the bar, so I ducked into the kitchen to get out of the noise of voices.

"Where are you?" I said. I thought, this is it: she's coming home on her own.

"Oakland." She asked me to meet her the next day at Bif's on Broadway.

"Two o'clock," she said.

Two-thirty, I was still waiting at the counter near the door. By three, I was sure she wouldn't show, but then there she was, coming in out of the rain, her hair frizzy, her nose running a little. We hugged awkwardly in the crowded counter area. "You're getting fat!" she said.

We took a booth by the window and ordered coffee. It was the middle of the afternoon, but most cars on Broadway already had their lights on.

"I'm glad you called," I said.

Lisbeth blew her nose in her napkin. She smiled. "I never thought I'd see you here." She looked around at all the bright and shining surfaces in Bif's. "This is one of the first places I came to here."

The waitress appeared at the table and asked us if we were ready to order. I remember her: a kind-eyed black woman, middle-aged, thin, her earlobes stretched by huge hoop earrings. Lisbeth shook her head and said she wasn't hungry. I told the waitress that I'd pass, too, but she wouldn't hear of it. If we wanted to sit in a booth, we had to order food. No food, and we had to move to the stools at the counter, so I ordered a burger I wasn't hungry for, and the waitress left us alone.

"Do you need money?" I said.

She shook her head, sniffled. "Nu uh." She slipped out of her parka and pushed the sleeves of her sweater up. I could see her scarred arm. Her burn had been worse than I'd imagined. It was flame-shaped, like Craig said, about six inches long, and at the wide end, near her hand, it went almost all the way around her wrist. I think she saw me looking at it.

Bif's was full of commotion, racket, noise I would never put up with in my place: plates crashing, the register bell ringing, drawers slamming shut. When a busboy dumped a load of silver into a tray right behind Lisbeth, she looked like she wanted to jump out of her skin. She couldn't drink her coffee, but she finished her water and mine before the waitress brought me my burger.

"Do you want a drink?" I said.

Lisbeth hesitated long enough for me to guess, yes she wanted a drink, so I ordered a beer for her.

When the waitress was gone, Lisbeth said, "I regretted it right after I called you." She brushed her hair with her fingers. "I almost didn't come."

"I'm glad you showed up," I said. "I've been waiting for you to call me."

"I wasn't gonna. I was gonna disappear." She looked at the window, not through it. She seemed to be watching a drop slip-sliding down the glass. "The rain reminded me of The Caves. You. Tommy's apple pie. I got sort of sentimental."

Her beer arrived: a bottle and a dingy-looking glass. "Everything all right here?" the waitress asked. She was looking at my untouched burger. I told her everything was just fine.

I said, "You still go by Gloria?"

She nodded.

"It's a pretty name."

"Gee el Oh are Eye aye," she said. "You remember?"

"Sure," I said. "Are you going home?"

"No, no. You know I can't."

"They're waiting for you. Earl and your boy. Brenda. Dad."

"I can't, Marvin."

"Come on. They were sick over you leaving. Brenda was as bad as when her baby died."

"I think about Brenda sometimes."

"You belong up there with Junior and Earl."

"They won't take me back."

"How do you know?"

"I made Earl crazy. He never knew what was going on. I can't blame him for hating me."

"He doesn't hate you. I've talked to him. Seriously, Lisbeth, he doesn't. He's hurt and pretty confused and he's worried about Junior, but he loves you."

She looked at me. "I never told Earl anything. You know, you're the only one who knows, Marvin."

"He'll take you back. I know it."

"You and Dad," she said.

"No, I lied to Dad. I told him I never found you."

"That's not what I mean."

I didn't know what she was talking about. I stared at her, waiting for an explanation. Sitting with her in that booth at Bif's, I felt as close to her as I did in Hank's truck. Why couldn't I see what she was trying to tell me?

She blinked a couple of times, stunned, and let out a little laugh. Then, without a shift I could see, she was crying into her napkin. Long, almost silent sobs rose out of her throat, and I remembered Sissy's fierce tears. She put her head on her arms on the table. All I could see was the top of her head, her hair, the dark roots, the wild ends. Her shoulders were shaking.

I felt like I'd done something terrible to her, like I'd betrayed her somehow. A couple of years later, when I sat with Donna in our kitchen with the blue-flowered wallpaper, I felt the same way. In a hungover haze of regret and self-pity, I confessed to sleeping with Barbara. Donna blinked in the same stunned way, put her hand in front of her face, then touch her forehead with the tips of her fingers. Like Lisbeth, she broke down and wept.

Lisbeth looked up at me, her face swollen from crying. Her napkin was in shreds. "You talked to me. You listened. I thought you knew. And after you let me go, and I went away, I was sure you knew."

I slid my napkin across the table to her. "Knew what?" I said. She kept on crying, so I reached out to touch her hand, and she pulled it away as though my touch burned her.

I'd never seen her like that before. In that trailer, in Eureka, she had seemed so controlled, so sure she wanted to go, that I couldn't stop her. If she had broken down then, I would never have let her go.

Our waitress sauntered by, glanced at Lisbeth and at my uneaten burger, and kept on walking. She leaned against the busing station, folded her arms, and glared at me. If I'd seen a crying woman and a man too uncomfortable to eat in my restaurant, I would have jumped to a conclusion, too. I learned a long time ago to leave quarreling lovers a lot of room.

I said, "Lisbeth."

She cried for a while; she couldn't stop. "You got me through. Then you left and I married Earl to get out of there. And now I'm here."

"What are you telling me?"

"About Dad and me. After Mom left. You had to know."

I looked away from her, out the window. It was so dark outside, I thought it had to be past opening time.

Lauren, do you remember your tour through The Caves? About halfway in, your guide stopped the group and turned out all the lights and said, Behold: absolute darkness. I sometimes gave that tour eight times a day in the summertime, but I always looked forward to that moment in the dark. I felt engulfed, submerged in it, totally alone in a darkness as safe as sleep.

What am I trying to say? I didn't want to see what Lisbeth was telling me. I didn't want to see it when she came to my room the winter after our mother left. I didn't want to see it when she started to steal, to run away. I didn't want to see it in that trailer in Eureka. I didn't want to see it at Bif's. And I didn't want to see it when I was living with you, Lauren.

But I see it, now.

I glanced at my watch. It was earlier than it looked, but I was still going to be late.

She said, "I shouldn't have called you." She stuck her arms in her coat sleeves, started to stand.

"Wait a second. Wait."

"Let me go, Marvin."

"No," I said, "let's go for a ride."

"No, Marvin. Please."

"Sit down," I said. "Just let me call my boss. I'll be right back. You want another beer? I'll bring you another beer."

On my way past our waitress, I asked her to give Lisbeth the beer, and I felt the woman's kind eyes go cold on me. I used the pay phone to call Barbara. I think I told her that my car had broken down.

When I got back to my table, Lisbeth was gone. The waitress arrived, beer in hand. "I'll be right back," I said.

"Hold it, mister."

I pulled my wallet out and handed it to her and ran for the door. I scanned the parking lot for taillights, a smoking exhaust, anything to tell me where Lisbeth's car was. I didn't see anything. I hurried up and down the rows, the rain battering my head, and looked into the windows of every car there, but she was gone.

I went back to our booth. Lisbeth's placemat was folded in half under my burger plate. Scrawled across it was, Sorry. I can't. But I love you. Lisbeth.

The waitress returned with my wallet. The fresh beer was on the table, so I sat down and watched the rain and drank it. When I paid her, the waitress wouldn't even look at me.

Lauren, it's going to take all my will to tell you the rest of this. Some things I think I remember, some I believe are true.

The only thing I know is that when I think about what happened to my sister, I feel like there's an absolute darkness in me, a cave. Lisbeth and Gloria, my father and Tunney, they're all together in this awful darkness.

After Tunney killed Rose Schiller, the frenzy that had carried him through January wound down. For days at a stretch, he didn't go to the office. Some days he called in sick, some days he didn't bother. He lay on the couch watching TV. He drank beer all afternoon, slept until ten or eleven at night, and drank vodka until the early hours.

When Tunney did go to work he looked sick to Scott Carter: thin, pale as a prisoner. His suits didn't seem to fit any more. Scott decided to ignore it. Things were generally slow that spring, cycles, peaks, valleys: it was the nature of the business. Tunney had earned a break with his December sales, the only sales in the office that month.

During this period, Alphie remembered that Gloria did their shopping. She signed Tunney's initials in the black book, which was technically not allowed, but Alphie let it go. He liked to see her come in the store. When he heard she'd gotten a job at the Ice House, he started to go there on his lunch break just to see her. He sat at the counter and she served him apple pie and ice cream and coffee. Sometimes she took a break and sat beside him on a stool and made small talk. She told him that she'd made the apple pie herself from an old friend's secret recipe. (Even then I kept getting glimpses of my sister, of little Sissy sitting with Tommy after school.) He remembered that she introduced him to a pretty high school girl who was working behind the counter. She said, "Carolyn, this is Alphie, the best boss in the world."

One day Tunney went into the C&M office with a new haircut and his tennis pro's bounce in his walk and asked Scott Carter if he could go on the draw. He said he was working on things. Spring was almost over and sales would pick up and he promised he'd break all records over the summer. Scott weighed and balanced his options. He'd heard about Tunney's cocaine days, but the two December sales gave him hope. And Tunney Sr. would make the debt good one way or another. He said, "How much do you want?"

This money, most of it, anyway, went down to Pat in Los Angeles.

Tunney began to feel better slowly. The weather turned warm. A few nice days in late April made him think about taking his pool cover off. He began to look forward to summer.

At the beginning of May, his father called him at work. "What's this about the draw?"

"It's standard practice."

"Ten thousand dollars?"

"It's not so much. One commission will wipe it out."

"What are you going to do?"

"Sell a house," Tunney said. "People seem serious about the Asilomar place."

"All right, but if it doesn't happen soon, I might have to sell your house."

"You can't do that."

"I don't want to. Don't get me wrong. It's a last resort. I'd even think about covering the debt if Gloria goes."

"I'm going to sell Asilomar any day now," Tunney said, which was not true. He didn't want to sell Asilomar. He didn't even want to show it. He'd locked the bedroom where he killed Lena and Rose and told the buyers that the owners kept some furniture, some personal property in there, he didn't know what exactly, but if they were serious about the house, he could get permission to show them that last room. I don't think he was afraid of people seeing anything; no evidence of violence could be found in there. He just wanted to keep it private. It was too intimate a place to parade strangers through.

He didn't want to let Gloria go, either. Ever since the night she ditched his car while he was burying Rose, he'd felt like she knew something. When she disappeared the next week, he thought, she's back in Seattle or wherever she came from, gone forever. And when she appeared at the door around midnight a few days later, he knew he'd never let her go again.

He went home at lunchtime after his father's call and found her lounging beside the covered pool. He leaned on the deck railing and called down to her, "You better enjoy it. They want you out of here bad."

Gloria raised her hand to her face and squinted up at him.

"He threatened to sell the house."

A magazine lay in her lap, a page shivered in the wind.

"For money I owe Scott."

She lowered her hand and closed her eyes and laid her head on the lounge chair.

Tunney walked downstairs and sat in the chair beside her, feeling hot and bothered in his three-piece suit.

"They'll make it good if you go," he said.

She knew he was testing her. She didn't dare say she'd leave. With her eyes still closed, she said, "Do you want me to go?"

Tunney leaned toward her. "Do you want to?"

She knew he'd never let her. She said, "No, I like it here."

He leaned closer. "No more mystery trips?"

"No."

Tunney stood up. "All right. I'll sell something. Make it good myself."

Gloria heard his hard shoes on the patio as he walked away. She heard his car start on the driveway, heard it swoosh through two or three turns on Snake. As soon as it was out of earshot, she wanted to run. Run and never stop. It took all her will to stay in that chair.

* * *

June 5, 1979, Tunney swung by the Ice House to pick Gloria up. She was sitting with Carolyn Cage on the brick planters in front of the store. When Gloria approached the car, Tunney said, "Your friend want a ride?"

Gloria slid in, shut her door. "No."

Tunney called out his window, "Hey. You want a ride?"

Carolyn said yes before Gloria could think of a way to stop what was happening.

She knew something was happening, the same way she might have known that our father was awake two floors below her in the Chateau. The sound of a door clicking closed traveled up the stairs, and down the hall, and through her closed door. The sound sent a vibration quivering along her spine.

Carolyn got into the backseat next to all the For Sale signs Tunney carried around. As they drove through Montclair, Gloria was quiet, while Tunney and Carolyn talked about their high school. He wondered if any of his old teachers were still there and listed some names Carolyn had never heard of. She listed a few Tunney didn't know. They came to the conclusion that no teachers were left from his day. "You make me feel ancient," he said.

They wound up Snake Road.

Liz sensed our father climbing the stairs. She imagined his slow progress by a series of creaking and groaning steps she knew by heart.

Tunney adjusted his rearview mirror so he could see into the backseat. He said, "Mind if I make a quick stop?"

Carolyn didn't mind.

Gloria receded into herself. She was the still center, and Tunney and Carolyn revolved around her. She told herself nothing was going to happen, and then the next instant she felt as though it had all already happened. She closed her eyes and pretended she was riding away from everything, she was never going to stop.

Liz lay as still as she could in her bed, listening, hoping the sounds she heard were the nighttime sounds of the old hotel, or the wind, or a restless guest. And then in her mind's eye she saw our father's bald head, his shoulders, the keys on his belt, as he climbed the last flight of stairs. She imagined riding away in a blue convertible.

Tunney drove down the long driveway. He stopped, set the brake, cut the engine. The car was quiet. He turned in his seat and said, "Do you want to come in a second? It's really some house." He smiled at Carolyn.

Gloria recognized the smile. It was the one he flashed her the first time she saw him at C&M Realty's window.

"Sure," Carolyn said.

Carolyn got out of the car and Gloria followed. She couldn't let the girl go in the house alone with Tunney. If she stayed close, maybe Tunney wouldn't do it. Maybe he was testing her to see how far she'd let him go.

Their voices bounced around the empty house. Light poured in.

"Beautiful," Carolyn said.

Tunney took off his tie, put it in his jacket pocket. He led Carolyn from room-to-room without saying a word. Gloria heard her tell him that she wanted to marry a millionaire so that she could live in a house like that. When Tunney headed toward the stairs to the lower level bedrooms, Gloria followed. They came to the locked door.

"What's in there?" Carolyn said.

"Ah," Tunney said, "I happen to have a key."

Liz heard our father's key ring, then the scrape of the key in the lock. The door swung open slowly letting the hall light in. The shape of our father filled the doorway for an instant, and then the door swung shut, and the room went dark.

Gloria felt the current rushing past her. She knew something was going to happen. Had she imagined this moment before? This moment is what she'd run away from, what she'd returned for. She watched Tunney insert his key, turn it. She heard the lock click open. Carolyn turned toward her and smiled in anticipation, like a child who was about to be shown a secret. How did Craig describe Gloria the first night she came to him? She had a look on her face like she didn't know what was going to happen the next second. An expectant look, he called it. That's the look Carolyn must have seen on Gloria's face. One word might have saved the girl, but Gloria kept quiet.

Liz knew where our father was by the sound of his key ring moving through the room. She heard it hit the floor beside her bed. In the dark, she saw the pale shape of his undershirt rising over his head. She kept quiet as he slid in beside her.

The door swung open on an empty room. Sunlight. Dust motes hovered in the air. Tunney went in. Carolyn followed. Gloria stood in the doorway and watched Tunney walk to a window and point outside at something. Carolyn went to his side and gazed down at the city. Did Gloria see the tie in Tunney's hand, or was he too fast for her? Did she scream?

Our father might have whispered her name. Liz closed her eyes and willed herself into Hank's truck. She felt the sweeping turns and the close heat.

I can't hear anything. I can only see what Gloria saw; Carolyn on her knees, trying to turn toward Tunney. He put his knee to her back and pushed to the floor. Did Gloria know that he was performing for her? What was he showing her? Make it true, Gloria Gloria. Her chest felt so tight she could hardly swallow. If this was a test, she meant to pass it. She wanted Tunney to believe she was Gloria. She wanted to believe it, too.

Our father rolled away. Could she hear his heart, smell the scent of his sweat? It would stay in her sheets all night. Was there a flash of a match? Our father's smooth head shined in the flame's light. She smelled cigarette smoke. She could tell he was getting up by the rocking motion of the mattress and the ember of his cigarette rising in the dark.

Gloria turned and climbed the stairs, holding tight to the banister. In the bathroom, she splashed water on her face and looked into the mirror. She said, Gloria. She listened, but she couldn't hear anything. It was like nothing was happening.

Liz saw his undershirt hovering in the room, the slow brightening of the cigarette as he inhaled. Why did it always take him so long to get dressed? She heard his key ring, his zipper. His knees cracked when he knelt to tie his boots. And then the tiny light rose and the door swung open and the whole room: the tangled sheets, the cluttered dresser, the mirror, the chair, were visible for an instant. The door closed and Liz was safely in the dark again. She shut her eyes and told herself that nothing really happened.

Tunney came up the stairs looking a little sweaty. His face was flushed and his tie was hanging out of his jacket pocket.

"Let's go home," he said.

At home Gloria barbecued burgers outside on the deck. Paul said his father ate at least three of them. He'd never seen Tunney so hungry. While Gloria and Paul watched TV, Tunney slept on the couch.

Gloria went to bed early. She took off her clothes and crawled under the covers and hugged her pillow. She felt like she was in her room at the Chateau, our father's scent in her sheets, his smoke in the air. A dull ache rolled up and down in the back of her throat. Her eyes burned with tears. She couldn't stop crying. How many nights had she buried her face in her pillow to smother her moans? Gloria screamed into her pillow. She rolled on the bed like she was on fire and she was trying to put out the flames. Exhausted, she lay on her side and rocked.

Tunney came to the door and turned on the bedroom light. She pretended to sleep until he turned out the light and left.

She listened to the garage door ride up on its rails, heard his car start and back out and drive away.

She got dressed in the dark. She found her purse, her keys. She had everything she needed.

As she passed through the family room, Paul asked the TV, "Where are you going?"

"7-Eleven," Gloria said, but she wasn't going to stop at the store. She was going to drive all night.

Lauren. Lauren. Lauren. Look where you led me.

TWENTY-FOUR

□

Last night, driving home from work, I saw a man on a ladder beside the dark marquee at the U.C. Theater. A woman stood on the sidewalk beneath him, handing him letters.

QUICK BLOOD
BLOOD SIMPLE

Then this afternoon, I noticed a short line for the early shows, but I didn't stop, I drove down to the restaurant and came up here to my office.

I thought I was finished writing this. I haven't written anything in months, and I can't say I missed it.

These are strange days. I live in the Oxford Street apartment with a woman who cooks at my restaurant. Her name is Marla Brody. I fell for her the day she came asking for a job. She showed up an hour before opening time a couple of years after Lauren left. She praised my menu with her dusky voice, her chapped fingers underlined her favorite dishes: smoked pheasant, poached salmon, lamb with aioli. After I showed her the kitchen, I surprised her—and myself—by taking her black braid in my hand and holding the heavy knot of hair for a moment before letting it drop. She had Donna's hair. She tossed the braid over her shoulder; she smiled, and I asked her to stay and start work that night.

Marla stayed. I thought she looked beautiful in her baggy whites, with her sweat-wet hair sticking to her forehead, her cheeks flushed. Most nights she was picked up by a balding man with glasses who waited for her at the bar reading in the dim light. Ronson called him The Professor. The Professor didn't talk much, and his silence made me worry that maybe Marla had told him about how I'd held her braid in my hand. Weeks passed, and the man never even ordered a beer. He gathered the bar candles around his book and read, as though at an altar, while Marla helped close the kitchen.

Then one night The Professor stopped coming for her. She rode her bicycle to work, and I let her park it in my office. After closing time, she knocked at the office door. She wore jeans and a gray sweatshirt, the sleeves pushed up to her elbows.

I looked up from my adding machine and said, "He's crazy."

Marla had her bike by the handlebars, backing it out of the room. She stopped and looked at me.

I said, "For not coming for you anymore."

"He's not crazy," she said. "I told him to stop."

"It's none of my business," I said.

Marla laughed. "It is your business. I told him to stop because you didn't like him. I could tell. The more I saw you didn't like him, the less I liked him."

"It shouldn't matter what I think," I said.

"Maybe I'm crazy," she said, "but it matters to me."

Soon Marla started spending her afternoons with me. She rode her bicycle through Berkeley to Oxford Street and locked it in the lobby and rode the elevator up to the apartment. It felt good to be with a woman who knew nothing about me but my work. Life was simple again. Before she moved in, she used to go to the restaurant by bicycle, while I followed in my car, for discretion's sake. Now my people know what's going on, and we don't have to show up separately anymore.

But that's not why these days are strange. My father died of lung cancer three weeks ago. Last summer, Brenda called and told me she thought something was wrong. She could hear him coughing all day through the loudspeakers. He wasn't eating like he used to, and he seemed weak. She asked me to come up and visit him and talk him into going to the doctor. He wouldn't listen to her, she said.

I said, No. I trusted he would go to the doctor when he was ready, and he did.

Brenda called and told me the news. Tumors. They couldn't operate and they didn't think chemotherapy or radiation would do any good. He was too far gone. The doctor gave him a bottle of cough syrup with codeine and sent him home. Brenda said Hank was with my father when he heard the news. He didn't flinch, Hank said. He thanked the doctor for his time and shook his hand good-bye. Brenda said my father was in decent spirits, considering, but he never talked about his illness, and he refused to go to church with her. She wanted to know if I wanted to come and see him.

No, I told her. I made up a story about being busy at the

restaurant and short handed and in the middle of training a new chef. I hadn't seen my father since I'd realized what he'd done to Lisbeth, and I didn't want to be in the same room with him yet. There were times when I could take some solace in the knowledge that he was suffering a slow and painful death. Other times, I couldn't help but feel sorry for him all alone up there with only Brenda to take care of him. I hoped he'd live long enough for me to be able to face him, if not forgive him.

Almost six months later, after Marla had moved into my apartment, Brenda called again. My father couldn't work anymore, he wasn't eating anything. "He's wasting away," Brenda said. "And he can hardly talk."

When Marla found out how long my father had been sick, she was outraged at me. "What's wrong with you?" she said.

Marla told me that I had to go see him. I couldn't argue with her without telling her the whole story, so I said I'd go.

When I got to The Caves, he looked skeletal. He couldn't talk at all, so I was spared talking to him about Lisbeth. I stayed there for a week, but I talked to Marla every night on the phone. I spent a lot of time during those calls describing his slow progress toward death.

Brenda and Hank and I sat by my father's bed through the last days. I held his hand and wept for Lisbeth.

When I saw that *Quick Blood* was back, I decided it was time. I was ready. Tonight, after the rush, I went downstairs and told Ronson I was going out for an hour or two, that I'd be back in time to help him close.

He gave me a wary look. "You're going to the show."

I was.

"You sure do love to suffer."

He was wrong about that. I don't love to suffer any more than a blind man loves the dark.

I looked into the kitchen and called to Marla, "I'm going to the movies."

She waved a pair of tongs at me.

There was no line at the theater. I checked the times: only forty-five minutes of *Quick Blood* left. *Blood Simple* would show again at eleven. The pouting girl slid a dollar and a torn ticket at me. She'd painted her short nails as blue as ink. The lobby was quiet. Worn carpets. The smell of popcorn and sawdust. I pushed open the door.

The screen was dark. Sudden headlights weaving over a road, through trees. I walked the gentle incline of the aisle and stood waiting for some light to hit the screen so that I could find a seat.

A garage door rides up on its rails.

The light inside the garage shined into a full theater. I had to go down to the front to find a seat in a short row on the side.

A Civic station wagon pulls in beside a Saab. A black and white movie: shades of gray. A woman sits in a car as the garage door closes behind her. The whine of the motor, the rattle of its chain. She opens her car door and gets out. Tall, thin. Bleached blond. I didn't recognize the actress. She had slightly buckteeth, like my sister, but she reminded me more of Lauren than of Lisbeth. Her hand flies up and brushes her hair out of her face. A man appears in the doorway. He must be Tunney. I recognized Joel Ahern. He was probably the reason half the audience was there. *Quick Blood* made the man.

Neither of them say anything. Music drifts out of the house. Faintly familiar TV music. He stands there as she walks past two bicycles and past him into the house.

When was this? After Rose. After she called me. Here was her homecoming, according to Lauren.

He follows her into the house, turns off the TV.

Two girls are dead.

He walks through the kitchen. A missing poster on the refrigerator. In the bedroom, he flops on the bed and watches the bathroom door. The sound of water running. He seems relaxed with his hands behind his head.

The door opens and she comes out with the towel over her face. She lowers it, sees him. You can see a flicker of fear on her face.

He pats the bed and she goes over and sits down. She takes off a shoe, a cheap, pointed-toe sneaker. She isn't wearing socks. The other shoe won't come off. She tries to untie it, but it seems to knot up. He bends down and takes the shoe in his hand and slowly unties the lace. He slips the shoe off as though it were a slipper, gently, and drops it on the floor.

He pulls her head to his chest and strokes her hair.

Then they're between times.

She walks through the doors of The Ice House. Through the window, you can see a man nod. Cheese sandwiches melt on a grill. She wipes her forehead with the back of her hand, wipes her hand on her apron. High school girls lean against a freezer cabinet making slow circular movements with towels. Boys walk out of the bright light from the street carrying skateboards.

The serene atmosphere of C&M Realty. A black-haired woman walks by his desk. He watches her, but she doesn't give him a glance. A phone rings. He listens while taking distracted glances at the woman who must be Lisa Bianche. He taps his pencil. "Fine," he says. "All right."

A second hand sweeps over the face of a clock. He hangs up and grabs his coat off the back of his chair and walks into the white light of outdoors. Sunglasses. He's behind the wheel of the Saab. Car radio music. A winding road. The quality of light seems to change. Long shadows. Dusk. The disk jockey announces the time: six-fifty-one. The Saab pulls to a stop in front of the Ice House and Gloria approaches the car and ducks into the front seat.

"Does your friend want a ride?"

"No," she says.

Carolyn squints in the direction of the car.

The Snake Road house. The garage door rises, but he stops on the driveway. "I forgot something. Be right back."

She gets out of the car and watches it take the first turn on Snake. In the kitchen, she picks up the phone, and hesitates and puts it down without dialing. She goes to the bedroom and changes into a tank-top and shorts and walks out onto the deck. The pool below shimmers. A web of light. She slides the door open again and goes back into the kitchen. This time she dials.

"Is Carolyn there?"

She closes her eyes, obviously relieved.

"Let me talk to her."

A long wait while she leans against the counter.

"What?" she says. "When?"

A tinny voice in her ear: "It's all right. Your husband gave her a ride."

He sits on the floor of an empty room. His suit looks like he's slept in it. The camera crawls along the floor and over the body of a naked girl. Shades of pearl and gray.

Gloria serves pizza to a blond boy who's drinking a beer.

He pulls Carolyn's panties on, wrestles her into her jeans. He pushes one arm, then the other slides into her sleeves. He grabs her and drags her toward the window. Her eyes are open, and for a moment, it looks like they're dancing.

Gloria goes to the garage and turns on the light and looks at her car. Two bicycles lean against the wall.

A grunt. He's down by the ditches in the dark. The scrape and slap of a shovel.

She walks through a room where the boy is watching television. Kojak sucks a lollipop. She returns with her purse and a sweater. The kid asks the screen, "Where are you going?"

"7-Eleven," she says.

Headlights snake up the road.

The garage door rides up on its rails. The Civic starts, backs out.

Headlights.

Her car takes the first turn on Snake, gathers speed.

Saab, Civic, Saab.

The cars pass in the night.

She looks in her rearview mirror and sees the Saab's bright brakelights. A curve. She glances up again and the Saab is behind her.

His face looks grim in the gray light.

A 7-Eleven sign.

She turns into the parking lot.

The Saab pulls in beside her.

She walks into the store without looking in his direction and moves under the lens of the surveillance camera. The over-the-shoulder angle makes it hard to see her expression. She slides the door of the cooler open and grabs a six-pack of beer.

Looking down on the transaction, money changing hands, beer being bagged. She crosses under the camera again and disappears.

He's standing beside her car.

"Good thing I saw you," he says. He points at a flat tire, then walks around to the passenger side of his car and opens the door for her.

They drive in the dark. He says, "Where were you going?"

"I was going to drive all night."

"And never come back?"

"Never," Gloria says. "Ever."

"You were going to another city. You were going to disappear."

She nods. "I was going to change my name."

"You have one all picked out."

Gloria doesn't say anything. She looks out the window at the darkness all around her. "Yes."

"What is it?"

"It's a secret," she says. "Nobody will ever know."

Two car doors slam. A flashlight beam sweeps over the front of a white stucco house. He's holding onto her elbow. The front door opens. He pushes her down the hall ahead of him. The beam shines on her white hair. She casts a long shadow.

The padlock. He hands her his keys and watches while she unlocks the door. The keys crash to the floor. He has his tie around her neck. She falls forward. They're in the narrow beam of the flashlight on the floor. She's on her back. Her face. Her eyes are closed and she arches her back and tries to roll, but he's on top, holding her down. Sweat on his forehead, at his temples. Their shadows go still on the wall.

He leaves her lying on the floor in the middle of the empty room. He staggers out. The camera moves from room-to-room following the beam of the flashlight.

He's in his car.

The boy's on his bike, leaning into a hard turn in the road, wild hair flying. He's caught in his father's headlights. Flies past.

The Saab whips into a driveway to turn around. It speeds up close behind the bicycle. Spokes flashing in the light. The bike slides, quivers, recovers.

The 7-Eleven sign. The boy pulls into the lot and rides right up to the front door. He ignores the listing Civic and goes in. We see him through the surveillance camera, rushing up to the clerk. A nod, a shrug, and then the boy runs back out of the range of the lens.

Into his father, who grabs him by his T-shirt, then gets ahold of his arm.

"Where is she?"

"Gone."

"Where?"

"She went away."

"That's her car."

He jerks the kid toward the Saab. "Get in."

"My bike."

"Forget it."

"That's her car, though."

"Get in."

"No."

"Get in if you want to find Gloria."

The boy looks at his father.

"Get in the car!"

The boy pulls away, loose jointed, his skinny arms shaking his father's grip away. He drops into the front seat and slams his door as hard as he can.

The road toward Asilomar. Silence. The white stucco house. The flashlight in Tunney's hand. He pushes the boy down the hall ahead of him. Shadows. At the end of the hall, the door is ajar. A quick glimpse of a body on the floor.

The boy stops and his father shoves him through the door. The kid falls to his knees beside her.

"What did you do?" he screams. He turns toward his father full into a flashlight beam in the eyes. He's crying. In a second, he's crying so hard he can't sit up. He's lying on the floor next to her.

"Pick her up," his father says.

The boy sits on his knees and looks at him. His face looks wrecked from crying. His disbelief, his grief have turned to pure hatred.

"Carry her to the window."

Fighting sobs, the boy grabs her under the arms and drags her across the room toward the window. The father puts the light on the floor and helps the boy lift her out. They stumble down the hill carrying her. The boy seems weak from fear.

By the ditches, the father finds a shovel hidden in the underbrush. He tosses it at the boy's feet. The flashlight plays over a ferny patch of ground between the water and the exposed root of a tree. "Dig," he says.

The flashlight goes out. The scrape and slap of a shovel. When the flashlight comes on again, she's lying in a shallow hole.

In the car, the boy has his eyes closed. He sits pressed against the door, hugging himself.

His father's voice: "Gloria went away. To another city. She changed her name. Nobody will ever find her."

Dawn light. The garage door begins to rise. You see the wheel of a bicycle, tennis shoes, Levi's. When the door is halfway up, the boy ducks under it and is pushing the bike, and then all in one smooth motion he's on it. He pedals down Snake through the early morning tree shadows, through the empty streets of Montclair past C&M Realty and LaSalle Market and the Ice House and carries the bike down the stairs by the tennis courts and into the park and then jumps on and pumps across the wide lawn to the fire station where he drops the bike and climbs the steps and pounds on the door.

The chopping whir of a helicopter. Below, a white car flashes through the trees on a winding road. Police cars follow, the numbers on their roofs visible. Higher in the hills, more police cars wind down toward the white car. They turn and form a roadblock. The white car emerges from the trees two switchbacks below. It seems to be driving at a leisurely pace, cruising. Behind, three cop cars follow. The white car slowly approaches the roadblock. It stops. The cars behind stop. The helicopter descends close enough to see hands emerge, see a man rise out of the car and turn in a slow circle. The copter veers away. Empty sky.

While the theater was still dark, I got out of my seat and walked up the aisle staring at the small white square of light on the back wall.

TWENTY-FIVE

A few weeks ago, a letter from the state came to the restaurant informing me of Tunney's execution. How they found me, I don't know. Lauren might have given them my address; it's possible.

At first, I didn't know if I wanted to go or not. Would seeing Tunney die stop me from thinking about my sister? Or would it just make it worse? After I saw *Quick Blood,* scenes kept flashing back to me for months. Driving, working, dropping off to sleep, suddenly I'd see some image from the movie in my mind. Empty rooms, shadows. That actress lowering a towel from her face.

Then, a couple of weeks ago, there was Lauren: on the late news, talking about Tunney. I hadn't seen her in nine years.

In the bright lights, I could see glints of gray in her hair, some lines around her eyes. Her neck didn't look so smooth anymore, but her voice sounded the same—sort of serious and whispery—and her hands still flew up.

That's when I decided to go. I wanted to see this thing through to the end.

I also thought somebody should be there to represent my sister. No matter what else happened, the man killed her.

I called Earl to see if he wanted to go with me. He's a full-fledged millionaire, now. He remarried about five years ago, and he lives on the coast near Brookings. He didn't want to see Tunney die. Water under the bridge, is how he put it. He told me that Earl Jr. was a racing car driver of some renown and that he was living in California in Bakersfield. He didn't think Junior would want to go, either, but he gave me his phone number anyway. Junior told me he would love to go, but he couldn't. He was recovering from surgery on his ankles after a bad crash and he wouldn't be on his feet for some time.

Since I had the phone in my hand, I decided to call Daniel and Donna. When she answered, she told me that Daniel wasn't home; he was working a summer job as a carpenter's helper. It was good to hear Donna's voice, so I kept her on the line by asking about life in Santa Fe. She complained about the rain, something she hadn't expected so much of in New Mexico. I didn't mention the execution, but she'd seen news of it on television, and she brought it up.

"I'm going," I said.

She was silent for a while. Knowing Donna, she was probably thinking that watching Tunney die would be the most horrible thing she could imagine.

"I hope that's the end of it, then," she said.

"Yeah," I said. But I knew that as long as I could remember Donna and Daniel, there would never be an end to it.

The hardest person to tell was Marla. To explain why I

wanted to witness the execution, I had to lay out the whole story for her: Lisbeth's early disappearances, her life as Gloria, Tunney, the girls, Lauren, the book, my father; everything. It took a whole afternoon.

When I was finished, she said, "I knew you had some kind of secret. I'm glad you could finally tell me."

I didn't tell her about these ledgers. I don't think she's ready to read about all the details, but who knows? Maybe someday I'll be ready to show them to her.

In the end, Marla gave me her blessing. "Go," she said. "Go for your sister."

Tonight was the night. July first, 1993, a minute after midnight. I worked all evening, thinking about Lauren, mostly, despite the fact that Marla was in the kitchen. At opening time, I remembered the first time I saw Lauren, her face cupped to the window, peering in. The candles around her mystery book on my bar. Her hair in the light. As the rush wound down, I began to feel the kind of anticipation I used to feel when I slipped out the back door and drove to the theater. I remembered the first cool touch of her hand in the dark.

Around ten o'clock, I sat at the bar and Ronson poured me my usual: soda with bitters, to soothe my stomach. I patted my jacket pocket to make sure my letter was there.

He said, "Peaches doesn't think they're going do it."

"They'll do it," I said.

"It's an ugly business. Why don't you stay here? When the time comes, we'll share a beer. Then we'll forget about it."

It was a tempting offer, but I told him no.

"She's going to be there? Your lady friend?"

"Good chance," I said.

The road near San Quentin was lined with TV vans, their satellite dishes pointed at the sky. People clustered on the foggy hills overlooking the prison. Some were carrying candles. A few guys stood at the side of the road waving signs at my car as I drove past. Thou Shalt not Kill, one of them said. I thought, what do they care? It wasn't their sister.

I parked and searched the crowd for Lauren, but I didn't see her. The guards were already herding the journalists onto a big prison bus. I searched the slit-like windows looking for Lauren's face, but it was hopeless.

A guard led me to a white van. Emerson Cage, Carolyn's father, sat in the rear seat, his head almost touching the roof. He must have recognized me, but he didn't even give me a nod. Did he come to believe Tunney, too? Then Lynn Jacobs, Lena's mother, climbed in, her head wrapped in a dark scarf that gave her the grave look of a peasant woman. Mr. Cage whispered something to her, and she gave him a weak smile. A minute or two later, Dolores Schiller, mother of Rose, arrived with a man I took to be her new husband. He had a hard grip on her hand. The van door slid shut and the driver and a guard got in.

I felt alone in there. I was one of them and not one of them. They lived in worlds of grief and loss at least as great as mine, but I envied them their daughters' innocence.

The van passed through the inner gate and stopped next to a closed door. As I climbed out, a gray government car pulled up next to us. Mrs. Tunney slumped in the backseat beside her husband.

The guards hurried us away from them and into a bright room that looked like an employee lounge: plastic chairs, vending machines. A man searched us. For what, I wondered, guns, cameras? Then he waved his hand-held metal detector at another door where another guard met us and led us into the chamber room. We stood against the wall behind a railing under dim light. The guard stayed with us. Nobody said anything. I never knew there were two chairs in there.

Through the window on the other side of the chamber, I

could see them leading Mrs. Tunney in. She shuffled like a blind woman in her dark glasses. Tunney Sr. had ahold of her arm, supporting her.

Then a long line of journalists marched in, looking as grim-faced as mourners, and filled the area between us and the Tunneys. There must have been twenty of them at least. I saw Lauren right away. Like everybody else, she was staring into the chamber.

Then she looked over at us. Was she looking for me? I gave her a small nod hello and she returned the faintest hint of a smile.

Beside me, Dolores wept. Her husband handed her his handkerchief.

Lauren looked at Mrs. Tunney, who had managed to raise her head. When she saw Lauren she stood up to her full height for a moment, holding herself up by the railing.

Then the chamber door clanged open. Sandwiched between two guards, Tunney was dragged in. They rushed him into the chair on the left, the driver's side. He didn't have time to resist or struggle, because the guards worked like they were being timed by a stopwatch. Tunney seemed to be in a daze as they strapped him in: his arms first, then his chest. The biggest guard hovered close behind him while two others knelt to strap his legs.

I couldn't hear anything. My mouth felt like it was stuffed full of cotton. My forehead felt hot. Suddenly I was sweating at my temples, in my beard. Time slowed.

Tunney's hair was as short as a recruit's and I could see the shape of his skull, his thin neck. Under the bright lights, his skin seemed to glow. He turned his head toward his mother and raised the fingers on his left hand. When his mother broke down, he turned away from her as though someone had slapped him.

He scanned the strange faces of the reporters. I could tell he was looking for Lauren. Then he saw her. I couldn't see his eyes, but I could tell he was glaring at her by the stillness of his head.

I looked at Lauren, too. Where had I seen that expression before? On the face of the woman who played Gloria in *Quick Blood.*

How many hours did Lauren spend talking with him? How many days did she spend listening to his tapes, thinking about him, writing about him? She knew him as well as she knew me. Maybe she knew him better. Listening to the tapes, I sometimes had the impression that he was more honest with her than I was. He lied about facts, the when and what of it all, but he told us the truth about how he felt about Gloria and what he wanted from her, which was something I couldn't do. But Lauren didn't believe him, and now he was going to die with her story out in the world.

When Lauren couldn't look at him anymore, she turned toward me. I'd seen that face before, too. The day I helped her move into her apartment. Dusk light. Her face framed by the gray mattress against the wall. *I'm at your mercy,* she'd said.

That's when I realized that she knew.

Before she ever left me, she knew Gloria was in that house when Tunney killed Carolyn Cage. But she didn't know why exactly. That was my secret.

Tunney slowly followed Lauren's line of sight toward us. Lynn Jacobs' scarved head was bowed. Mr. Cage gripped the railing beside me. Tunney stared at me as though he were trying to figure out who I was.

"I'm sorry," he said. I heard his voice so clearly, it shocked me. It had been so quiet for so long, I'd thought the chamber was soundproof.

Before I could say anything or even nod, I heard a hissing sound. Tunney looked between his legs. His head whipped back toward his mother. He said, "I'm sorry," again even louder.

I could see a pale vapor rising to his knees.

He looked down again as though in disbelief.

Don't breathe, I thought.

His hands twitched. He raised his head toward the ceiling. His eyes were open. His chest rose and fell, rose and fell.

Don't breathe!

His eyes rolled back, then his chin dropped.

He's dead, I thought.

Suddenly, he strained against the straps as though he were trying to stand up. Then his head jerked back, stayed very still for one, two, three, four seconds and then slowly fell forward. A vein on his forehead rose almost as thick as my finger. His jaw dropped, his face went red, then almost blue. His body looked limp. His hands relaxed. Then slowly, he raised his head again, like a man waking from a nap. He gagged. A line of saliva shined at the corner of his mouth. Then he went still.

I felt like I'd watched everyone I'd ever known and loved and lost disappear again.

My sign is dark. The lot's empty. Ronson's gone. If he were here, he could tell me the time without looking at the clock. Three-thirty in the morning.

I don't want to go home. I know I won't sleep. I keep thinking about Lauren. Tonight, I saw her step off the bus into a swarm of TV people and stood in the darker part of the parking lot and watched her talk under the bright lights. When she finished her interviews, and the lights went out around her, she saw me. She walked over to where I was standing. We hugged. We held each other for a long, still moment. I could feel her hair through my beard. I said, you knew, and she nodded into my neck. I didn't have to say anything else.

I keep thinking about all of them, everyone I lost. My mother sliding into the front seat of Mr. Spenser's convertible. Lisbeth picking at the ragged fringe of bandage at her wrist. Donna at the garage door in her robe, waving good-bye. Daniel. I remember Lauren dancing under the low ceiling of the Rathskeller. The shape of Tunney's skull, his thin neck, the way his skin glowed under the chamber lights: I'm surprised how much I wanted to save him. I can feel my father's cold bony hand. When I imagine his cough coming out of the loudspeakers, it's hard to go on hating him.

Why did I let them all go?

I'm more like my sister than I ever realized. She left and I let her go: two sides of the same coin.

We all told lies. Lisbeth tried to live a lie as Gloria. Lauren couldn't face the truth about her any more than I could. Tunney lied so much, it was hard to see the truth in what he was telling us.

Lies, fears, silence, secrecy: they cost me everyone I ever loved. I've tried to tell the truth here. Writing this, I felt closer to Lisbeth than I ever did while she was living, but it led me to lose her more deeply, and this loss is harder to live with. How did I forget this simplest thing, this feeling for the importance of truth? Now it seems like the most urgent thing in the world. If I had felt this in that trailer in Eureka, I would never have let her go.

It offers little comfort, but the truth is the only light I have to find her with. Filling these ledgers was all that I could do for her, but it's not a small thing. My sister's not completely lost, because I remember her in the light of truth, and I still love her.